Tabula Rasa

Filip Forsberg

Tabula Rasa

ISBN: 978-91-984746-3-3
Published by FF Publishing

Costa Rica
1048

With great strain, he worked the hard and unforgiving soil. It was AD 1048, the year of our Lord, and the humidity was intense. It lay like a wet, warm blanket draped over the landscape; now, when the sun was at its peak, it was almost unbearable. An intermittent cooling breeze swept down from the great volcano in the west. Although the moving air would normally help keep the temperature low, today it was weaker, and the heat of the sun burned straight down from the clear blue sky.

Adsil, who worked the field, was dripping with sweat. The strong muscles of his bare back tensed and relaxed as he rhythmically drove his pickax through the soil in front of him. Time after time, he lifted it up and then plunged it deep into the ground, digging deeper with each swing. The ground was like brick but it was fertile, and it needed a strong man to keep it in check.

A young boy came running down the path that led to the field where Adsil worked, shouting as he bounded along.

"Dad!"

Adsil put the pickaxe in the ground one last time. He stretched his arms across his body, then wiped the sweat from his forehead. He smiled at Cirro, then, as fast as a panther, he raced toward him across the uneven ground. Adsil caught the child as he had done many times before, lifting him up and throwing him high into the air; his son felt almost weightless as he fell back into his arms. Cirro howled with laughter.

"Dad, I'm flying!"

Adsil laughed. He ruffled the boy's hair and gave him a long embrace before setting him back down on the ground.

4

"How's it going back home?"

Cirro smiled widely, his eyes aglow with pride. "You know what happened?"

Before Adsil had time to answer, the boy continued, "We killed a snake!" Cirro measured it out with his hands and held them out high. "It was this long! It was so big. Jaco and I were collecting fruit for Mom, and on our way home it came out from behind the shrubbery."

His small voice spoke quickly, and he gestured wildly as he told his father about the snake. Adsil crouched down, listening attentively. The boy's pride and excitement were clear as he relayed the day's events to his father. Adsil lovingly nodded at him and smiled.

"I will finish working the field, and then when I come home, we will have a feast. We will celebrate that my sons are strong warriors, capable of killing one of the most dangerous animals in the jungle."

He paused while Cirro beamed with pride. "Tell your mother to prepare the snake and we'll grill it together."

Cirro jumped up, hugged his dad, and then set off across the field at a gallop. Adsil grinned as he watched his son disappear. When he stood, his back creaked a little; the intensity of the heat didn't help at all. He massaged his aching shoulder muscles. Then he stepped over to the shade of a large tree and sat down for a much-needed break.

* * *

Adsil didn't know how long he had been sitting there when he felt something change inside him. An ugly feeling of vague discomfort had sparked in his gut and was growing. He opened his eyes, blinked a couple of times, and very slowly looked all around. A thick, dull

5

sound rang out, but it was difficult to determine exactly where it was coming from. The sun was razor-sharp. He rubbed his eyes back into focus.

Looking up again, Adsil couldn't quite work out what he was seeing. He stared upward, astounded and astonished. Ever so slowly, he started to rise from his seated position. The sky, which only a few moments earlier had been clear and light blue in color, had now been replaced by a strange, shimmering light that seemed to originate from above sparse clouds.

The light shone weakly at first, yet before his eyes, it grew stronger and stronger. Time seemed to stand still. Captivated by what was unfolding in front of him, Adsil watched the spectacle; he felt just a hint of apprehension, but it was increasing by the millisecond as the shimmering light started to change color, slowly transforming into an oceanic, greenish hue.

His surroundings bathed him in a blue-green light, and the usual shades of the forest now looked almost completely alien. Adsil stood as still as a statue, gazing intently upward, while the sky changed color from blue to purple, and then steadily transitioned through all the colors of the rainbow. He heard his son's voice.

"Dad! Dad!"

Adsil blinked in surprise.

"You must come! It's Mom—something's happening to her! Jaco is there—quick, come quickly, now!"

Adsil's brain raced. The surroundings now had a yellowish shine and made Cirros' face look sick. His words penetrated like needles into Adsil's head. He ran.

*   *   *

Adsil arrived at the clearing where their house stood.

He shouted, "Gisa! Where are you?" He looked around desperately. The timid, weak voice of his son Jaco came from inside the house.

"Here, Father! Come quickly!"

Adsil rushed into the house and was immediately struck with a bolt of terror. Gisa, his wife, was on the floor, shaking uncontrollably. Her beautiful face was caked with dirt and distorted by a grimace; from the corner of her mouth, a string of saliva trickled down across her cheek and to the floor. Jaco sat at her side, tears streaming down his face as he tried to help his mother. He sobbed uncontrollably.

"She's sick! Something is happening to Mom!"

Adsil rushed to her side and put his hands on her body. She was hot—burning hot.

"My love, what is happening to you?"

She didn't answer but continued to shake violently; the muscle contractions that swept through her body made it stiff as a board. Adsil stared uncomprehendingly at her. The shifting light outside pierced through the cottage windows, giving the interior a surreal glow. Gisa's face was distorted by pain and looked almost ghostly.

Adsil shuddered. He glanced over at his wide-eyed sons and thanked the gods that they hadn't been affected by . . . whatever this was.

"Help me carry her to the bed," he shouted.

Gently, his sons grabbed hold of their mother, and together they carried her to one of the corners of the cottage and cautiously placed her on the straw bed. Gisa's body was still shaking, and her mouth opened and closed in soundless words.

Outside the house, the dull sound changed character. Adsil froze. He turned his head and looked through the open door to the ground outside. The shimmering light had changed color. It was now reddish; everything looked like it had been doused in blood. Fear grabbed hold of him. The sound lifted and fell in intensity, and it was like the noise was calling out to him.

He rose and took a step toward the door, hesitated, then took another. Jaco shouted behind him.

"Father, stay! Don't go out there!"

Adsil turned around, a confused look on his face. He stared at his sons and saw tears in their eyes; they begged him not to venture out into the blood-red world outside their home. He tried to stop himself but found he was unable to do so. Then, raising his hand to his children in an almost greeting-like manner, he turned and went outside.

The red glow warmed his face. As he gazed upward, he saw half a dozen suns slowly falling to the ground. Captivated, he stared as the shining suns eased downward. They did not fall uncontrollably—it was as if they were being lowered by an invisible rope.

Completely engulfed by the eerie red light, he raised his hands slowly and looked at them. As he did, he felt himself become warm inside. It was not fear that filled him; it was neither fear nor love. It was something else, something he had never felt before. A warm, soft feeling arose from somewhere within him, replacing the abyss of darkness he had felt just a few minutes ago. Looking up at the shining spheres, he stretched his arms out and reached up toward them.

Adsil heard Jaco's voice behind him but didn't understand what he had said. He turned around and looked directly at his son. Jaco pointed toward the cottage, and Adsil's gaze followed the older boy's outstretched finger. In the opening stood Gisa—dirty, weak, and sweaty, but sane. She smiled at him. He rushed to his wife and took her in his arms.

"How are you doing? What happened?" he said, his voice trembling.

She rested her head against his chest. "I don't know what happened." She paused. "Perhaps the gods have come to show us something." Her voice was low but strong. Adsil looked in bewilderment at her.

"What do you mean? Why do you think that?"

Gisa shrugged and looked up at the hundreds of spheres falling from the sky.

"It may be so, and maybe not. It doesn't matter really."

Gisa lifted her hands and saw them now in the new bluish light. Her voice was calm in a way that Adsil had not expected.

"What do you mean, it doesn't matter?"

Gisa shook her head and gently grabbed hold of her husband's arm. "It does not matter," she repeated. "But I know something else." Her eyes sparkled with expectation.

Confusion took hold of Adsil's thoughts. "What?"

Gisa leaned toward her husband and hugged him tightly. "They are here to help us. They have come to show us the way. They have come to open our eyes, and they are with us to lead us into the light." She lifted her arms, and the warmth of the spheres radiated over them.

Death followed them with a cold, calculated gaze. The light-blue helicopter rose smoothly and continued along the coast toward the northern tip of Madagascar. Its large rotor chewed through the air and kept the speed at just over two hundred knots. The slender airframe glided across the sky, unaware of the watchful eyes that followed its journey.

The sun sat low, just above the horizon, and the sky glowed as they approached the end of their long, drawn-out journey. They flew at an altitude of a little more than 1,100 meters, and the thin, sparse clouds drifted lazily next to them. Beneath them, the dramatic coastline of Madagascar continued for mile after mile.

Inside the helicopter, Malin Persson tugged at her seat belt so that it wouldn't grip her too tightly. The soft seat enveloped her and absorbed the deep vibrations coming from the engine. She peeked out the window, past both the pilots. Far in the distance, something glittered on the horizon. Like a sparkling grain of sand, Tabula Rasa reflected the bold rays of the sun. Malin's pulse quickened. It was there they were going—Tabula Rasa, created by the legendary businessman John Vendrick III, who was as skittish as he was mythical.

John had not been seen in public for more than seven years, and it had been more than eight years since the last time he'd been interviewed. Malin smiled. She was close. She had fought hard over the past year to come here, and with sharp elbows and a little luck, she had done it. They were on their way to an interview with one of the world's most sought-after subjects; this, she knew, would take her career to new heights.

After nearly twenty hours of traveling, both she and her colleague, Denver Mikkelsen, were completely overwrought with exhaustion. They had boarded a plane in Paris, then flown ten hours south to Harare in Zimbabwe. After the obligatory delay there, they had continued toward the east coast of Africa, and after that, they had set a course toward Pemba, westward from their destination in Madagascar.

Malin shook her head and rested her chin on her fist as she looked out the window. She was nervous. Tense. This was her chance. She had struggled so hard to reach this point. She would be someone, she would make her name known, and she would rise from the anonymous masses.

They'd been sent from the journal *International Life*, and their mission was to be as easy as it was exciting: to interview John Vendrick III, the creator and designer of Tabula Rasa.

She looked toward Denver and smiled. They had worked together a lot in recent years, and they had a great professional relationship. Denver had a friendly face, was quick-witted and intelligent, and always had a good solution to any problems that arose. He smiled at her and winked. He was just about to say something when he abruptly closed his mouth.

The helicopter bounced into an air pocket, and Malin gripped the armrests. She held her breath for a couple of seconds, but then forced herself to relax, easing her grasp. She did not like flying, but it came with the job.

During one of her first flights, there had been smoke in the cabin, and breathing masks had dropped down from their holders above her head. It had turned out that the smoke was harmless and had arisen because of some burned toast in the small kitchen, but the experience had nonetheless left a deep mark within her.

She had known even then that she had to do something about her newly created phobia because her dream was to become a journalist. Either she would need to overcome her fear (as air travel was inevitably a part of trekking all over the world), or she would give in to it and opt out of her dreams.

Malin had chosen the former. She had signed up for and completed several courses about how to control the fear of flying; she could now relax—mostly—when she flew, instead of white-knuckling the armrests at the slightest hint of turbulence.

More air pockets put her thoughts out of her head, and she instinctively pulled the belt tight again. She rubbed her hands, and the tension within her continued. The bumping continued for a couple of minutes, but soon the helicopter calmed down and continued its way forward.

A voice crackled in her earphones.

"How's it going back there?" Asked André Liss, one of the pilots.

Malin pressed the helmet microphone against her mouth. "Well, we're still here. A little unusual to ride in a helicopter, though. How far is it?"

André gave a thumbs-up. "Five minutes, no more. Straight ahead."

Denver pointed out through the side window. "It's interesting that it's 2048, but when you look out at the landscape from this altitude, you can't tell if we're here now or a million years ago." He paused, staring out at it. "I like the view, but it'll be really nice to finally get there and stretch our legs." He sighed. "Doesn't it look beautiful?"

Malin nodded, but she knew better. From the helicopter, the landscape looked untouched, but she knew that the past decades of environmental degradation and industrial disasters had also imposed their impact on remote, isolated areas like Madagascar.

After all, it had been no more than three years ago that the supertanker Maxim Hoy had capsized during a storm less than a hundred nautical miles away from here. Maxim Hoy had been one of the world's largest ships, and when she had sunk, more than seven million barrels of oil had leaked out into the ocean. It had been an unprecedented environmental disaster, and even today there were still cleaning teams working to remove the oil, which had spread as far as India.

Malin's eyes were irritated, and she rubbed them gently. It had been a long journey, and now she was running on empty. A headache had taken a firm grip of her neck; every hour, it crept like a wet, cold blanket further and further up the back of her head. She rubbed her temples, and while the pain eased somewhat, she wished she had thought to bring some aspirin with her. Things had gone too quickly when she'd packed. She hadn't brought half of what she usually traveled with.

Malin reminisced on the conversation she'd had with her boss. She had called Malin up on the video link and ordered both her and Denver to leave at once. It had been unusual—her boss didn't usually behave like that—but she had been keen that Malin leave quickly.

All Malin's hard work to get permission to interview John Vendrick III had apparently paid off. Exactly how the permission had been granted, she did not know, and she hadn't had the opportunity to investigate the matter any further.

The blood vein in the boss's forehead that would throb when she got excited or angry had looked like it was going to burst. During their conversation, Malin had instinctively taken a step back, even though they'd been thousands of kilometers apart at the time.

The memory of her beloved uncle Laurent, who had inspired her to become a journalist, appeared in her mind now, along with all his stories of the crazy bosses he'd had throughout the years. Malin chuckled.

Their destination, Tabula Rasa, was a new type of mega-complex. Such developments had begun to establish themselves around the world in the middle of the twenty-first century. The first had been projects of the major Chinese business areas that had grown up around the turn of the century. Different countries had decided their own laws and rules regarding mega-complexes, and some were more advantageous than others when it came to the establishment of these new types of society.

Most were located in Asia and South America; however, in the last decade, Africa had experienced a boost in mega-complexes. Basically, the mega-complexes were independent cities concentrated in a minimal area to make every square meter more efficient. Nearly a million people lived in the largest of them, and in the smallest, there were barely a hundred thousand.

The soft seat embraced Malin, and the muffled sound from the engine soothed her. She looked over at Denver.

"Yes. It will be nice to arrive, and even more exciting to meet Vendrick. It'll be a real scoop. Promise me we won't mess it up."

Denver smiled. "Of course we won't mess it up. This will be the best one we've done so far. It'll put our names on the map for sure."

Denver didn't have the same desire for fame that Malin had; he was quite content with a more anonymous existence. She found strength in his confidence and was grateful that he was her colleague. She returned the smile and started to bend over to remove something from the bag under her seat when she was interrupted.

A small red lamp in the middle of the pilot's control panel began to flash angrily. Malin and Denver exchanged glances. Half a second later, a loud noise cut through the cabin, and the hair on Malin's arms stood up.

"I didn't think there were any active warnings," the copilot shouted.

Some parts of Africa's coasts were more hazardous than others, and for the most dangerous areas, regular warnings were sent out that highlighted the various threats that were current in that region. By far, the most common warnings regarded pirates. Nowadays, the pirates were outfitted with the latest equipment technology could bring: speedy boats that allowed them to come out of nowhere, strike, and then disappear just as quickly. They were as well-equipped as they were cruel; rarely did anyone survive a successful attack.

André replied, "No, I didn't think so either—I haven't heard anything."

The copilot thumbed the communication button. "Tabula Rasa approach. This is flight tango-tango-five."

A few seconds passed. The radio crackled, and a calm female voice came online.

"This is Tabula Rasa approach. How can we be of service, flight tango-tango-five?" The voice's tone stood in stark contrast to the rising turmoil in Malin's head.

"We have two civilians for delivery and are four minutes from arrival. We are being followed by a ground-based tracking radar. At least two immediately requesting assistance."

The angry beeping from the warning lamp continued and filled the cabin with howling sounds. The radio was silent for two full seconds.

Then, "Stand by. Assistance is on the way. One minute."

The pilots looked at each other, and Malin's feeling of unrest grew.

"I hope they don't *shoot* within a minute, then," André said with acid in his voice.

Malin resumed her tight grip on the armrests, leaned forward, and began her controlled breathing.

* * *

One kilometer down and seven kilometers away from the helicopter stood a heavyset man holding a portable rocket over his shoulder. The rocket was heavy, but he carried it without any visible effort. From the east, a faint, warm wind blew over the small hill on which he stood in the vast, rugged landscape. Fine-grained sand was driven in front of the wind, gliding slowly over his shoes.

The powerful man held the launcher with both hands and stabilized himself by placing one of his feet upon a stone in front of him. The rocket was the latest Bofors model. Laser-guided. High-precision, and capable of firing a rocket toward its target at more than three times the speed of sound.

"You have them?" A second man, slim and thin with horned eyeglasses spoke while pushing a phone against his ear. The powerful man nodded briefly.

"Yes, I have them. Eight kilometers. I shoot?" His gaze followed the helicopter moving across the sky.

The man with the glasses shook his head. "Wait. I'm awaiting confirmation from the other team. Stand by."

Seconds dragged on. The powerful man smiled to himself. Their goal was in sight; he couldn't miss. His heart rate increased.

"Confirmed?" the bespectacled man said gruffly into his phone. He was silent for a few seconds and then nodded. He lowered the phone and looked at his companion, whose eyes sparkled with expectation.

"Okay. Take them. Shoot."

The powerful man nodded imperceptibly. Clutching the warm metal hard in his hands, he gently squeezed the trigger.

Disco Bay, Greenland
2048-12-26

Fate breathed down his neck. Jonathan Jarl's legs burned as, exhausted, he approached the end of the winding stone staircase. At the last moment, he slipped and struck his ankle against one of the hard, crooked steps. The pain temporarily distracted him from his other, more serious, injury.

The wound high on his left arm burned like fire. Thick blood pulsed from it. Jonathan kept his right hand pressed against it to slow the flow.

The wound was not long, but it was deep. Raddick's knife had penetrated almost through to the bone. He clenched his teeth and pulled the belt out of his pants loops. He quickly strapped the belt above the wound, just over his biceps, before pulling hard.

Tiny stars in all the colors of the rainbow flashed before Jonathan's eyes. He stumbled as the pain tore through his arm. He bit down on the excess leather so as not to scream.

The contaminated rain lashed down around him and rattled against the stone steps. He tried to avoid getting the rainwater in his mouth, but it was difficult not to. He turned around and glanced down the stairs from where he had come. Shadows moved, and Jonathan could sense two men moving upward toward him. There was no time to hide.

He looked around. The stone staircase had led him up to a short ledge on the top of a hill. The hill was on a cape just north of Rodebay in Disco Bay on Greenland's west coast. This was where Jonathan and his partner, Eric, had located and managed to steal back an artifact that contained a unique astrological calendar.

It had been his first real mission—to repatriate the antique that Raddick and his team had stolen.

Jonathan and Eric had traced Raddick to a warehouse just outside Rodebay.

During the night, they had broken in and found the antique, which they'd removed and taken with them. The mission had been successful, but their escape had been discovered by Raddick who had unexpectedly returned to the warehouse when they fled. Raddick had thrown a knife that had hit Jonathan's arm. Eric had bashed Raddick's head with a wrench; they'd expected him to pass out, but it had only resulted in making him angrier.

It had been terrifying. That blow would have knocked any normal person out, but for Raddick it had seemed like a mere mosquito bite. Eric had hit him with the wrench again, harder this time, and when Raddick finally stumbled to his knees, they had run. However, Raddick had recovered fast and immediately went after them.

Raddick had thrown another knife, and this one had struck Eric in the back. Eric's mouth, open in a soundless scream, and how he had fallen—the vision was stuck in the forefront of Jonathan's mind.

Jonathan looked out over the bay and saw shapeless darkness. The rain poured down, and the sky was broken apart by heavy bolts of lightning. The dirty rain mixed with the sweat from his forehead and trickled down into his eyes. Faint nausea rose within, and he did not know if it was because of the rain or his injury—or perhaps a combination of both.

Raddick's voice was closer now. He came running up the stairs, followed by his partner. The sting of fear crept up Jonathan's spine, and he struggled to not let panic completely take over. He slipped on the wet stone floor, caught himself, and spun around. All his muscles were ultra-tense, nearly to the breaking point. His pulse roared in his ears, and although he was exhausted, his senses were on high alert. The towering

19

Raddick stepped onto the ledge, and his partner followed a second later.

Jonathan saw that Raddick had a deep gash on the side of his head, just above the ear where Eric had hit him; blood ran down his ear toward his neck. The blood coagulating in his dark hair mixed with the rain, turning into a disgusting sludge.

But despite his injuries, Raddick was a formidable opponent. His well-trained, iron-hard physique gave him an aura of invincibility, and a shiver passed through Jonathan's skin.

Next to Raddick stood his smaller but heavily built partner—a man with the longest arms Jonathan had ever seen. They reached down to his knees, resembling a gorilla's arms. His hands seemed just as powerful; the fingers looked like small, thick steel hooks. The man's face was rough and hard, and he had a nose that appeared to have been broken many times. A fat scar on his cheek twisted his face, making him look somewhat like a sadistic clown.

The three men were silent as they studied one another. Raddick gave a sign to the powerful man, and they both began to move away from each other in a semicircle while looking at Jonathan.

Raddick glared at Jonathan and growled, "You bastard. Give me the disc now, and I'll kill you quickly." His voice dripped with contempt.

Jonathan did not answer. Instinctively, his hand was drawn to his inner jacket pocket, and he checked that the disc was still there. It was. He had not come this far only to give it back.

Raddick took a step forward. A knife flashed in his hand. It was a hunting knife with a blade that was a little more than ten centimeters long; along the top of the blade was a serrated edge. Jonathan could tell that Raddick was accustomed to fighting with a knife. There was a light, panther-like flow in his movements—to the untrained eye, this was hard to detect, but Jonathan had seen men such as Raddick fight before. When you had survived a couple of knife fights, you gained a newfound respect for the damage a blade could do.

"Give it to me. Give it to me now, and I'll do it quickly," repeated Raddick. Jonathan chuckled.

"Do you promise? Do you swear?"

Raddick's eyes gleamed with evil. "You don't know what pain is. But if that's how you want it, I'll be happy to show you."

Raddick gently flicked the knife in the air in front of him. The rain still whipped down, and water dripped from the tip of the knife as it hovered in front of Jonathan's face. His mind was racing. He had to get Raddick off-balance, had to agitate him so that he made a mistake. Otherwise, it would be over soon.

"Come on, you're too slow." Jonathan's voice was slow; each word slipped out of him with as much contempt as he could muster. He moved backward while Raddick and his henchman moved toward him. One slinked left, and the other right, trying to catch Jonathan right between them.

"You bastard," Raddick said again. "You're going to die."

"Stop talking about it and just do it."

The powerful man had moved in a complete arc around Jonathan, who was now almost square in the middle. The three of them stood silent and tense, like prey and predators. The rain sliced hard into Jonathan's eyes, and he blinked rapidly to get rid of it. His body felt light. It was if, at any second, he would levitate from the ground and fly away.

Jonathan took a step to the right, pretended to slip, and tensed his body like a spring. As if on a given command, the two men rushed at him. He spun around and, in one movement, grabbed Raddick's knife hand and pulled it upward. Jonathan pivoted on his right leg and hit Raddick's lifted arm with as much force as he could.

Behind them, the stronger man rushed forward to grab Jonathan's head with his beefy arms. His powerful fingers slipped around Jonathan's neck just as Jonathan pushed Raddick's hand to the side and then up, hard. The knife sunk deep into the powerful man's chest.

The man coughed, and his heavy body slumped toward Jonathan's back. A thick coating of blood sprayed over him—the man's lung had been pierced through.

The chaos in the cockpit accelerated at a rapid pace. The sharp sound and the angry flashing of the lamp continued to cut through the helicopter. Malin stared, terrified, at Denver. His eyes were gaping wide.

"What's happening?" he gasped.

Before she could answer, the copilot shouted, "We have a missile coming at us!"

Surprisingly calmly, André said, "Mayday, mayday—we are being fired upon." He looked down at the dashboard and said, "Seven seconds to impact."

Far below them, a missile screamed through the sky with a deafening roar. In less than eight seconds, it would consume the distance between itself and the helicopter. The two kilograms of high explosives, together with the five thousand small bullets of tungsten, which was packed into the warhead, guaranteed that even if it missed its target, the bullets would perforate everything within a hundred-meter radius when it exploded.

"One more! Dive, dive! Activate countermeasures!" André shouted into the microphone while giving full throttle. The copilot pushed the buttons for countermeasures, and thousands of small, mirror-coated bullets sprayed out of the airframe. Their task was to confuse the rockets that approached them.

Diagonally below the helicopter, the two rockets hurtled toward them. The first one would reach them within five seconds.

André pushed the control stick forward, and the helicopter's nose pointed steeply downward. Malin almost vomited out of sheer terror. The ground was approaching alarmingly fast and filled the cockpit window in front of her. The two pilots were working frantically to escape the rockets that were after them.

"Malin!"

Denver screamed her name, and she looked over at him. A wild and terrified face stared back at her. His eyes begged any and every god that might listen for an escape from this terrible moment that had come about so quickly. Seeing his horror, Malin's own fear struck with full force. Panic screamed within her, but she couldn't do a thing. She sat there, strapped down, at the mercy of the pilots' skills.

"Two seconds!" André yanked hard on the control stick, and the helicopter braced against the air and turned sharply up. A silver arrow, the helicopter heaved from its descent and rose quickly until its position was almost vertical. To Malin, it seemed like being locked up inside a living creature that was struggling to survive and trying desperately to steer away from the wolves chasing behind. She closed her eyes and saw her uncle.

Five hundred meters behind, the rockets continued straight toward them at a furious speed. They had the helicopter clearly in sight, and the small mirror-balls had not deceived them. The temperature of the rockets' casings had reached several hundred degrees due to air friction, even in the few seconds they'd been flying. They were designed to withstand the heat without effort; the rocket engine consumed several kilograms of highly concentrated solid fuel every second.

* * *

Six kilometers away, a black-painted combat helicopter followed what was happening. Its pilot pressed a button, and a laser weapon folded itself out just below the nose. The pilot typed in a series of commands on a screen. A sophisticated guiding system followed the roaring rockets and their journey toward the light blue helicopter.

The laser aimed with millimeter-precision at one of the rockets and burned a hole in the outer rocket casing. Half a second later, the rocket lost its steering ability and exploded.

* * *

"It's gone!" André pointed at the radar screen and turned his head to get a better view. He could see a cloud behind them and just below it, the second rocket. He shouted and made the sign of the cross.

"Here comes the next one!"

* * *

Six kilometers away, the pilot repeated his actions; the second rocket disappeared in a deafening explosion.

* * *

Malin and Denver sat numbly in their seats. Malin barely understood what had happened. She had heard both explosions—it had sounded like they were just outside the window next to her.

André checked his instruments.

The radio suddenly came to life: "Tango-tango-five. This is four-nine. Over."

André's eyes stung, but he ignored the pain. "This is tango-tango-five," he answered. "Who is this?"

"Flight four-nine here. We're from Tabula and heard that you were in trouble."

A couple seconds' pause.

Four-nine went on, "Both missiles destroyed. No more threats detected."

André pressed the button. "Thanks for the help. It's really appreciated. It was the last second."

"No worries, mate. Yes, it was a close call, but everything is okay now."

The cramp in Malin's shoulders slowly released its grip. Her heart gradually began to pump blood throughout her body again, yet she still felt a little light-headed. Her shirt was dripping with sweat. She looked over at Denver. His face was pale. He stared out the window and held firmly to the back of the seat in front of him.

"Oh my God," Malin whispered.

Denver took her hand, his voice also a scratchy whisper. "Yeah. Really."

"That was close," she said. "A few more seconds, we would've been dead."

André adjusted their course and put the helicopter on a straight trajectory toward Tabula Rasa. He confirmed that there were no more threats in the area. Malin and Denver looked at each other, their eyes still wide with shock and gratitude that they had survived. Slowly, their pulses returned to normal, and Denver could let go of his grip on the seat. Malin leaned forward.

"Have you experienced this before?" Her voice was still shaky, but she fought hard to get it under control.

"Yes, a couple of times, actually. There are pirates and robbers along the coast—they make their living attacking the ships and flights to Tabula Rasa." André smiled at Malin and continued, "In recent years, however, staff from Tabula Rasa have conducted regular clean-up operations along the flight routes used to minimize the threat, and I thought they had succeeded. But when we get to Tabula Rasa, we'll report that they are not done with their work."

Denver had followed the discussion and leaned forward. "So you mean there is special staff at Tabula Rasa who get out and clean up?" He paused and narrowed his eyes. "By the way, what do you mean by 'cleaning up'?"

André laughed. "Just what it sounds like. They send out teams assigned to clear an area of pirates, villains, and other riffraff. You know, shoot first and ask questions later." He gave a thumbs-up, and Denver nodded doubtfully.

Denver glanced over at Malin, and they looked uncertainly at each other. Less than five minutes later, André pointed forward.

"There it is—Tabula Rasa."

Both Malin and Denver leaned forward in their seats. A spectacular sight unfolded in front of them. Malin blinked a couple of times; it was hard to absorb the sheer size of their destination. She stared, wide-eyed.

"Oh my God, how big it is," she whispered.

In front of her stood three huge pyramid-like structures. They were like the pyramids of Egypt, though on a far larger scale. They reached several hundred meters into the air. The sun glared off their surfaces; Malin had to protect her eyes with her hands so as not to be blinded. She couldn't tell whether the pyramids were covered with glass, but whatever their surface, the reflection made her squint. André laughed.

"Yes, that's usually people's first reaction. It's a little different to experience Tabula Rasa than to see it

on a picture." He turned to look at it again.
"Impressive, right?"

The three pyramids were placed in each corner of a triangle; each pyramid marked one of the tips. Malin estimated the height of each of the pyramids to be more than a kilometer. Several different crafts circled in the air like flies around an elephant. She looked down, to the right side of the helicopter, and saw two runways that cut through the surrounding jungle.

Denver had been sitting speechless. Finally, he said, "Yes, that's amazing. Imagine building something that big. How many people live there?"

André thought about it for a moment. "Just over a million was the last I heard. They usually talk about an increase of between fifty and one hundred thousand per year."

Malin blinked. "A hundred thousand? You're going to double the number of people within ten years?" She could hardly hide her surprise. "There must be complete chaos in there. How can you manage such a tremendous population increase? Is there even the physical space to accommodate so many?"

André nodded thoughtfully and flashed a dazzling smile.

"Oh, yeah, that's actually the least of the problems." He raised his eyebrows in a playful smirk. "But it's better if I don't say any more right now. It'll be more interesting once you arrive and experience Tabula Rasa for yourself."

Disco Bay, Greenland
2048-12-26

Raddick's arm was locked between Jonathan and the powerful man, and all three stumbled backward. Jonathan pushed off with his legs, and they fell in a big pile. As they tumbled, the powerful man's body was pushed underneath, and the knife plunged even further into his body. With his dying breath, he plunged his thick fingers into Jonathan's neck like living pieces of steel. The long fingernails ripped and tore at his skin.

Jonathan screamed and threw his head back; instantly, he felt and heard the crushing of a nose. He turned and watched as, with a gurgling sound, life left the man.

Raddick beat feverishly to get loose. He managed to pull his arm back and quickly got on his feet, the bloody knife stretched out in front of him. Jonathan rolled away on the hard ground and came up two meters in front of Raddick, bloodied and gasping. The powerful man lay dead on the ground. His shirt was soaked with dark red blood. Only the whites appeared in his eyes. Raddick spit.

"You bastard. I'll kill you."

"Come up with something new to say," Jonathan answered wearily and slid gently to the side, opening some distance between himself and Raddick. The pulse in his ears sounded like a drum. His breathing was erratic and hard. The fight had lasted less than a minute, but his power was already draining. The rain had eased, but the stones were still dangerously slick.

The knife flashed in Raddick's hand. Jonathan twisted his body, and when the knife came against his stomach, he bent his leg and kicked. The kick hit the underside of Raddick's arm, and the knife fell to the ground. Raddick shouted and leaped to the side. His arm was hanging loosely at his waist, apparently broken. His face was contorted in a grimace.

"You bastard, I'll cut your heart out."

Jonathan's body reacted to the adrenaline flowing through his veins. The belt he'd pulled around his arm had come loose and slipped off. Thick blood oozed from the wound, but there was no pain. Gently, he raised his hand and touched it, and his fingers became sticky with blood.

Raddick charged suddenly in an effort to end the fight. He began hitting Jonathan with short, quick jabs with his still-functioning arm, while the broken one flopped wildly. Raddick aimed at Jonathan's midsection and moved toward him.

Jonathan was surprised by the violent attack and blocked it as best he could; even though Raddick only had one working arm, he was still a fierce opponent. Raddick's muscles danced under his shirt, and he hammered hard against Jonathan's stomach.

Jonathan threw his head forward to head-butt Raddick but missed. Raddick continued, and in desperation, Jonathan slapped his hands against Raddick's head, hitting both ears simultaneously. Raddick screamed and staggered backward.

Jonathan felt the familiar metallic taste in his mouth, spit, and saw blood. His hair was glued to his forehead. Blood ran from a corner of his mouth down his chin, and he was leaning to his side, where his kidney had taken a beating. Raddick's non-functioning hand seemed to have swollen up in just a few minutes and was now heavily enlarged. Jonathan glanced at the hand and then to Raddick's pulverized face. If he could throw Raddick off-balance and get him out of focus, get him so angry he'd make a mistake, he thought, he could finish this.

Jonathan smiled and pointed. "Maybe we should buy you one of those foam rubber fingers people use at basketball matches for your other hand. Then they'd match."

It did the trick. Raddick screamed.

"You bastard! I will roast your heart over an open fire!"

Jonathan responded in an excessively sleepy voice, "Do you see any fire here, you idiot? If you haven't noticed, it's been raining. It's quite difficult to make a fire in the rain, you bonehead. Didn't you learn that at school?"

He dragged it out, letting the sarcasm flow in every word he said.

Raddick opened his mouth and tried to reply, but no words came out. Instead, a strange, animalistic sound gurgled from his throat. His lips pulled back, and his teeth seemed to want to attack Jonathan on their own. He rushed forward like a locomotive, roaring, with his arms swinging wildly.

He used the broken arm as a weapon, spinning it surreally in the air like a broken propeller. Jonathan ducked and kicked hard at Raddick as he came charging. He made contact just above the left knee, and a soft, disgusting *crunch* was heard. Raddick fell.

Jonathan got up to his knees and looked toward Raddick. He lay on his side and struggled to get up. One of his legs was broken, and blood slowly trickled from his crushed nose into his mouth.

Despite his injuries, Raddick managed to get to his feet. He leaned against the stone wall and stared at Jonathan with pure hate in his bloodshot eyes.

Jonathan regarded him skeptically. An ordinary man would have remained on the ground with such injuries; Raddick said nothing but continued to glare at Jonathan.

Jonathan fingered his inner pocket and froze. The disc was gone. Raddick's mouth drew back into a sly smile.

31

"Missing something?" He held the disc in his hand and waved it teasingly in front of him. In all the chaos, he had somehow managed to get the disc. Rage filled Jonathan, burning like fire, but he tried to remain calm.

"Keep it. I'm in no hurry. I'll take it later."

"Is that so? Later? You think I'll just give it to you . . . later?" Raddick's mouth contorted into a vicious smile.

"Yes, you will. You just don't know it yet."

"And how exactly would that happen?"

"You see over there?" Jonathan turned slowly and pointed into the darkness. "Up there on the hill? There's a sniper rifle that has you right in its sights."

Raddick laughed hoarsely. The sound that came out was more of a wheezing than an expression of mirth.

"You idiot. Do you really think I believe that?"

"No, obviously not. It's ridiculous that he hasn't shot you already."

Jonathan put his hand to his wound, which was throbbing like a hammer hitting an anvil. The pain had burned off the adrenaline and now loudly made itself known.

"But actually, I wanted to see if I could beat you, man to man. That's why the sniper and I agreed on a sign I would give if you were too strong."

"Really. And what sign was that?"

Jonathan formed a V-sign with his left hand and stretched it high into the air.

"This."

Raddick smiled grimly and stared at Jonathan. Nothing happened. Several seconds passed. Raddick's smile widened. He knew there was no one out there. Still, for some reason, he made the mistake of looking down at his bloody shirt for a fraction of a second to see if there was a laser marker on him.

In that same second, Jonathan jumped into a tiger leap against Raddick and drove his knee into Raddick's crotch. Raddick's smile froze when his manhood was crushed, and the disc fell clattering to the ground.

"You bastard." He groaned and fell to his knees, and turning his head up toward Jonathan, glared at him. Jonathan's left arm was pounding with pain, and his hands were wet with blood. He took a step forward.

"It didn't have to be like this," he said, and with a hard punch, he crushed Raddick's larynx.

Tabula Rasa, Madagascar
2048-12-26

The helicopter began its gentle descent from its cruising altitude. It bounced a couple of times on its way down, and both Malin and Denver held their breath, hoping and praying that there was to be no repeat of their earlier adventure.

On Malin's left hand was a ring she had received from her mother many years ago. The slender, silver ring held a beautiful, deep green emerald. She had always treasured it. She fingered it as they approached the landing pad, and the familiar feel of the ring calmed her. The previous experience had been enough excitement for both Malin and Denver, but even as it had been chaotic, it had also filled them both with strange energy afterward. It was as if their near-death experience had somehow made them more alive. Malin savored every breath, and her body was filled with an inner, warm light.

She peered out for the hundredth time through the window and gasped.

In front of them, Tabula Rasa stretched out in all its splendor. She had read the reports about it and other similar mega-complexes. She had visited a couple of Tabula Rasa's counterparts around the world, but none of what she had seen could compare with this. The actual size of Tabula Rasa was much larger than anything she had ever witnessed.

The helicopter was now just a couple of hundred meters above the entire complex, and she could, in principle, see the entire area from where she was. The sides of the pyramids shone with the sun's reflected rays and gave rise to a kaleidoscope of colors. The pyramids seemed to be covered in silver and gold, and their shiny surfaces glimmered magically in the sunlight. Large, arched passages connected the pyramids, and Malin could see vehicles moving through them.

Small crafts glided in the air between the pyramids, and while Malin watched them curiously, Denver laid his hand on her shoulder. He pointed past her and said something she couldn't hear. Malin followed his pointing finger — on the side of a pyramid, a large panel was starting to slide to the side. Out of the opening rose a large, crescent-shaped platform. She heard Denver laugh with delight.

"Shall we land there?"

André gave a thumbs-up and answered, "Yes, it's for us! But we're doing a sweep over the area so you can get a bird's eye view. You'll be here for three days, and I don't know how much time you'll have to see Tabula Rasa from the air. Take the opportunity to enjoy it." André smiled and directed the helicopter in a smooth turn. Malin pulled at Denver's arm.

"Look, that's incredible."

Along the edge of one pyramid, myriad antennas reached up toward the sky. Malin estimated they were over a hundred meters tall, but as they stood beside the pyramids, they looked like toys. It was fascinating. Malin saw a crowd of crafts floating softly and sliding around in what looked like a choreographed dance.

She glanced over at Denver and giggled when he winked at her. She felt giddy—high, even. Malin had studied everything she had managed to get her hands on about Tabula Rasa before they'd left.

She knew each of the pyramids had different functions. They passed the western pyramid—Cibus—which specialized in ecology and producing food for the entire complex.

Cibus slid out of their field of vision, and the northern Primus moved under them. Malin had read that Primus was the one that provided the energy supply and generated most of the power. She had

35

understood that the latest in power supply innovations was here, and Tabula Rasa had earned big money in licensing some of their technology to other mega-complexes around the world. The problem of generating enough power and energy on a small surface was what usually restricted these types of communities.

Typically, mega-complexes used a combination of renewable energy, such as solar, wind, and geothermal heat, to produce what was needed, but it wasn't always like that. The first mega-complexes had used nuclear power, but after a catastrophic accident in northern Japan near the end of 2032, an international ban had been established against the use of nuclear power in these communities. The meltdown had destroyed large parts of the mega-complex and made the rest of it completely uninhabitable.

More than thirty thousand people had perished on that fateful day in December many years ago, and a further forty thousand had died of radiation-related injuries and diseases in the months that followed. Malin shook her head. If Tabula Rasa was this big already, it must mean that they had a new way of generating power.

Denver touched her arm and pointed east toward the third pyramid, Gaudium, glittering in the sun. Malin squinted and looked at the pyramid that largely consisted of housing modules and parks. It was in that one that most of the social life, like sports and cultural events, took place; more than eighty percent of the population in Tabula Rasa lived in that pyramid. André tapped his headphones and pointed to the crescent-shaped platform.

"The names of the pyramids are in Latin. 'Primus' means the first—it was the first of the pyramids to be built. 'Cibus' is Latin for food. That one basically produces everything that's consumed and exported.

'Gaudium' means joy, and it's primarily in that structure that the social interaction takes place." The corner of his mouth pushed upward in a half-grin. "One minute to landing. I hope everyone is feeling relatively good despite our experience back there?"

Malin leaned forward and smiled. "Oh, yes. We'll be fine."

André pressed a couple of buttons. "Super. There are four different landing places for helicopters at Tabula Rasa. There's also a large harbor and two smaller ones, and two runways close by. You probably saw the runways when we began our approach. Even though we're pretty far away from the rest of civilization, there are lots of transportation opportunities here."

Malin nodded thoughtfully. "How long have you been working here? You don't strike me as the kind of person that would live in the wilderness and fly transports."

André laughed and smiled broadly. "Almost two years now. It's the best job I've ever had. I mean, look around you. Every time I come back, something new has been built or something has changed." He pointed at the huge, glass-like pyramids growing ever larger as they approached. "A couple of years ago, I was down at the bottom. I mean really at the bottom. Divorced, unemployed, and with the bottle as my best friend. It's so stereotypical that you'd think I was kidding. But now it's completely different." He did his boyish half-smile again and said, "And when you're employed, you can join the stock option program they have. A really good deal, I might add."

Malin didn't reply but let André continue. It was one of the first lessons you learned as a journalist, to keep quiet and listen.

"For some reason, I was approached by someone who worked for Tabula Rasa, and they offered me the opportunity to go through their pilot selection process. To make a long story short, I passed it, and here I am today."

Malin nodded. "Was it difficult to get through?"

André kept his eyes focused on the landing pad and said, "Yes and no. I've never experienced so many different types of questions and investigations. I mean, they didn't just check me out. They also investigated my family, my ex, and my previous employers. Tabula Rasa means business. But it suits me well. I completed the process, and here I am."

Malin was about to continue pumping André for more information, but the copilot, who had sat quietly during their overhead tour, finally spoke.

"Miss Persson, it's time for landing. Please sit back and check your seat belt."

Godthab, Greenland
2048-12-26

The heat relieved the pain in his body. As he took another unsteady step into the tub, the warmth began to alleviate some of the aches. He moaned quietly as the hot water embraced him.

Very carefully, Jonathan sat down. His hand touched his chest, where two ribs were most certainly cracked. His left pinky finger was broken, and his body had received numerous scratches and cuts. The doctor had stitched up the deep wound on his left arm, and the sharp pain there had shifted to a deep pounding. The wound on the arm would leave a scar he could show off at the bar; the broken ribs, he knew, would make his every breath feel strained for the next couple of days.

Jonathan had also taken two tablets of oxycodone to help combat the pain—at least, that's what he told himself, anyway. The pain. That's why he'd taken them, not because he was addicted to them. The last months had been particularly hard, and the tablets did give him relief. A few more days and he would stop. Yes, that's how it was. A few more days, then he would quit.

Curls of steam rose from the water, and the oil he had poured into the bathtub helped give his body some welcome relief. He had been picked up by the Amber Group's helicopter shortly after fighting Raddick, and the doctor had patched him up during the trip back. However, Jonathan had insisted on being dropped off at his apartment instead of being transported all the way to Paris, where the Amber Group had its headquarters.

The Amber Group's protocol dictated that he would debrief immediately after completion of the assignment, but that would simply have to wait. He needed to take a few hours for himself after the round he'd been through. It could not be helped that Backmann would get bent out of shape about it, but that honestly didn't matter right now.

Raddick had been inhumanly strong. Their battle played on repeat in Jonathan's mind, and he turned and twisted it, analyzing it in the smallest detail.

It hadn't been the first time he had been in a knife fight. He had a good grasp of different techniques in combat. Various techniques had their own strengths and weaknesses. Raddick hadn't shown there was any special technique he relied on; instead, he'd trusted on his strength and power.

There were some of these types of fighters around, but not very many. Most of them met their fate early, in bar fights or down a dark alley. But the strength Raddick had shown was astounding.

Jonathan remembered how Raddick had used his broken arm as a kind of propeller when he'd attacked. Jonathan tapped lightly against the edge of the bathtub with his fingers. The pain must have been overwhelming, he thought, but Raddick hadn't seemed to feel anything. A nagging feeling pecked at Jonathan's brain; had he missed something? Was there a detail he'd overlooked?
He shook his head while he pondered the questions.

His apartment was old and was located on the outer edge of Godthab, Greenland. It was a surprisingly large space. It had old windows with glazing bars, heavy carpets, and an overall rustic sense of charm. His family had owned it for two generations, and because he was the only child, he'd had to take it over when his mother passed away.

She had been a strong woman. Together with three other women, she had undergone and passed the French astronaut training. Jonathan had never met his father, but he knew he'd been from Sweden. His mother had seldom talked about his father. Through the years, he'd found out fragments, but had gotten no clear picture. His mother had accidentally said too much once, after a few too many glasses of Feteasca, and he'd found out that his father had been posted as a Swedish air officer to train English and American pilots stationed at the Thule Base. In retrospect, he regretted that he hadn't pushed his mother for more information. Now, it was too late.

Soft music by Vivaldi sounded from the living room; Jonathan could hear it through the closed bathroom door. His cat, Gustavius, was stretched out like an accordion on the floor a few feet from the tub.

He reflected on the past few days and all that had happened. The briefings last week with Backmann and the nervousness before he had left. His first official mission had, on paper, been a simple affair, but the infamous Murphy's Law had shown its ugly face. The preparations, the mission, the fight against Raddick, Eric. Everything tumbled around in his brain. Their mission had been seemingly simple—recovering the famous Skydisc that had been stolen from its museum near Nebra in Germany.

The Skydisc had been found in the late nineties in Germany by two men, Henry Westphal and Mario Renner. Henry and Mario had been out with a metal detector and shovels to look for treasures in the mountains near Saxony-Anhalt, as they had heard rumors and thought it would be fun to check it out.

They hadn't had permission to be there, and knew that anything they found would need to be handed over to the authorities if they were caught—otherwise, it would be regarded as theft. They'd been out there looking when they'd hit the jackpot. The metal detector had given a reading, and they had loosened the ground with the shovels. From the earth, they

41

uncovered one of the most remarkable findings in modern times.

It had been an antique bronze disc that weighed a little more than two kilograms and had inlays of gold. The disc had been affected by verdigris and was a beautiful, shimmering green. The gold inlays were amazingly detailed renderings of a full and half-moon, solstices, and stars in the sky. The use of the disc was unknown, but it was assumed it had been used in astronomical contexts.

The day after they'd found it, Henry and Mario had sold the disc to a shady dealer in Cologne for thirty-one thousand D-mark. The dealer had then sold it to someone else, and the disc changed hands several times in the following years, each buyer shadier than the next. With each sale, it became more and more expensive, and finally, the price was over a million D-mark.

After tips from the public, the police had found out that a valuable, archaeological artifact had been uncovered that had not been correctly reported to the authorities; after two years, they conducted an operation that successfully recaptured the disc. It was then sent to its rightful owner, the museum in Saxony-Anhalt.

The disc had stayed there while the debate about its authenticity ensued. Most researchers agreed it was genuine, but there were a few who believed the disc was a forgery.

And then, in the fall of 2041, it had been stolen from the museum. The police investigation almost immediately became stuck, and although the police and Interpol had collaborated with police forces all over the world, the disc had been missing from the earth's surface for many years.

Through contacts, however, the director of the museum in Saxony-Anhalt had met the Amber Group and its director, Nicholas Backmann. In silence, the museum's director had hired them to locate the disc and to recover it a second time. After a lot of hard work, they had managed to trace the thieves to Greenland.

It had been Jonathan, the Group's newest member, who, together with a more experienced agent, Eric Stolt, was awarded the mission to recover the disc.

Fury and sorrow welled up inside Jonathan now as he pictured Eric's dead, blank eyes staring up at him. He closed his eyes and let the pills spread their soothing effect over his aching muscles.

The doors on the side of the helicopter slid open, and Malin rose to step outside. After the flight and the trip, her legs were unsteady, and she wobbled when her feet touched the platform; she sat down on the edge of the cockpit.

An overwhelming scent of greenery greeted her, but also something else—a faint, sour odor she couldn't recognize. A strong gust of wind ruffled her hair, and sharp, penetrating sunlight embraced her so intensely that she had to hold on to the door frame to keep her balance. She squinted, trying to focus, and heard Denver's concerned voice behind her.

"Are you okay?"

She nodded. "Yes, I'm okay. It's just a little bright," she lied.

Ever since she'd been young, Malin had suffered from episodes of migraines that could make her feel so awful that she had to lay in bed for hours, unable to do anything.

Denver put his hand on her shoulder, and his touch was soothing. She wasn't sure how much of the tension she felt came from her migraine or from their frightening experience before; after all, it hadn't been more than ten minutes ago that they had escaped death. She smiled.

"It's okay. It'll pass."

A troubled look slid over Denver's eyes, and he let go of her shoulder. They got out of the helicopter and continued to unload their gear, which took them less than three minutes.

After making sure nothing had disappeared during the trip, Malin looked around quizzically. She had expected that someone would be there to greet them, but they were alone. She went over the details in her head, trying to figure out if she had overlooked something.

She glanced up. The sky above them was beautiful, truly amazing—far better than the heavy gray clouds she saw more and more of through the windows of her apartment back home in New York. Several times over the last few years, the rain clouds had contained toxin levels that exceeded the limits set by global authorities. When it was at its worst, you couldn't go outdoors at all.

A sting of jealousy rolled over her that her city was not surrounded by the same beautiful sky as here. But on the other hand, New York didn't have problems with giant, sinking oil tankers. You can't have everything.

She shrugged, inhaled deeply, and tried to identify the source of the weak, sour undertones in the air. Before long, her thoughts were interrupted by a wheezing noise.

Two elevator doors on the platform slid open and out stepped a short, stocky man wearing thick glasses, followed closely by two guards. The small group came directly toward Malin and Denver. The bespectacled man walked with surprisingly quick steps—he was clearly overweight, contrasting sharply with the two guards who followed him. Both of the guards appeared to be near-perfect physical specimens.

The man approached them and bowed deeply. Malin could see the beginnings of a thin-haired crescent on the top of the man's head.

"Bonjour, welcome to Tabula Rasa, Ms. Malin. My name is Derek Lamm, and I will be your guide while you're with us." He paused for a momentary gasp of breath and went on, "but we do not have to be so formal. You can call me Derek."

His voice was half an octave higher than she had expected, and his heavy French accent made her smile involuntarily. On Derek's outstretched hand, a thick gold ring glimmered in the sunlight.

"Thank you, Derek. It's nice to meet you. My name is Malin Persson, and this is Denver Mikkelsen, my colleague from Life."

They shook hands. Derek gestured to the guards behind him to take care of the luggage. The two men moved like one, and without a word, they lifted all the luggage in sight. Denver, who was a strong man, was surprised to see one of the men lift a bag full of camera equipment—weighing more than thirty kilograms—with just one arm, without a shred of effort and gently hang it over his shoulder.

Lamm continued talking, but Malin barely heard a word of what he said. She was fascinated by how the two men had managed to carry all the bags at one time.

"Is everything okay, Ms. Persson?" Lamm's voice sounded genuinely concerned.

Malin blinked. "Yes, I . . . I was just surprised that your men could carry all of our luggage like that."

Lamm looked at her endearingly and chuckled. "Don't worry. They have no problem with physical effort."

Lamm took Malin's right arm and Denver's left and began guiding them toward the elevator as he continued speaking.

"You are so welcome here, and I know that Mr. Vendrick will be very happy to meet you."

Malin, who hadn't expected anyone like Derek Lamm, glanced over his head toward Denver with raised eyebrows; Denver seemed just as surprised. Lamm's arms barely reached above their waists. Malin thought the whole thing must have looked quite comical.

They entered the elevator, and Lamm made a sign to one of the men. Denver glanced back at the two guards, who stood silently at the back of the elevator. Lamm nodded and smiled as he studied Denver.

"Yes, I know. They are very strong. I'm so used to them that I don't notice such things anymore. Many of those who work here at Tabula Rasa have talents that are beyond the ordinary. You'll see more during your guided tour here later." He gestured with his arm that they should follow him. "This way, dear friends."

Malin followed Derek, throwing a little shrug in Denver's direction. The silver-colored doors of the elevator slid shut behind them with a snake-like hiss. The silence that surrounded them, and for the moment, Malin lost her sense of orientation.

"We have really been looking forward to your visit here," Derek repeated. "There is so much the world has misunderstood about our work here, and I know Mr. Vendrick would like to correct it."

"Yes, we're looking forward to it, too. When are we scheduled to meet John?"

An almost imperceptible change came across Derek's expression, a dark shadow gliding over his eyes. He looked straight at Denver and said with emphasis, *"Mr. Vendrick* is a busy man, and you will meet him when *Mr. Vendrick* has time."

Derek continued to look straight at Denver. Denver shifted uneasily.

He stammered, "I apologize; it wasn't my intention to insult anyone."

After a few long seconds, Derek's face softened again, and a wide smile spread over his face.

"Don't worry, dear friend. It was me who overreacted. We all have the utmost respect and reverence for Mr. Vendrick, and as such we should address him as Mr. Vendrick."

"Of course. It was entirely my fault."

Derek smiled broadly and gestured that they should follow him.

47

"This way, dear friends. Your apartment is quite close. It's among the best we have for our guests." His smile stretched from cheek to cheek.

Malin and Denver followed Derek, and close behind them, the two men followed with all the equipment.

"So, Mr. Lamm, how long have you worked here at Tabula Rasa?"

"Call me Derek, dear. I've been here for almost twelve years. I was fortunate to come here as one of the first. In the start, there were only a couple thousand of us. Then, of course, Tabula Rasa was not as developed as it is now. But even back then, I saw the potential of what Mr. Vendrick was trying to accomplish. Now, there are just over a million souls here and we have the highest valuation of all mega-complexes listed on the world's stock exchanges."

Malin nodded. "Yes, I heard that," she said. "It's impressive, both in terms of value and that you've managed to grow so much. How do you manage to produce enough energy to maintain a population of so many?"

Derek chuckled. "We are far ahead in development, and on some fronts, we're further ahead than all the other mega-complexes." He made a sweeping movement with his hands. "Here, things are not about quantity but quality—you will discover this during your stay. Tabula Rasa is humanity's last hope, and to achieve what we set out to do, we need citizens with high potentials rather than a bunch of mediocre people."

"Mediocre? What do you mean by that, exactly? Do you think people who aren't in Tabula Rasa are inferior?"

"Interpret it however you want. Compared to the quality of the people at Tabula Rasa, the future of humanity will inevitably be shaped here. After all, here we have the resources and the capacity to take humanity's next step."

Malin kept her voice soft. She caressed the emerald ring on her finger with her thumb and smiled her most understanding smile.

"What do you mean by the next step of humanity?"

Derek Lamm smiled back radiantly. "That, my dear friends, is something I know Mr. Vendrick will tell you more about."

Godthab, Greenland
2048-12-26

In the quiet stillness that surrounded him, the sound that came was surprisingly loud. Jonathan had not been in the bath long before he heard the faint click of the front door. He stiffened instantly and opened his eyes. Small droplets of moisture glided lazily down the bathroom mirror.

Silently, he stood, pulled a towel from the steel rack, wrapped it around his hips, and got out of the bathtub. Gustavius didn't move but simply observed him semi-curiously. Jonathan tiptoed to the old wooden door, stood behind it, and listened. A couple of seconds passed. He heard weak, tapping steps in the next room. *High heels?* he wondered.

A moment later, the bathroom door opened slowly, the hinges whining, and a dark-haired woman tentatively stepped in.

High heels indeed. The woman's pumps clicked gently against the hard tile floor. Jonathan lunged forward. The woman noticed the movement behind her a second too late. Unable to pull her head away fast enough, Jonathan's arm slid beneath it while his other arm locked her head in a firm grip. The woman twitched and moaned.

"No, Jonathan, wait."

Instinct took over. He spun her around and glimpsed her face in the bathroom mirror between the drops of moisture. The woman's hands struggled against his arms, and her nails dug into his skin. It burned in the wound on his arm.

A split second later, he relaxed and smiled. It was Marie L'angi, his direct supervisor.

"No need to knock anymore?" He released the pressure on her throat and she rubbed her neck, making an annoyed face at him.

"You're sharp. That's not a way to welcome one's boss, is it?" Her voice was hoarse, and her eyes flashed. Jonathan took a step back and gave her some space.

"Sorry. You could've said you were coming instead of sneaking in like a cat."

Gustavius mewed as if on cue, then laid his head back down on the bath mat.

He smiled and pulled up the towel that slipped from his hips to the floor. He gazed at her. She looked amazing. Her hair was cut short, in a page-style haircut. Her tall cheekbones and sharp, sensual traits framed a beautiful face. Her dark eyes pierced him.

"Sure, but I thought I would surprise you. Apparently, it was a bad idea." Her voice was more acidic now that the shock had subsided.

"Don't get angry. I said I'm sorry."

"Yes. It was probably also my fault. I should have said something before."

He walked closer, put his arms around her, and pulled her to him. "I've missed you." His eyes gleamed. The heat between them was immediate. The spark between them had been strong from the first second they'd seen each other. She was the older and more experienced of the two. He, the younger, more impatient.

50

"I've missed you, too." Her eyes were big and soft but still hesitant. Her gaze slid down to his arm, and she gasped.

"You're hurt; why didn't you say anything?"

Jonathan looked down to his arm and saw a thin streak of blood running from the wound down to his elbow. He shrugged.

"Don't worry, I can barely feel it."

Marie rolled her eyes. She pulled some toilet paper from the roll and began to wipe away the blood. Once she was satisfied with her work, she nodded to herself.

"There were three things I was going to talk to you about."

He took a step back and sat down on the edge of the bathtub.

"What kind of things would they be?"

Her body language became more professional. She raised her eyebrows and placed her hands on her hips. "The first is your stop here. You know that the debriefing should take place directly after the mission. No exceptions. We went through it before the mission started, and that was no more than four days ago. Backmann is more than a little pissed that you took the liberty of making a stop instead of going directly back to headquarters."

Her eyes were authoritative and attempted to transmit severity. He met her gaze.

"Sure, I understand. But it was my first mission, and the battle with Raddick took its toll, you know."

She sighed. "I knew you would say something like that. But this is the first and last time you do something like this; once more, and you're out. Whether you think you're immune or not."

Jonathan nodded briefly. "Got it."

She glanced over to the sink and the opened pill jar that stood there: oxycodone. She had certainly seen what it was, Jonathan observed, but she said nothing.

Instead, she turned around and walked into the living room. He followed, then walked into the adjacent bedroom and opened the closet. Marie could see Jonathan as he slowly began to get dressed.

She walked to the window and looked toward the street below. There wasn't much traffic at the moment. A couple of older people walked with bags in their hands, probably on their way home to make supper. A light rain had begun to fall and colored the asphalt dark, and the small drops drummed rhythmically against the windowsill. On the news over the past few days, it had been reported that the pollution levels in the upcoming days' expected precipitation were below the limit and that no curfew was in force.

"The second is John Vendrick. We intercepted the communication two days ago."

Jonathan put a leg in his jeans. "Between?"

"Between two technicians who worked at their communications department. It was about one of their satellites."

He pulled a thick, knitted white sweater over his head. "Which one?"

"Atlas."

Jonathan wrinkled his forehead and tried to remember.

"Is that the one that has to do with long-distance surveillance?"

"Yes, it is."

"I remember I read a memo about it. It was developed in the 2040s and was launched a couple of years ago, I think. A real badass. I think it was even armed—some sort of laser cannon capable of destroying any kind of meteorite."

She nodded. "Yes, that's the one. And that's also all we know about it."

He took a comb and began fixing his blond hair. Some unruly curls were doing their best to fight back.

"What were they saying about the satellite?"

Marie grinned at him as he tried to work against his unruly curls. Finally, they won, and Jonathan gave up.

"It was encrypted," she said. "We're working to decipher it, but it'll take time. The cryptology department is putting all its resources on it, but still, it won't be done quickly." She dragged the words a little.

He threw his comb on the bed.

"How much longer?"

"At least a day more, maybe two. It depends on how lucky they are."

"Okay," he said. "And the third thing?"

"This."

She pulled him toward her.

His body was taut and strong. He didn't have a lot of bulky muscles, but his body's agility made him resemble a panther when he walked. He and Marie had met almost three months ago. He'd been focused on his studies with such a level of commitment that it bordered on mania. He'd studied at Lund University, and she'd seen him in the corridor. Jonathan had been studying astrophysics.

Marie had been there for another matter, a meeting, and as she'd been leaving, she had stumbled on the stairs. Jonathan had caught her when she fell.

She had been deeply embarrassed, but Jonathan had pretended like it was nothing. They'd started talking and had stood there for ten minutes. He had asked if they could go and have a cup of coffee in the cafeteria, but she had declined. After all, he was only twenty-four years old; she was closer to forty. But two days later, he called—she never did find out just how he got her number.

They had gone out a couple of times. Marie had been hesitant about letting it develop into anything deeper, but the chemistry had been too good. They had become lovers, and she had experienced a passion that eclipsed everything else.

"What are you thinking?"

She smiled and blinked back to the present. "That night in Madrid," she said. "Remember the grumpy waiter at the restaurant?"

Her hands stroked his hard shoulders. Her touch was warm and sensual, and his body reacted.

"Yes, he was strange. It must have been a bad day for him."

"He probably didn't get any that morning." She winked at him.

"Probably. They say people actually perform better at their jobs when they get some in the morning."

"Then we'll make sure you can perform well today, right?" She pulled him closer.

* * *

They lay together, tightly entwined in bed. He groaned when she touched the damaged parts of his body. Her soft kisses took away some of the pain, and her body took away the rest.

She stopped for a moment. Thoughts swirled through her head. She wanted. He wanted. That's all. That was all that was needed—for now. Afterward, she would regret. Almost certainly.

His lips pressed against hers and his hot body lay beneath her. She sat astride over him, letting him imbibe her femininity. His admiring gaze danced over her neck, her shoulders, her breasts. Her nipples stiffened, and he took them in his mouth. She shivered with pleasure.

Some part of her knew it was stupid that they continued with their love affair. Chance had wanted Jonathan to be recruited to the Amber Group, where Marie had already been working. It had been one of those strange coincidences that life sometimes came up with.

She looked down at him where he lay under her, and inside, she fought the urge for him with her professionalism. After a while, his body tensed and they climaxed together. Sweat ran off them both in little streams, the warm, dampened sheets spun between them. Marie knew Jonathan had been married and that he'd had a child, despite his young age; she knew that he and his wife had lost their child and the grief had doomed their marriage. He didn't talk about it much; she could count on one hand how many times he'd opened up about what had happened.

"You're absolutely amazing," she mumbled.

His tendinous forearm caressed her back. "You're not that bad yourself." He groaned as the pain in his body made itself felt again. Marie turned her face up toward Jonathan.

"Do you have a lot of pain?"

Jonathan shook his head slowly and said, "Don't worry. Nothing that a couple of days of good sleep and good food can't fix."

"Is that really all you need?"

"Maybe."

She let her fingers slide down his chest.

"Raddick was hard on you?" Her eyes were soft.

"Yeah, he was a tough one."

Marie hesitated. After some silence, she asked, "What are you thinking about?"

Jonathan closed his eyes. "I'm thinking . . . there's something that bothers me about the mission."

She wrinkled her nose. "Raddick?"

He nodded. She waited for him to continue.

"I've been thinking about it ever since I got home. Something isn't right." He paused, staring at the cream-colored plaster of the wall. "I mean, Raddick was a hardened killer. A real dangerous type. What would he do with an antique like the Skydisc? It makes no sense."

Marie thought for a few seconds, then said, "Maybe he just liked it so much that he had to get it?"

Jonathan grimaced. "Funny." Marie laughed.

"Don't be so grumpy. It doesn't suit you."

He tried again. "But seriously, think about it. What would he use it for? It doesn't make any sense. The Skydisc from Nebra is valuable for sure, and it was good that we managed to get it back, but I still don't understand why Raddick and his cronies stole it."

She bent down and placed her hands on his shoulders. "He must have been hired by someone," she said. "That's the only explanation."

"Yeah, it must be something like that. It sounds strange to me that a mercenary killer would turn into an antique thief."

"Yes. That sounds strange."

"And how could he be so damn strong? When I was fighting him, it was like he was made of stone."

Marie leaned close to his face and smiled sweetly at him, showing off two perfect rows of teeth. "A little jealous or what?"

He put his hand on her back and pushed lightly.

"No, not at all. It is not like that. But I mean it. When I hit him with punches that should've floored him, he wasn't affected at all. It was just like whatever I did meant nothing to him."

Marie nodded while her hands continued to caress Jonathan's chest.

"Well, I don't know how badly injured Raddick is, but I know we can do something about *your* injuries."

The pain from the broken ribs suddenly resurfaced, as if Marie had woken it up by talking about it.

"How?" he asked.

She looked him in the eyes. "A surprise." She got up and retrieved the bag she had brought with her from the floor next to the front door. She opened it and took out a gold-colored syringe. Jonathan cocked his head and narrowed his eyes.

"What's that?"

Marie smiled. "Something amazing."

Jonathan shook his head, grinning.

"It's a synthetic drug that accelerates the healing process," Marie elaborated. "Small, intelligent robots that are microscopic in size. They find their way to where the damage is and repair it. After an hour or two, you'll be like new," she said, paused, and then told him with a grin, "but only if you want to."

He returned the smile, and she sat down beside him.

"No side effects?" he asked.

Marie shook her head. "No. Just make sure you don't get a similar injection the next month. It takes about thirty days for them to pass through your system. And if you mix injections, it can be a problem—a big problem."

Jonathan listened and nodded. "I'm ready."

Marie patted his leg and then turned to rummage through her bag again. She pulled out two foil packets. She tore the tops off both, set the larger of the two down on the bedspread, opened the smaller one, and removed a sterile cotton ball saturated with rubbing alcohol. She wiped the top of Jonathan's arm with it, and the cool cotton made him shiver. Marie smiled at him, held up the gold-colored syringe against the lamp in the ceiling, and tapped on it with her fingers a couple of times. She nodded—looked good.

She grabbed the flesh of Jonathan's arm from below, found a vein, and expertly slid the needle into it at forty-five degrees. She pressed the plunger slowly and then pulled the needle out. A dot of blood began to grow at the injection site, and Marie quickly reached two fingers into the other packet, pulled out a small patch of gauze, and applied it to the site.

"Hold this here and press," she instructed.
Jonathan did.

Heat spread through his arm from where the needle had been. It moved up through his shoulder and down through his chest. He blinked a couple of times as if trying to see the microscopic machines through his skin.

"How does it feel?" Marie asked.

Jonathan blinked again, staring at his body. "Warm." He paused for a few seconds, looked up to meet her eyes, and continued, "It feels warm."
Marie put her hand on his chest.

"Good, that means they're active. Right now, they're flowing through your body to analyze where to start. They compile your injuries and prioritize them. Just remember, do not mix injections. Do you promise?"

Jonathan chuckled. "Maybe you could've given me the syringe before we made love?"

Her eyes gleamed, and she shrugged playfully. "I think you were quite enjoyable even though you're hurt."

Jonathan smiled and closed his eyes. "You were pretty lovely yourself," his said, his voice becoming sluggish. A wave of fatigue poured over him.

Before she could answer, Marie saw his eyelids drooping. His breathing became deeper and slower. She nodded to herself and watched him as Jonathan fell into the darkness of deep sleep. She sighed, gently laid down beside him, and closed her eyes.

* * *

Marie woke up with a twitch of panic, but the warmth of Jonathan's body next to hers calmed her. The smell of him was close—a weak mixture of man and . . . something undefined but that she enjoyed. She shook her head, trying to bring clarity to her thoughts. Over the last several days, she had been wrestling with her feelings for Jonathan and their future, but now she had decided. Their relationship must end.

Now that he'd started with the Amber Group and she was his supervisor, they could not continue. The Amber Group had a stated policy that relationships between managers and employees were not permitted.

As she lay beside him, she agonized over the inevitable conversation. She stared at his face, at the thick, dark eyebrows that turned upward on the insides, giving him a perpetual expression of mild piteousness, like a lonely puppy. It was her favorite feature.

Jonathan's eyes fluttered open and he smiled at her. "Hey, good looking."

She stretched and placed her hands on his legs, braced herself, and squeezed.

She sighed and said, "You know this can't go on, right?"

Jonathan glanced at her, then averted his eyes. "Why not? We have fun at work. Have you never done anything like this before?"

She got up on her elbows and with half-acted and half-genuine indignation.

"No, never! What do you think of me?"

He smiled broadly and blinked. "Only good things, believe me."

Now she was serious. The immediate desire had been satisfied and she was in control; it was time to say what she had come to understand in the last few days. It wasn't easy, but their relationship simply could not continue.

"This was the last time; it won't work anymore. I can't risk anything now. Not when I've come so far. These past few months have been amazing, but we've got to end it. I'm your supervisor, and now that you're working with the Amber Group, we need to have a professional relationship. It . . . it has to be like this. Backmann won't allow it. It'll end with us both being fired."

Jonathan raised an eyebrow. "Well, the fun really didn't last too long, did it?"

"No, I know. I feel terrible, but I've been thinking about it a lot and it really can't work."

"Okay, I understand."

Marie stared at him, head slightly tilted. She was glad he'd responded how he had, glad he hadn't made a scene, but at the same time she was somewhat offended by the fact that it had been so simple.

With one smooth move, Jonathan rolled over to the other side of the bed and stood up. He reached for his clothes. He could feel her gaze on his back—it practically burned his skin. He smiled for himself. If she was going to play hard to get, that wasn't a problem. It was a game they both could play.

Marie glared at Jonathan's back and said with an angrier voice than she wanted to, "Good. Then it's settled. Get to Paris and talk to Backmann. He'd like to talk to you."

The jungle, Costa Rica
2048-12-27

The ordinary sometimes conceals the amazing.

Near the border between Costa Rica and Nicaragua lies the Cordillera de Guanacaste mountain range. It stretches for more than a hundred kilometers along the northern part of Costa Rica and lays like a dragon with its nose pointing down to the southeast.

The highest point is the Miravalle's Volcano, which rises just over two thousand meters above sea level. Lush rainforests cover the slopes, and the temperature at these altitudes is not as aggressive as further down.

Dr. Lisa King sat on a wobbly plastic chair in front of her computer in a worn tent and listened to the sound of the jungle outside. Faint noises of cicadas and crickets echoed rhythmically. The stomped earth floor was relatively smooth, but the table and the computer still wobbled regularly.

She was in the process of recording an introduction for her scientific report, her responsibility in the excavation they were now running. Lisa adjusted her headset so that it didn't press too hard against her ears. She closed her eyes for a moment to clear her thoughts and then continued with her dictation while the words softly slid across the screen in front of her.

"During the 1930s, the American business known as United Fruit Company was in Costa Rica clearing areas for the creation of banana plantations. United Fruit controlled huge areas of Central America and had a constant need for new areas to expand their business. In the international market, United Fruit fought against many other companies, but in some parts of the world, the company had essentially developed a monopoly.

"After a brief period of planning, heavy machinery and thousands of workers were sent into the area to begin clearing all vegetation. Soon after, they came across the first stone ball, and then there were more. Each one weighed several tons. Later, they would be known as Costa Rica's famous stone balls. Nobody knew where they'd come from or who had made them. Some speculated that they had been placed there by aliens, others that they had been crafted by the native population who had placed them there for reasons that had been lost in time."

The chair wobbled, and Lisa instinctively grabbed hold of the table. She looked at the screen and read through the piece, nodding with satisfaction. She continued.

"At the start of a project to clear the way for a road, the stone balls were pushed aside by bulldozers. As time passed, a rumor arose that they were full of gold and precious stones. Several enterprising men in the clearing patrols began to drill holes in them and stuff the holes with explosives.

"When the dust had settled, the men investigated the destroyed balls, but no treasures were found. The only thing the explosives achieved was the destruction of copious numbers of these mysterious stone balls. As the years went by, the stone balls achieved mythical status in Costa Rica, and finally, a museum opened for the purposes of preserving them and seeking to find and protect as many of them as possible. Many of the stone balls had already been moved from their original locations, and since no one had notes of where they'd been found, no one could reconstruct their original positions."

She fell silent, read through the text, and nodded again.

*   *   *

Lisa was just over forty years old and was an archeologist with specialization in Central American culture. This mission was a joint effort partly was sponsored by herself and partly by the Amber Group. She had worked with Backmann in the past, and each of those missions had been successful.

But yesterday, Backmann had called with some unusual information. He had recounted strange stories about shining spheres that had been seen under two completely different archaeological excavations—on two separate continents.

At first, she'd thought Backmann was joking with her, but he had assured her this was not the case. Backmann had asked her to keep a lookout in case she discovered something similar during her excavation. She hadn't understood what it would be, but nevertheless, she had promised to be aware.

Ever since she'd become a student at the university, she had been fascinated by Costa Rica's mysterious stone balls. Over the last year, she had managed to scrape together enough money to fund a research mission in Costa Rica where she could investigate their origin and purpose. It was a struggle, but for Lisa, the difficulty made the challenge even more attractive. And to work in such a dramatic landscape as this—with the great volcano Miravalles in the background—was amazing.

Lisa got up from the desk and left the heat and humidity in the tent behind her. She approached the entrance of the cave system they had explored in recent days and placed her hand on the cold stone wall. It dripped of moisture, and the cold penetrated her hand.

The cave path in front of her led slightly downhill; she squinted at the pitch-black opening. Darkness— and not just any darkness but compact abyssal darkness, like a black hole devouring all incoming light. The opening before her was just the right height that she could enter without ducking.

Lisa wasn't very tall—barely over one and seventy centimeters—but she was agile as a cat. Her long blond hair was pulled back in a tight knot, and the powerful fabric of her overalls fit her body snuggly, emphasizing her well-trained contours. Her heavy hiking boots kept a strong grip on the rocky, uneven ground.

It was colder here than she'd anticipated. The thermometer had displayed barely twelve degrees Celsius half an hour ago at the camp.

She stared into the opening. Cold air poured out of it like a dragon with icy breath. Her exhalations formed small veils of smoke that rose and dissipated into the air.

Lisa had been on-site for eight days, and this cave seemed to be the most promising so far. She and her team had, in recent days, investigated seven sub-tunnels in what appeared to be a larger tunnel system. Four of the sub-tunnels had led more than a hundred meters into the mountain's interior; two of them had led more than three hundred meters. But in none of the tunnels had they found what they were after.

"Lisa, are you okay?" The voice behind her was dark and deep.

She turned around with a jolt. "Yes. Tim. Everything's fine." She chuckled. "Just looking into the dragon's mouth to see if he has our treasure."

Tim Pedersen smiled. His white teeth flashed, and at that moment he reminded her of an actor—someone famous—but she'd forgotten the guy's name. The actor had been in all kinds of blockbusters back in the nineties. She grinned. It didn't really matter what the doppelganger actor's name was; it was Tim's voice that was his most distinctive feature. It had that deep tone that women all over the world loved.

It had been a rare stroke of luck that Lisa had met him. Otherwise, someone else would have taken him. And she'd been tired of waiting. Tired of sitting on the sidelines and putting all her effort into her work.

Kevin Costner! That's who it was. She laughed, causing Tim to wrinkle his forehead in confusion.

Lisa had undergone a heart-breaking divorce three years ago and had buried herself in her work—as many other heartbroken people had done before her. She'd worked hard and documented several new discoveries in Central American archeology. But the years without any sort of closeness or intimacy had taken its toll. She and her ex-husband had no children together (as the divorce proceedings had progressed, she'd thanked her lucky stars for that). Now, with everything done, she realized more and more how much she regretted not having children yet.

She turned her head back toward the cave and chuckled sadly. It had been so long. She'd met Tim two months ago, and the spark between them had been like fireworks. All the air in her lungs had vacated the moment she'd seen him. He had been introduced to her during a mingle at the Swedish embassy in Costa Rica, but during the first twenty seconds of his talking to her, she had lost herself in his voice.

It was soft but not too weak. Warm but not too hot. It had gone straight into her interior and touched a place no man had reached before. After the mingle, the two of them had slipped away together without anyone noticing, and they had made love on the embassy roof under the moonlight.

She blushed ridiculously as she thought about it. Just imagine if her sister had found out! The wholesome Lisa meets a man for the first time at a party and goes up to the roof to have sex the same evening.

"What in the world do you keep giggling about?"

Tim's warm eyes studied her. She blinked away a tear of joy, turned back to him, and stroked his cheek.

"Nothing really, good-looking. I was thinking about when we met. On the roof. You know, that was the first time I'd done something like that. Don't think you're with a loose woman."

He rolled his eyes playfully and crossed his arms. "I'm glad you brought it up. I've thought a lot about what happened that night, and actually, I was completely surprised that you were so forward. One could almost say that you caught me off guard."

Her eyes wandered over his face. High cheekbones, bright blue eyes, and a dark fuzzy hair that had its own life every morning they woke up together. She pinched him lightly on the cheek.

"You can't take advantage of a willing party, you know. And when we were laying on the roof, you actually seemed quite willing."

She leaned forward and kissed him softly on the lips. He opened his arms and held her tightly while they kissed in front of the cave's darkness.

The sound of a throat being cleared interrupted them. Lisa and Tim turned toward the voice simultaneously; it was Lars, their trainee. He was on loan from the embassy, and Lisa had been told to return him in mint condition. Embarrassed, the lovers let go of each other, grabbed their equipment, turned on their headlamps, and with sheepish smiles on their lips, began the slow descent into the opening.

Lisa led the way and Tim was in the middle; Lars went last, keeping an eye on the rope that trailed them deeper and deeper into the cave to ensure it didn't break. Slowly, they moved forward into the cold, black space.

67

Tabula Rasa, Madagascar
2048-12-27

The electronic buzz of the computers penetrated Elisabeth Snow's head. She thought she heard something and glanced over her shoulder, but nobody was there. She blinked a couple of times as she let her eyes glide across the room. Her shawl had slipped off the back of her chair; she bent down, picked it up, and laid it distractedly on the desk.

Her breathing was fast. Elisabeth was alone in the computer lab, which was in the western sector of Cibus. The walls were covered with screens, and in the middle of the room, the advanced control computers were set up. The weak humming of the computers—and their heat—were like a physical presence. The air in the room smelled stuffy despite the active ventilation system.

A wide, rounded screen on the wall showed a live news broadcast from Hong Kong. The report was about the riots that had broken out in both Hong Kong and Macau over the last few days. The riots, which were growing in size and intensity every day, were a reaction to China's decision to recapture both areas. Even though everyone knew it would happen, people still seemed surprised. Elisabeth shook her head; some people would never learn.

Elisabeth's red hair was up in her usual ponytail. She wore an old thin, teal-gray sweater, and her white lab coat was unbuttoned. Her forehead was dotted in beads of perspiration, but it wasn't the heat in the room that made her sweat; it was what she was doing. Her heart pounded in her chest and moisture trickled down her temples. She leaned toward the screen.

She had to hurry; time was of the essence. She would only get one chance, and it was now or never. She took a new hologram cube from its packaging, tore off the transparent protective paper, and loaded the die-like chunk of technology into the computer. She typed a few commands on the keyboard, uttering a silent prayer. It must succeed; it must. She pressed "Enter" and the copying started.

A dialog box appeared on the screen, and the status bar began to grow slowly from left to right. Her pulse pounded so hard in her ears that she could hardly focus. She wobbled, lightheaded, and grabbed the edge of the table, forcing herself to take deep breaths.

After a few seconds, she regained control. She reopened eyes she'd squeezed shut to keep herself from vomiting. The screen in front of her displayed the meter indicating the copying completion percentage—it was at barely twenty-five percent. It moved nerve-rackingly slowly.

Thirty percent.

Thirty-five.

The indicator teased her, freezing in its tracks. The electronic sound seemed to be gaining intensity, and she cursed.

Elisabeth had come to Tabula Rasa just over three years ago and had initially been convinced that she'd made the right choice. She was smart, highly educated, and had a burning desire to put her mark on the world. She was determined to make a name for herself in the astronomy world.

It was her passion. Ever since she was young, she'd thought of space as infinitely exciting; after university, she'd gotten the opportunity to work in the field at Tabula Rasa—the place where the future would be created. It was where they had the resources, where the limits of humanity would be pushed and moved forward, and she wanted to be part of it. It had seemed like that for the first few years, anyway. As time went on, she had discovered more and more sides of Tabula Rasa that she couldn't come to terms with, like their need to control, their focus on profit, and their drive to satisfy the stock markets.

All the planet's mega-complexes were listed on the global stock markets, and they were all driven by profit. Discoveries made within the mega-complexes were patented and used as weapons in the eternal struggle for wealth.

A crucial step had come the previous week when the amazing discovery had been made. It was a discovery that, in Elisabeth's eyes, belonged to the whole world for the simple reason that it would affect all people on earth. It wasn't something that should be patented and used to generate profits. Her sense of justice had always been too strong to ignore; she'd spent long nocturnal hours anguishing over how she would act on this issue.

She'd realized that John Vendrick III had no intention of sharing anything with anyone. What he and the team had discovered would be kept within Tabula Rasa, whatever the cost.

A couple of Elisabeth's colleagues had argued that the United Nations must be invited and informed of the discovery; they had been brutally silenced. After only two days, both colleagues had inexplicably disappeared. Elisabeth had not seen them since, and that had happened three days ago. The explanation she'd been given was that her colleagues had been posted on assignments, but Elisabeth knew better. She was convinced they'd been murdered.

Now, she knew without a doubt that she had to do everything she could to find a way out of Tabula Rasa—and take enough information with her about the discovery to convince the outside world.

Her eyes focused again on the indicator on the screen, which continued to mock her with its unhurried pace.

There wasn't much time—no one was ever alone for long. Normally, there were three people in the control room, but today both of the others had come down with acute stomachaches. Elisabeth allowed a smirk as she pictured them at home, stuck on their toilets. It was amazing what a few drops of laxative in a cup of coffee could do.

Sixty-seven percent.

Sixty-nine.

A sound from outside the room made her look up, and she stared, hyper-alert, at the gray metal door. Fear pounded in her stomach, and a creeping wave of nausea was building up inside of her. The indicator stopped short of seventy-four percent—Elisabeth's breath stopped with it—and then continued.

She waited for the door to open. The seconds crawled by, but nothing happened. After another minute, the indicator finally showed that copying was almost complete. She turned toward another screen next to her and dialed her father's number.

"Dad, are you there?" A couple of seconds passed before Richard Snow replied.

"Hello, Elisabeth. Yes, I'm here." Her father's voice was comforting. His face hovered just in front of the hologram screen.

"Are you at home?" she asked.

"No, I'm down at the power stations in Primus. Is everything okay?" Richard's hologram flickered. There were often disturbances in the signals from the lower regions where her father worked. She hadn't told him that she planned to escape from Tabula Rasa, and even now, she still hesitated.

"No."

"No? What's wrong?" His voice was at once concerned.

"Something . . . came up at work, and I don't know how to handle it." Elisabeth hadn't said anything to her father before when she hadn't been sure what she would do, but now she had to include him.

"Sounds serious. Is there something I can do?"

"Yes, I think so. I need a favor." She spoke quickly.

"Tell me, and I'll do it. You know that."

"Thanks, Dad. You're a rock. I'll send you a holocube with data. A level four cube."

He hesitated. "Level four? Why so much space?"

"Actually, I wish I had something bigger. Level four isn't nearly enough, but that's all I have here. I'll figure out how to deal with the rest. What I'm going to send you is big enough—bigger than I thought." She was rambling nervously.

"Okay, wait. I'll run in and see if we have any level four in the office. Two seconds." His voice disappeared. She waited.

"I'm back," he said a bit winded, "I have one. Stina forgot to return the one we borrowed from the archive."

"Okay. Upload it, and I'll send you the data."

There was a pause, and then Richard said, "All right, ready. Go for it."

"I'm sending it now. Do you see it?"

A couple more seconds passed.

"Yes, I see it. What is it?"

"It's from Atlas, the Tabula rasa satellite—"

"But I mean what kind of data is it? Why are you sending it to me?" he interrupted.

Elisabeth swallowed. "I don't know where else I can send it."

"Well, what should I do with it?" His voice sounded anxious.

"Put it away and do nothing with it for now. It's my insurance."

"What do you mean, 'insurance'?" Audible worry had crept into her father's voice.

"It's a suspicion I have. I want to be on the safe side. If something should happen to me so, send it to CNN."

"Now I'm actually worried," he said. "What do you mean that something might happen to you? Are you in trouble?"

"Oh, no," she lied, "As I said, it's a little insurance, just in case."

*   *   *

Computer technician Djing Shin sat two levels below Elisabeth in a hermetically sealed room. He carefully studied the computer monitors in front of him. The sharp light emanating from the screens gave him a pasty look. He lifted the colorful plastic cup and took another sip of his homemade mixture of Coca-Cola and caffeine tablets.

Two monitors and a hologram screen were set in a semi-circle, with Djing in the middle of them like a conductor. On one screen, the security system for the entire data processing department showed all inbound and outgoing data traffic from the department. The usual, even flow that the department used to generate had begun to change five minutes ago, but Djing hadn't noticed.

On the hologram screen, he watched the broadcast of American football. The holographic football players floated a few centimeters in front of the screen.

A few minutes later, at a quarter to eight, a sizeable step increase in data traffic was recorded and a warning tone sounded. It got Djing's attention. He was on-call for the weekend; usually, there wasn't much to do at these times, and he had been expecting a calm and relaxing evening. He'd been looking forward to calling his fiancée in Bombay—they had gotten engaged just last month and would marry next year.

His calm, however, had unexpectedly been torn apart by the warning signal. Djing let his eyes slide across the screens. They showed a steady increase in outgoing traffic flowing from the lab. The information was pouring out of the lab's data cable.

Djing's fingers flew over the keyboard. He worked quickly, trying to isolate the event and understand what was happening. Had it been a hacker attack? Those happened now and then. The Tabula Rasa cyber defense was among the most effective in the world, but sometimes an exceptionally talented hacker—more often than not, a college kid—managed to get through the firewalls and the other defense mechanisms they had in place.

Djing flashed his teeth in a wild smile. He studied the screens, and after a few minutes was able to rule out an attack. The data wasn't coming from the outside but from inside the lab. He shook his head, bewildered. What did it mean? Djing knew he should contact his boss, but she was always edgy these days.

He drummed his fingers on the desk. If he were to sound the alarm, and it turned out to be nothing, he would surely regret it. Perhaps permission to travel to Bombay to get married would be delayed. Or maybe his future wife would be denied a residence permit at Tabula Rasa. He leaned forward, covering his mouth with his hand, and debated what he should do.

* * *

Elisabeth tapped the screen, trying to force the stubborn indicator to move faster.

"Have you gotten everything?" she asked her father hastily.

Richard replied, "Not yet. It's at ninety percent. What should I do when it's ready?"

She thought for a minute. "Hide it somewhere in your house and pack a bag for yourself and Marina. I'm going home to get some things, and then I'll come to your place around midnight and tell you everything."

* * *

Richard worked quickly. Holocubes could hold a vast amount of data, but he saw that the copied information filled the entire cube. He lifted it and held it against the light. Its faint blue sheen gave his hand a ghostly look. The cube was small, barely three cubic centimeters, and it weighed basically nothing. Richard looked into Elisabeth's hologram eyes and told her it was done.

"Okay, good. I'll come over when I'm done here." Elisabeth replied.

"All right, honey. Listen, that was quite a bit of data you sent. And what do you mean about packing a bag?"

"I mean pack the most necessary things you and Marina own." She hesitated. "We have to escape."

Richard gawked at her silently for a long while. Then, "Why?"

"You wouldn't believe me if I told you."

"Try."

She sighed and licked her lips. She hadn't wanted to explain it on a call, but Elisabeth saw that her father needed to know what was going on—at least, a little taste of it.

"We've discovered something," she said. "Something that will change everything. Just over a week ago, we discovered a sphere coming up from inside the moon."

Richard had heard what she'd said but did not fully register its meaning.

"What?"

"I don't know how to explain it, but I can say that it seems we've discovered that we're not alone in the universe. The sphere came up from the moon's surface and placed itself in its orbit. Tabula Rasa already had a space station in place—they've managed to establish contact with the sphere and all the data the space station has collected so far. They sent the data to our analysis center for investigation the day before yesterday."

Richard hesitated, eyes narrowed. "That's incredible. But I haven't heard anything on the news about a discovery. Why haven't NASA or ESA said anything?"

Nodding slowly, Elisabeth said, "No, that's precisely the problem. I don't know if any of the other global space authorities have discovered the sphere yet, but it's only a matter of time before it's uncovered by someone else. For now, Tabula Rasa seems to be doing everything it can to ensure that nobody else discovers anything. They want to keep the sphere and the communication a secret for as long as possible to get as much of a head start as they can."

"And what you've sent me—is it all the information about this so-called sphere that they've managed to gather?"

Elisabeth grimaced lightly and shook her head. "The holocube I sent to you?"

"Yes?"

"It's a fraction of it."

* * *

Right beneath the floor under Elisabeth's chair, Djing was sweating profusely. Things were going straight to hell. This was nothing he was prepared for. He hadn't received any training about how to handle this type of event. Djing was quick and smart, but he was also afraid of doing something wrong and wanted instructions before taking any kind of action. The pulse in his head pounded hard, and his stomach tied itself into a hard knot.

The amount of data that had left the lab was too big for something not to be wrong. Djing made up his mind. He had to do something. If he didn't sound the alarm and it turned out there had been an intrusion and valuable data had been stolen, he would be held accountable. He swallowed hard and lifted the handset, tapping the speed dial to his boss. After a couple of signals, a hard female voice responded.

"Yes?" The woman sounded annoyed.

"It's Djing. At sub-central K."

"Yes?"

"There's something going on in lab fifteen. The data traffic has increased exponentially in the last three minutes. The level is now at eighteen hundred gigabytes per minute, and it's growing as we speak."

The line was quiet for a few seconds. Then,

"Eighteen hundred? You must have read it wrong. It can't possibly be that much."

Djing did not hesitate. "No, no, I'm sure. The levels all day have been between a half and one gigabyte, just like normal. Without warning, it began to spike."

"Who's in the lab now?"

"A technician."

"*Who?*"

"Elisabeth Snow."

"Position?"

"Not sure, but I think she works with Atlas."

"Level of competence?"

"I don't know. I can check if you want me to."

"Do it," replied the female voice.

Djing's fingers flew over the keyboard. "Level two-seven," he said.

"Two-seven. There should be nothing in her duties that would require so much bandwidth." She said it more to herself than to Djing.

"No," Djing answered. "It's absolutely impossible that she'd need that much—and it's still increasing. The flow is now over two thousand gigabytes."

"Two thousand?" The female voice sounded doubtful.

"Shall I shut it down?"

"I'm not sure. I don't know exactly what Atlas' specifications are, but I've never heard of them needing so much."

After a moment's hesitation, Djing asked again, "What shall I do?" At first, he wondered if their connection had been lost. "Ma'am?" he asked the silence.

"Cut it."

*　*　*

Elisabeth stared at the screen in horror.

The connection signal was indicating that all communication had been cut off.

Her fingers worked the keyboard. After a few seconds, she realized that it had been cut from outside the lab. Someone had discovered her. She had almost managed to send everything. Her brain worked frantically; it could still be done. She could still get out of Tabula Rasa—but it would be difficult.

There were a couple of large main roads in and out and a handful of minor points where one could leave the mega-complex. But to do that, one must be approved in the scan. And if she were discovered, it wouldn't take long before they locked her ID—and without ID, it would be impossible to pass the scan.

She thought of Backmann. He was her contact person on the outside that she'd been in touch with over the past few days, and he would help her. Her mind raced. Elisabeth quickly opened a communication program on another screen and dialed Backmann's private number, the one he strongly instructed her to use only in case of emergency.

After a couple of seconds, the holoscreen flickered.

"Yes?" Nicholas Backmann responded.

Elisabeth leaned close to the screen, nearly touching it with her forehead.

"I'm compromised. I need help to get out." Her breathing was erratic.

"Okay. Take it easy." He raised his hand in a calming gesture. "I'll help you. Get to your apartment as soon as you can. We'll send someone."

And with that, a massive stone fell from Elisabeth's chest.

"Thank you," she said. "Sir, I have amazing information. It changes everything."

Backmann nodded at her, and a weak smile pulled the corners of his mouth. "Good. Make sure you get to your apartment. Help is on its way."

Elisabeth returned Beckmann's nod and smile.

"Understood." She paused a few seconds before she continued, "and my father and his girlfriend. They need to come too. It won't be long before he's discovered."

Backmann gave a single nod and replied, "Okay, transportation for three."

"Thanks again," said Elisabeth, and she ended the call and pushed back her chair.

Immediately, she started a cleaning program that would sweep the tracks after her. The program began systematically destroying data on the servers. It would be all but impossible to recreate processes after the program had cleared the servers, she thought. At least, she hoped so.

It didn't matter. It would take time for them to try to recreate what she'd done if it would even succeed at all. That would be all the valuable time she and her dad would need to escape. She wiped her sweaty hands on her pants and looked around the room.

She would not come back here. They had discovered that she'd been about to steal the greatest discovery in human history; she had been caught. A cold drop of sweat slid down her spine, and despite the heat in the room, she shivered. She pulled the white lab coat tighter around her. She abruptly stood up, and the chair clattered to the floor behind her.

The room was spinning. Elisabeth had to hold onto the desk for a few seconds while everything stabilized. She glanced at the screen; the cleaning program continued its work. It would chew through all the data that existed on the local servers, and after they were cleaned, it would also clean itself. If someone were to try to restart the system after it had been cleaned, all they would get was a system prompt. Everything would be gone, all evidence of her betrayal.

The understanding that her career at Tabula Rasa was over was bitter, but Elisabeth did not hesitate. What she had done was right. The discovery was not only Tabula Rasa's, and it was her duty to make sure it was shared with the world.

With a twinge of sadness, she looked around a final time and left the cleaning program to work in silence.

She wrapped the shawl tightly around herself, and then she disappeared through the door.

Sydney, Australia
2048-12-27

The glowing heat from the fireplace filled the room with a cozy, crackling sound, and the pleasant warmth spread throughout the room. The fireplace stood on one of the long side walls of the expansive, well-appointed room, and an extended oak dining table stood regally in the middle. The walls were covered with modern artwork, and the parquet floor had been newly refinished. The aroma of expertly-cooked food lay like a comfortable veil in the room.

Lawyer Dennis Topp was enjoying himself to the fullest as he sat with his beloved wife in their dining room. Their apartment was their fixed point in life, their home base, the place where he was safe. There, he could retreat and take a break from his pressing work.

Dennis looked up at his wife, who sat opposite him, and smiled. Kathy was beautiful, so beautiful it almost hurt. She'd always been so. When they had met almost twenty-five years ago, his first thought had been that she was the most beautiful woman he had ever seen. She had a cute upturned nose and a smile that could make a man feel blessed with eternal happiness.

From the very first moment he'd seen her, he'd been hooked. When they had met, she'd already had a boyfriend, but the day after she'd met Dennis, she had broken up with the other guy, and Dennis and Kathy had begun dating regularly. It had been a whirlwind. They'd been obsessed with each other, and if it hadn't been for Kathy holding back as much as she could, they would have been married within a month.

He considered himself the luckiest man in the world. There were probably not many people in life who could say they were as happy as he was. He had a wonderful wife, an important job, and a fantastic apartment. Life was a gift, and he had truly won the lottery of life, the gamble all people participated in. Dennis grinned at his wife as he put his glass down, then smacked loudly with his lips.

"That was probably the best salmon I've ever eaten, my beloved wife. You've outdone yourself again."

Kathy Topp smiled warmly at her husband. She had been the chef in this relationship the whole time they'd been together, but she still felt gratified when Dennis praised her cooking. And he'd always made a point to do so.

Kathy liked spending time in the kitchen, putting together delicious dishes and pastries. At the moment, she was inspired by the Nordic cuisine, and so she and Dennis had enjoyed both Swedish meatballs and Danish butter bread over the last week. It had been with her cooking that she had caught Dennis when they'd originally started dating; she thought of it now as they sat over their empty plates, and the memory made her giggle.

Dennis smiled at her quizzically. "What are you laughing about? Don't you think I'm telling the truth? The salmon was actually amazingly good."

She took his hand and kissed it lightly. "My Dennis. Of course I believe it. I know you like my cooking—I've known that since I warmed up that lasagna on our very first date."

"Yes," he agreed, grinning, "that lasagna was probably the most capable lasagna in the history of the world. It's not often that so much good comes from a lasagna."

Kathy laughed and sipped her wine. "By the way," she asked, "how is it going with the compilation of testimonies?"

"It's going pretty good, actually. We expect to be ready in a couple of days, and then it has to be officially cleared with the prosecutor if charges can be brought." He paused and said, "If we proceed, which I really hope we do, then we can count on it that there will be a couple of turbulent months ahead of us."

"I'll be there for you all the way, you know that. Not only because you're my husband, but you're also a shining knight for many women, women who have passed on. They don't have a voice, but you can fight for their justice."

The past months had already been turbulent. Dennis and his colleague, Mary Thompson, had worked on something that truly was something of a bombshell. In addition to their work with the prosecutor, with the help of a journalist, they would be publishing a series of articles exposing the dark, dirty parts of John Vendrick III's career and the bloody trail he'd left behind him.

The month ahead of them would be tough, but Dennis had to do this. It was a calling born a few years ago, when an awful event had taken place.

In his mind, it was just like yesterday. A woman had contacted him; she had been desperate for his help. The woman had been named Louise Dorr, a young woman from Canada. Louise had contacted him because she had seen his name in the newspaper in an article that described Dennis' pro-bono work.

Her story had, at first, seemed too strange to be true; it had been a while before Dennis had accepted her tale as true. Louise had told him how she'd worked for one of the middle managers from Tabula Rasa, a man stationed in Toronto to take care of the Tabula Rasa application center there. Louise had worked as a sort of assistant to the man, and in the beginning, the job had been exciting and interesting.

Her tasks had been to plan and book various meetings and to help him with other small things that needed to be arranged. But after a couple of months at work, John Vendrick III had made a visit to their application center and had met Louise himself. He had taken a liking to her, and in the evening, he had knocked on the door of her apartment, where she had lived in downtown Toronto. He had forced his way into the apartment, and despite her screams and attempts to fight back, he had raped her.

Afterward, she had threatened to press charges, but John had promised to ruin her life if she did—and Louise had believed him. Her boss had persuaded her not to go through with the charges. John Vendrick III had been a rising star and moved in the finest social circles.

Louise had tried to forget the whole thing and move on with her life, but John hadn't let her. He had forced her to stay at her workplace, and slowly but surely, he had broken her. Gone were her job responsibilities and tasks. John began to lock her in at his apartment, and after a while, she was completely in his power.

With psychological and physical terror, he had taken control over her. He had started to rape her on a regular basis, comforting her afterward when she cried. Louise had soon lost all perception of time and space. But one day, John had made a mistake. He'd dropped a key to the hallway floor, and after he was gone, Louise had managed to escape. Panicking, and with only the clothes on her body, she fled without any idea of where to go.

Dennis shuddered thinking of the fear she must have felt. He had just closed the door to his office when he'd heard footsteps behind him. It had been Louise Dorr who stood there, scared and with an expression on her face that Dennis would never forget. She had sold a tiny diamond ring, and with the money, she'd been able to get out of town.

He could still see the desperate expression on her face. Dennis had helped her, and Louise had told him everything. She had told of her background and about the man who had done this to her. Dennis had promised to help. He helped her find a place in a sheltered accommodation where she could live until they were able to find a more permanent living situation.

Everything had gone the right way, but soon they found out that Louise was pregnant with John Vendrick III's child. Despite all that had happened, she had decided to keep the baby.

Ultimately, though, that's not how it would turn out. One early morning, Louise had taken a walk near the sheltered accommodation. As she'd been crossing the street, a car had run her over. Witnesses later said that Louise had crossed the street on a pedestrian crosswalk, and the walk light had been green. The car that hit her had not braked but rather had seemed to accelerate. Neither the car nor the driver had been found, but Dennis knew John Vendrick III had been behind it to avoid being involved in a scandal.

Louise had been thrown twelve meters away and had broken fourteen bones. She'd still been alive when the ambulance had delivered her to the hospital, but two hours later, while Dennis stood by and held her hand, both she and her unborn child had died.

After that, he had sworn to give Louise Dorr vindication. He'd contacted various colleagues and made some inquiries. After a year of investigation, Dennis had learned that what John had done to Louise, he had also done to several other women. All these women had either died or disappeared in one way or another.

John Vendrick III was a monster, Dennis had realized; behind the presentable facade hid a psychopath and a sadist who enjoyed tormenting other people. Dennis and a colleague had collected a considerable amount of evidence, and they would soon go to court with it.

Dennis and Mary had worked obsessively in recent months, and now they would present their evidence to the prosecutor. They'd already had some initial meetings with the attorney who assisted them. The prosecutor was known as a hard but fair man, and Dennis had an optimistic attitude. They had done everything they could. They had searched and found seven other victims who had all encountered Vendrick, and now his rampage would soon be stopped.

Dennis smiled at his wife and took her hand. He was proud of her. Proud that he had her as his wife—not only because she was the most beautiful woman he'd ever seen, but also because of her sense of justice, her unconquerable attitude that evil must be fought, whatever the cost. He turned his face toward the fireplace and watched the flames dance. Then he turned back to Kathy.

"That's the reassurance I need, my dear." He smiled, but his smile was concerned. "John Vendrick is a powerful man. If we get the go-ahead in the meeting with the prosecutor and he chooses to go through with it, we can expect a minor storm—not only because we'll have to endure the inevitable media chaos, but also because of all the top lawyers who will do everything to crush us."

Tabula Rasa, Madagascar
2048-12-27

Offense is the best defense.

Sweat beaded on Elisabeth's forehead, and she used her shawl to dry it. She was sure they were coming after her, but she could not give up. The alarm must have gone off in the control room, and that was why they had shut her down. Her thoughts raced. She had to get out of there as fast as possible. It was her only hope; she must get out, and she must find her dad.

She raced up the metal staircase that led from the control room where she'd been. The staircase was deserted, and she thanked her lucky stars. The sterile light from the fluorescent lamps gave the skin on the backs of her hands a sick, pasty look.

She stopped on the third-floor landing; just beyond it was an operations room she had to pass through if she was going to manage to get out of the lab. She peered at the closed door—above it shone a green sign labeled *Exit/Sortie*. (All signs at Tabula Rasa were labeled in both English and French.) She wasn't sure how much time she had, but it couldn't be much. Elisabeth took a deep breath, clenched her fists, and sprinted to the door. Softly, she touched the sensor. The door slid sideways, and she walked in.

Inside the room, computers buzzed as usual, the screens all illuminated, but no one was there. She exhaled heavily. Elisabeth tried to regain composure, but the room felt unreal, hostile. She had spent countless hours here, sometimes together with other technicians, but usually alone. Data monitoring wasn't the sexiest of tasks you could have, but she rather liked it. She enjoyed the feeling of seeing data from all Tabula Rasa's satellites streaming down to operations rooms like this.

But now the surroundings felt unfamiliar. Her hands trembled when she lifted them. She balled them into fists again and pulled them to her belly. She stood there a few seconds, took a deep breath, and regained some of the control she had lost. As she'd fled, she had lost orientation of where she was. Her body had gone into shock, but she knew if she could get out to the public sections of Tabula Rasa, her chances of staying hidden would increase significantly.

With more than a million people in Tabula Rasa, Elisabeth would have a chance to stay out of sight, and if she could get out to the main parks, she could buy some time. The officials weren't able to track each person directly. In the beginning, when Tabula Rasa was new, all residents had a tiny computer chip implanted under the skin—it provided authorities the precise location of each person—but after a while, it turned out that this wasn't an optimal solution. After the system had been in place for a couple of months, they had seen a violent increase in paranoia and mental breakdowns from the constant surveillance.

After this traumatic time, the mega-complex's leaders had chosen to change the system. Instead, a voluntary system had been implemented that allowed each resident to decide whether the system could follow where he or she went. Everyone had been given a hologram bracelet—an H-band—which monitored all biological functions as well as communications of the carrier and his or her location.

But if the carrier took off the H-band, the system lost the exact position. In the first year, officials had naively believed that almost everyone would voluntarily wear it at all times. When only half the residents had been reported as wearing it on a regular basis, the policy changed again and it became a requirement to wear the H-band. It was forbidden to take it off. Predictably, mental illness had increased again.

After a couple of months, Tabula Rasa's inhabitants and the whole of the complex had experienced another traumatic period with fires and riots. Afterward, they concluded that every person needed a certain amount of freedom and that the system could not enforce one hundred percent control. Vendrick and the management of Tabula Rasa wanted to avoid similar problems in the future at all cost and had permanently switched back to a totally voluntary system.

Now, Elisabeth looked at her H-band. The time read a quarter to nine. As she tried to decide what to do, the operations room door opened and her colleague Mike came in. Mike was tall—over one meter and ninety centimeters—and his big, wild hair stood straight out on end. His glasses were pushed so far down on his nose that he had to tilt his head back when he looked straight ahead.

"Hi, you." He smiled as he walked, coffee cup in hand, toward a desk.

Her mind raced. "Hello." She flashed what she hoped was a convincingly "Elisabeth-like" smile.

Mike set the coffee cup down and pushed aside a few books that lay dangerously close to the edge of the table.

"How's it going?" Mike asked. "You look like you've seen a ghost." He laughed lightheartedly.

Elisabeth struggled to sound normal but heard her voice come out a few pitches too high, a few beats too fast. "No, not at all. A couple of problems with the data transfer, but nothing serious. I tried to fix it by downloading a couple of new protocols from the main system."

Mike raised his eyebrows and nodded thoughtfully. "Okay, good." He picked up his coffee and continued,

"It'll be great when headquarters finally takes some time to update that entire part of the system. It's ridiculous that it's taking so long for them to get it done."

Mike turned to her with a meaningful look, obviously expecting her agreement. Elisabeth gave him a strained smile.

"Yes, absolutely ridiculous."

Mike pulled out his chair and sat down at the desk. Elisabeth walked over to another desk, picked up some papers, and pretended to read. A couple of minutes passed. Her thoughts swirled. She had to get out of here, but she couldn't just leave before their shift was over—Mike would be suspicious. But she must get out, out and up to the parks. From there, she could get to her apartment unnoticed, and then on to her dad's place.

Mike had picked up a small scanner, apparently working to debug it. Elisabeth sat no more than five meters behind him, watching his back while he worked. The small cameras embedded in the ceilings rotated in their normal rhythm, but she knew she couldn't continue to sit there like a petrified penguin. She rose and pretended to read something on her phone.

"Oh—I have to get up to the control room on seventh to get a pair of crypto keys to install the new protocols." She shrugged her shoulders theatrically and muttered, "Damn it."

Mike glanced at her doubtfully. "Can't they just send the crypto keys?"

Elisabeth grimaced. "No idea, but it's probably best I go up, don't you think?" She pointed to the scanner in his hand. "How is it going with that?"

"Well, a bad data chip. Nothing I can't fix." He looked at the broken device in his hand. Before Mike could say anything else, Elisabeth disappeared through the door, calling over her shoulder, "Good luck with it."

Mike looked up at the closing door and frowned.

* * *

The big elevator slowed softly and stopped. The doors opened with a fizzling sound and Elisabeth stepped out. The murmur of human voices reached her, and she instinctively took a step back. She was at ground level now; the doors had opened to the outdoors, to central park, which was shaped like a figure eight and was more than six hundred meters at its widest point. It was filled with people talking and laughing. Her pulse calmed down as she looked at the tall trees stretching upward.

The air was pleasantly warm. It would have been a great day for a walk in the park, and maybe she would have gone down to the two lakes if she hadn't been on the run. Now was not the time for a relaxing trip.

She stood with her back to the elevators. Ten or twelve people moved around her, some on the way into an elevator, others on their way out. A group of people, all dressed in dark red monk-like suits with gold-colored belts and bare feet, slowly shuffled as one through the crowd of people.

She recognized them as Undicier. The crowd opened for the group and the robed men walked through it. All the Undicier were smiling with arms outstretched as they approached people, ready to embrace them. Elisabeth froze when a tall one came up to her and took her in his arms. The tall man looked down at her and beamed.

"How is my child doing? Are you ready for salvation?"

93

Elisabeth looked up at his pockmarked face and grinned awkwardly. "Thank you, but I think it's too late for me."

She took a step back and hurried on. In front of her was the oval-shaped road that surrounded the central park. On the road in front of her, traffic flowed clockwise. Small, silent vehicles slid in and out of the traffic—they pulled over to drop off passengers or pick up new ones, and then slid out again.

There was no need to have your own car in Tabula Rasa. The traffic system was structured so that with a payment card you had access to all the transport systems available. You could use all vehicles, cars, boats, slides, and elevators. You paid only for the distance you traveled. The system was used to its fullest, as almost no one owned a vehicle; personally owned cars just would simply sit at home collecting dust. Only a few of the very highest positions in Tabula Rasa had access to private transportation, except for the police and rescue services.

Elisabeth's dad lived across the park, just over a five minutes' walk from where she was. To get there, she could either go through the park on foot or use one of the many taxis that circulated on the main road, but she had to hurry.

They were after her, and both she and her father were in danger.

She took off her H-band. When a taxi slowly slipped past, she held her breath and tossed it in the direction of the car's luggage rack. It was a good throw—it landed in the rack and got lodged on a bar. She smiled with satisfaction as the taxi glided away, then she swiftly walked across the main street on foot and disappeared into the park.

Sydney, Australia
2048-12-27

The salmon's delicious aroma lingered in the room.
Dennis and Kathy both helped clear the table, and
when they were about to set it again for their dessert,
the holotelephone rang in the living room.

Kathy continued to lay out the plates for the
fragrant tiramisu she had prepared. Dennis went into
the living room, sat down on the couch, and then
noticed that the dessert spoon was still in his right
hand. He held onto the spoon as he pressed the
button to activate the holophone, which was built into
their coffee table.

Four thin, arched metal arms had been installed on
the edges of the coffee table; above them, when you
used the holophone, a hologram was projected of the
person you spoke with. The lamp under the
holotelephone flashed green to indicate that it was
active.

"Hi, it's Dennis."

Silence. The space above the metal arms was
empty. He wondered if the holotelephone could be
malfunctioning—it did that at times—so he moved his
hand in the air where the hologram would normally
be. His fingers sparkled with the projector lights; the
phone was on. Slowly, he leaned forward.

"Hello? Is anybody there?"

He waited. Nothing. The seconds passed by. He
thought he heard someone breathing, but wasn't sure.
No shadows moved, no face appeared. There was no
clicking sound to indicate the call had ended, either.
The silence dragged on. Just when Dennis was about
to press the button to hang up, he heard a faint
sound. He listened for a couple more seconds.

The sound came again. It was weak, but it was
there. There was still no hologram in front of him, but

he heard something that resembled a voice—that he was sure of. He couldn't understand what the voice said, but it was clearly saying something.

Dennis struggled to understand and leaned even closer. It sounded like the voice was repeating the same words over and over. No matter how hard he focused, he couldn't understand what it was saying. He sat there for several seconds, looking intently in front of him at the empty air. Nothing moved. The green light continued to flash.

"Hello?" he tried again.

The voice was thin and shadowy as if someone were talking into a box.

Without warning, the holotelephone clicked, the green light went out, and the call was lost. Dennis pursed his lips and wondered if someone was trying to play a joke on him. But somehow, instinct told him it was not a prank. The discomfort within him grew. He stayed seated for a few seconds, uncertain of what he should do.

"Who was it?" Kathy called from the kitchen.

He shook his head and hesitated.

"Nobody. Wrong number."

He stared at holophone as if it might ring again at any moment. Kathy stuck her head out through the doorway.

"That was a long conversation with someone who dialed the wrong number," she said, her face skeptical. Dennis looked at her, wearing a puzzled look, and rose.

"Yes, it was. There was definitely someone there, but I couldn't hear what she said."

"She?"

Dennis nodded. "Yes, it was a woman. I'm sure of it."

He hesitated a couple of seconds. That had been weird. He stood to leave the living room to help Kathy but had only taken three steps when the holotelephone rang again.

Kathy poked her head around the corner with a cheeky smile. "You can tell your mistress to call another day," she teased. "You're busy having dessert with me."

She giggled. He wrinkled his nose and shook his head as he walked back to the couch and sat down again.

"How could I have a mistress? My heart belongs to you."

Dennis pressed the button again but said nothing this time. The green light was illuminated a second time, but the air above the holophone arms was still empty. A mute, hollow silence spread out in the room. It spoke to him but said nothing. Kathy was still standing and leaning her upper body through the living room doorway. She looked at Dennis.

"Who is it?" she asked, sounding more serious now.

Dennis didn't answer. He stared at the empty air in front of him and lost himself in it. Fascinated, he watched something dark and glittering materialize in front of him. Weak, thin shadows moved hypnotically above the coffee table. He tried to make out what the shadows were. There was a strange pulsating sound now, like the voice he'd heard earlier, but a little bit different somehow. It was faint, like a whisper, all but inaudible. As the seconds passed, however, it became clearer and clearer.

It was a voice—a woman's voice. The same voice he'd heard before.

Dennis stared, enchanted, at the swirling shadows and he leaned forward to listen more closely. He couldn't distinguish the words, but the voice sounded scared, frantic. It kept repeating the same thing as a robot stuck in an infinite loop. Kathy now stood behind Dennis. She put her hand on his shoulder.

"What's happening?" An edge of worry had crept into her voice.

Dennis shook his head slowly, his eyes squinted in confused concentration. The voice sounded like it had something important to say. Something that could not wait. It was pushing, becoming more and more agitated. More desperate to be heard, he thought.

He turned to Kathy and saw her eyes widening. She lifted her hand and pointed past him at the shadows above the coffee table. Her lips moved, but he couldn't understand what she said.

Dennis turned back to face the shadows that had now adopted a more solid shape. He froze. A creeping feeling of horror grabbed hold of him, and he looked down and saw that he was still holding the dessert spoon in his hand.

The shadows were coming together, forming the shape of a face in various shades of gray.

It was a face filled with terror. A woman's face. Her eyes were wide open and wild; Dennis clearly saw the whites surrounding her pupils. The woman looked to be dark-haired, maybe around thirty years old. Pretty. But her beautiful features were disfigured with fear, and her lips moved silently, frantically.

Then, suddenly, Kathy and Dennis were thrown back as the woman's voice penetrated the darkness of the shadows with full force.

"Help! Help me! Please, please!"

The jungle, Costa Rica
2048-12-27

In this place, the light was no match for the darkness.
The sharp beam emanating from Lisa's flashlight made
no impact on the gloom in front of her. She took a few
deep breaths and continued her descent into the cave.
The silence was almost deafening.

She walked with bent knees, and Tim followed right
behind her. The uneven surface forced her to move
carefully so as not to stumble. Her backpack
contained several glow sticks—the kind that emitted a
green light when activated. She stopped and pulled
out three of them, snapped them, and threw them in
front of her. Three green spots of light landed on the
path ahead, revealing that the surface was a mixture
of rocks, stones, and smaller pebbles.

"How does it look? Do you see a good way
through?" Tim asked.

Lisa studied the terrain in front of her. "Yes, I think
so. There seems to be a slightly better passage near
the left edge. If we walk about ten meters along the
cliff wall, we'll arrive at that plateau over there."

She pointed, and Tim nodded. Slowly and with
extreme caution, she pushed on. Each step was well-
balanced. She slipped once but managed to stay
upright.

"You good?"

"Yeah," she called back, keeping her eyes on the
ground.

Finally, Lisa had covered the ten meters to a small
ledge. Behind her, with experienced hands, Tim fed
out the rope, which now lay like a long snake between
them.

"What's it like over there? Is there a passage?" Tim's
voice echoed faintly against the walls. He usually liked
caves and enjoyed exploring them, but this one gave

him the creeps. There was something about it he couldn't quite put his finger on. Normally, you could hear the echo of the sounds that bounced against the cave's hard walls, but in this one, Tim could barely hear any echo at all.

Lisa squinted at the darkness. It was even more compact than before. No matter how much she moved the flashlight back and forth, she saw no contours of anything in front of her.

"Maybe," she replied. "It's so dark that I can't see anything. Wait just a minute—I'll throw out some more glow sticks." She cracked three more of them and tossed them ahead. Two of them hit the side walls, and the third ended up a little further along than the others.

The ghostly green glow gave the passage an almost supernatural appearance. The narrow passage continued from the plateau she was on, and in the weak light, she could see that it continued for about ten meters before tapering off slightly to the right. The roof and walls sloped downward and inward, making the passage resemble a narrowing tube. Lisa shivered. It was colder than this type of cave ought to be. She was experienced. She had explored quite a few cave systems in the past, and she had always enjoyed the challenge they presented. This one did not feel as exciting. She turned to Tim.

"Tell Lars to bring a couple of our floodlights so we can see more of what this really looks like."

Tim nodded. "Back in a minute." He doubled back, speaking into his radio. After about five minutes, he returned with Lars and two powerful lamps that were each about a meter high. Tim found a relatively flat surface and set the first one up; when he turned it on, it spread a bright light to a distance of fifteen meters. Lisa heard Lars struggling with the second lamp. Tim laughed.

"Take it easy, young man."

Lars was panting. "Yeah, that's probably a good idea."

They continued on, Lars in the rear, carrying the second lamp. The three of them spaced themselves out as they walked.

Lisa had rounded the corner and gone just ten meters further when she saw a faint glow. It wasn't from the floodlight; this light looked supernatural. She'd never seen anything like it. She was several meters in the lead, and as she got closer, she clearly saw a faint blue pulsating light in the distance.

"Do you see that?" she asked the others.

"What?" called Tim.

Lisa, her attention rapt ahead, didn't answer. She continued forward and stopped when she was two meters from the source of the light. Here, at the end of the cave, a blue aura poured from a sphere. Lisa froze. She heard Tim speak, but didn't comprehend what he'd said. It was like she was immersed in a pool, and Tim stood at the edge of it as he spoke to her.

She stared at the sphere, unsure whether it was even real. It was small—maybe thirty centimeters in diameter. She couldn't tell what it was made of. At first, she thought it was metal, but when she saw the weak light that played over its surface, she knew it was made of something else.

The light that moved over the surface of the sphere seemed alive. It danced, forming different patterns that disappeared as quickly as they had appeared.

Lisa took a step closer; she wasn't afraid. Instead, she was filled with a sense of calm. The sphere would not hurt her, she was sure about that. A few seconds passed before she realized that the sphere wasn't resting on the cave floor, and she gasped. It floated weightlessly a hand's breadth above the ground.

Tim was beside her now. He didn't say anything as he stared at the sphere floating in front of them. Lisa also stood silent, unmoving, a statue.

As she stared at the sphere, it seemed to talk to her, except without words. It was a feeling unlike anything she'd experienced. It was like a voice, one she didn't understand, that spoke to her from within herself.

She turned to Tim and tilted her head, as you do when listening for something. How long they stood there, she did not know. She heard Lars shout. His voice seemed far away. Blurry. Unclear. She tried to turn toward the voice but did not know where it had come from.

In a voice louder than Lars', but that only Lisa could hear, it called her; she stood there, nailed to the floor, unable to move.

Lars had called for Lisa and Tim to wait, but when nobody had answered, he'd overcome his fear of the deep darkness and headed into it after them. Now, he discovered them both standing in front of a bright, shining sphere hanging in thin air.

Slowly he moved closer to Tim and Lisa. He said their names, but neither reacted.

"Tim, you hear me? Lisa?" The supernatural light from the sphere gave the cave a surrealistic appearance. Blueish light flicked over the rough stone walls, and shadows danced over the floor where they were standing.

Small puddles of water on the floor were filled with a ghostly shine. Slowly, Lars leaned forward, grabbed Lisa's shoulder, and squeezed lightly with his hand. She didn't move. Lars squeezed harder. He saw something glimmer on the ground under the sphere—a disc of gold with green inlays. The sphere floated directly above it. Small strings of glimmering stars glided between the sphere and the disc. The sight was hypnotizing.

"Lisa!"

Lisa shook and seemed to come to life beneath his hand. She turned around and looked blankly at Lars.

"Don't you see?" she asked distantly.

Lars gave her a surprised look. "Yes, I see. I see that you and Tim are completely gone. It's time to go. We have to get out of here."

She answered with a soft voice, "Lars, it's all right. It's really all right."

Lars shook his head. "Lisa, it's really time to go now. You and Tim have got to turn back and get out of here now."

Lisa smiled at him. "Tim, too. He's coming with us." Lisa gently grabbed Tim's arm.

"Tim, honey. It's time to go."

Tim was mesmerized by the sphere, and at first, Lisa's voice did not affect him. To her surprise, Lisa saw tears running down his cheeks.

"Tim, baby. We need to go. It's time to leave."

Tim wobbled and nodded weakly. "Yes, you're right." He faced Lisa and a feeling of joy rose within him.

Outside Paris, France
2048-12-28

The decay of the society was not apparent, but it was
there, like a concealed disease waiting to break out.
The sun had descended below the horizon, but the
remaining heat in the air still made the evening feel
hot. It had taken Jonathan half a day's traveling to get
here, and now he was in the countryside just outside
of Paris.

The sound of crickets chirped vaguely in the air and
mixed with the twittering from some swallows racing
past. A little further down the long, dusty dirt road
where he was standing was a huge bakery that
delivered artisan bread to exclusive parts of Paris. The
bakers were in full swing preparing for the night shift.
The bakery's products were only for society's elite, and
in the past few years, they had needed to hire guards
to chase off intruders and thieves.

On a dented sign, the road name read *Rue de
Maincourt*. Jonathan studied the aging, seemingly
abandoned barn that loomed in front of him.

The delectable scent of freshly baked bread mixed
with the weak odor of burning tires that rolled in from
the west. Although it had been forbidden for many
years, some smaller, shady industries still illegally
burned their waste. It was strictly forbidden and came
with hefty fines if they were caught. But the
authorities couldn't be everywhere, and there were
plenty of factions that fought over power in general
and money in particular.

Jonathan shook his head and continued to walk
toward the barn in front of him. He had been recruited
by a friend of his mother's. The friend's name was
Nicholas Backmann, and he led a small but profitable
enterprise called The Amber Group. The name had
originated from the first mission the group had carried

out—to locate and return the original Amber room to its rightful owner.

The Amber Room was something truly amazing, regarded by many as the eighth wonder of the world. In 1716, the Prussian King, William I, had given the room as a gift to the Russian Tsar Peter the Great. It had been assembled in the Catherine Palace outside of St. Petersburg. The room was made of amber, gold, precious stones, and mirrors; it had taken more than fifteen years to build. When visitors entered the magnificent room, they were overwhelmed by an explosion of various shades of gold and extravagance.

During World War II, the room was dismantled by German soldiers, transported away, and hidden. All attempts to relocate it had failed. But at the beginning of 2042, a German businessman had contacted Backmann to continue the search, and he had been interested in the assignment. It turned out that the businessman had access to secret information from World War II that allowed the group to focus their investigations on a narrow area where the Amber room might be hidden.

It had been found in an abandoned mine in eastern Germany, and Backmann and his group had, together with the businessman, delivered it to the Russian and German authorities. From that first successful mission, the seed of business had grown and today they had ten employees. The group he belonged to was not big, but they had considerable resources behind them.

Although the worst heat that had reigned during the day had passed, Jonathan would probably never really get used to the warmer climate that covered these parts of Europe, turning it into an oven for the last months of the year. It was at that time of the year that millions of people fled the big capitals and searched for a refuge at coastal cities.

In the last decades, the heat that was normally retained in Africa during the summer months had started to crawl further north later in the year. This had cause shifts in the seasons. Small, isolated areas in southern France had started to appear more and more like deserts.

Jonathan frowned. His shirt clung to his back. He took off his sunglasses and put them in his shirt pocket. The barn in front of him was shabby, worn, and seemed mostly to contain laid-off agricultural machinery and old industrial materials. It was long, maybe thirty meters along the side. He looked up at a row of broken windows on the upper floor; it looked like a vandal had systematically smashed every glass pane that could be destroyed.

Rust had taken a firm grip on the sheet metal, and the red, dark paint was flaking from it. Small cracks had gotten hold between the pieces of sheet metal and seemed to tear the building to pieces.

But he knew it was all a charade. The Amber Group employed some of the world's best camouflage experts, and they had been given free hands. The house was designed to appear as anonymous as possible, resembling hundreds of other barns in the area. The dirty paint peeled from the walls and rust and weeds were allowed to spread as much as their hearts desired.

Under the surface, however, there was something else. The whole place was packed with the latest technology, and the four floors contained equipment that would make any spy organization in the world green with envy.

A narrow dirt path stretched from the road and winded its way up to the gates. The gravel crunched lightly under Jonathan's feet. He walked up to a rusty speakerphone that hung from a gate. It looked like it could fall off the wall at any time. He pressed the only button there was and waited.

He knew that scanners were sweeping over him, that at least two pairs of eyes were watching him at that very moment. Small, invisible rays swept over him and searched his body for weapons.

A few seconds passed, and one of the small, rusty doors opened with a click. Jonathan entered. It was noticeably cooler inside—the hair on his arms stood up. He passed another scanner and went through a hall, and a metal door opened automatically. The room he entered was bright and decorated in a contemporary style. Two glass walls reached from the ceiling to the floor, leading the visitor to a long, modern reception area. A middle-aged, cheerful woman stood waiting for him. She smiled.

"Hello, Jonathan, everything okay?" said Dolores Lee. She was the receptionist and the individual who knew all the gossip about everyone in the Group. Dolores wasn't fat per se, but heavy-set in a way that makes female shapes more accentuated. Her dark hair swayed; it was easy to see that she liked to toss it around.

Jonathan opened his arms. "Hello, Dolores. Yes, thank you, everything is fine. How's it going with such a beautiful woman as yourself?"

She smiled even wider and slapped him playfully on the arm.

"You charmer. You know how to handle women."

Dolores was the kind of person who had a strange ability to get people to confide in her. This trait helped feed her limitless appetite for gossip, fueled by the Group's social life.

He laughed. "No, not at all. My romantic conquests are probably not as impressive as yours."

She hugged him again and pulled him closer, this time a little more seriously. "How's it going with Chantelle?"

He'd known the question would come, but it still hurt. Chantelle had been Jonathan's wife for two short, wonderful years. They'd had a child, Kristina, and their little family's happiness had been limitless. It had been the most joyous time of his life. He and Chantelle had laughed together, they had grown together, and they had done everything a young couple on the threshold to adulthood would do.

But when Kristina was eight months old, she had become sick. It had started as a cold that didn't seem to go away; after a couple of weeks, both Chantelle and Jonathan knew that Kristina was sicker than they had originally thought.

It had been cancer. A rare, aggressive form of leukemia. He had screamed and cried. He had punched and slammed the walls until his fists were bleeding. Chantelle and he had done everything to protect their child, but it hadn't helped. Approximately half of those diagnosed with leukemia survive. Children have a better chance of surviving than adults, and they had put their hope in that simple fact. But it hadn't mattered.

Their beloved Kristina had fought bravely, but the cancer had been so powerful and malignant that it had taken barely five months from the appearance of her first symptoms to her passing. Jonathan had been sitting with her in the hospital bed. Her body had been broken after all the chemotherapy and radiation, and she had lain in his arms, light as a feather. The chemo had melted away half her body weight; he could feel her bony skeleton through the hospital robe. Chantelle had been sitting beside them. Petrified. Immobile. Beyond grief.

Kristina had lain in his arms soundlessly. She'd been so dazed by the toxins and cancer that she could no longer open her eyes. Endless minutes had passed. He had listened to her weak breathing become shallower and shallower until he'd wondered if he hadn't noticed that she'd passed away.

At that point, the tears on his cheeks had dried a long time ago. He had sat there, as a father. A father who'd had his heart torn out of his chest. Kristina had twitched. The little girl had opened her eyes, looked at him, and taken a deep breath, defying life and death and all the pain she had to endure. Jonathan had known the poor child just didn't want to feel out of breath anymore, even for just a few seconds. She had smiled at him and placed her head against his chest, and he knew, he knew she'd left him just then, right there.

The days after that had been a blur. He and Chantelle had supported each other, but as the weeks and months went by, they drifted further apart. They did not find their way back to each other but were reminded of their loss every time they looked at one another. He had tried, she as well, but they had not been able to find that special connection again. Something vital had been lost—an innocence, perhaps. Jonathan wasn't sure.

He had lain on his bed sleepless for many nights, tossing and turning and trying to find a way out of the maze they had gotten into.

They had divorced six months after Kristina's passing. In less than half a year, Jonathan had lost his wonderful family, and the grief still tore up his insides. It was two years ago now, and he had thrown himself into his studies. He and Chantelle had tried to continue to see each other, but it had been difficult. They met sometimes for a cup of coffee or a walk, but he got the feeling that every time they met, they were even further away from each other.

His eyes met Dolores'. "It's going okay," he said shortly.

There wasn't much more to say. He had experienced the whole gamut of feelings this past year, and it wasn't until now, over the last few months, that he had slept an entire night.

There was compassion in Dolores' eyes. "Tell her that she's in my prayers."

"I will," he said and looked away.

Dolores gave him an extra hug and pointed over her shoulder. "He's waiting for you."

Jonathan smiled and walked toward the heavy elevator door, grateful that she'd let it rest.

After another scanning and more voice samples and fingerprints, another set of elevator doors opened. It went down three floors. After yet another fingerprint scan, he finally arrived at Backmann's office. It was located at the bottom of the complex; Jonathan knocked on the door.

"Come in," a voice sounded from inside the office.

The jungle, Costa Rica
2048-12-28

It wasn't an easy choice. In the tent sat Dr. Lisa King, deeply absorbed in her thoughts. The soft, damp scent of the jungle surrounded her. She sat at the work desk, and in the light of the small but strong battery-powered lamps, she looked at the floating sphere in front of her, fascinated.

The surface of the sphere was bizarre—silvery, yet not silver. Small swirls moved over its face, gliding in and out of each other and creating one incredible pattern after another.

She went over the last day in her head and what it had implicated. They had dragged a metal box into the cave and had placed it under the sphere. She'd had no idea how they would get the sphere down into the box, but it had worked out by itself. While she, Tim, and Lars had been talking about how they would do it, the sphere itself had, without warning, started to descend. The three of them had stood still, hypnotized, while the sphere had sunk down and placed itself inside the box. It had almost been as if the sphere itself demonstrated intelligence.

Lisa reflected on the potential consequences what they'd done would have for them. They had obviously discovered something amazing. The question now was how they should proceed. They couldn't stay there in the jungle. She had spoken to Backmann the day before, who had asked her to bring the sphere to the Amber Group in Paris, but Lisa wasn't sure if that was the right choice. Of course, she trusted Backmann, but she was still uncertain.

Maybe, she thought, it would be best to give the sphere to the local authorities. After all, they were responsible for the area. But she suspected that if the authorities were informed, they would take over the excavation and Lisa and her team would be shut out—or worse. She simply couldn't be sure.

They could go to the press, but then it risked becoming a media circus they could not control. No matter how she approached the problem of how to proceed, Lisa couldn't find a workable solution.

Her thoughts were interrupted by Tim's entrance.

"How's it going?" Tim asked, walking up to her and putting a hand on her shoulder. The warmth from his hand penetrated the light fabric of her top.

"Well, it's all right I guess," she replied with a smile. "I'm glad you're here."

The warmth in his eyes could not be misunderstood. Tim gave her a gentle squeeze, then bent down and gave her a kiss. He pulled out a chair and sat down beside her. The shiny sphere lay in a box in front of them, and Tim gazed at it. There was something supernatural about it. The only somewhat similar thing Tim had seen had been in science fiction movies.

But even after all that had happened, he was not afraid. There was nothing in the experience with the sphere in the cave that made him feel alarmed. Curious, sure. Interested, no doubt. But not afraid.

It was warm and humid in the tent. The hot Costa Rican sun heated up the surroundings so much during the day that by late in the evening, it was still warm and comfortable.

Tim studied the sphere with fascination. "What do you think it is?"

Lisa chuckled humorlessly. "What it is? I haven't got a clue what it is." Her voice carried a hint of frustration. "What do *you* think it is?"

Tim glanced at her and back at the sphere. "Something we haven't seen before. Something that's not from this world."

Lisa shook her head and tapped the table softly with her fingers. The sphere was still floating—it hovered a couple of centimeters above the bottom of the box. Small, shining swirls moved on the surface of it like clouds gliding in the sky. The swirls seemed to rise from inside the sphere and swim along the surface, only to be replaced by new swirls.

Tim's voice was soft. "And now what? What do think we should do now?"

Lisa's thoughts raced. Which way should they choose? There were pros and cons with all the alternatives. The Amber Group was contributing to a large part of the excavation, so it was natural that they'd want to be part of this discovery. She had also promised Backmann she'd bring it back, but she was reconsidering.

If they turned to NASA instead, or to one of the other space authorities, it would be complicated and maybe more dangerous. The Costa Ricans would be offended that they weren't informed, and if they found out they'd been intentionally left out of the loop on this, Lisa would surely be thrown out of the country, her excavation shut down immediately. And if they were to go to the press, it would all explode. Her mind spun.

*   *   *

In the second tent on a folding chair, Lars sat by his computer. A battery-powered lamp hung from the ceiling and spread its warm light. A fly buzzed angrily around him, and Lars slammed it with his palm when it landed on his leg.

He turned his eyes back to the screen in front of him. The last few hours had been spent surfing social

113

media sites and major news agencies. On CNN's website, he clicked on the latest live broadcast from Flor Fria. A small holo video faded in on the screen.

A light rain fell over the female journalist who stood in a red raincoat and spoke directly into the camera.

"Behind us, the riot continues in Flor Fria and the surrounding areas. Over the last twenty-four hours, several thousand people have been injured and over two hundred killed. Two of the factions have joined forces and are now combating the regular Chinese forces sent in to reclaim Macau and Flor Fria. Similar scenes are also playing out in Hong Kong, where confirmed reports mention up to one hundred and ten people killed."

As the reporter continued her monotonous relay, Lars stopped the video. For the next half hour, he continued to read and gather information, and then he shut down the computer. He swallowed nervously.

From his elevated position, John Vendrick III felt like a lion surveying his kingdom. This was what he was telling himself, anyway. The gnawing feeling of doubt in his own ability was kept well hidden, as always— even from himself.

The pleasant tones of Wagner's Tannhäuser overture caressed the room; he closed his eyes and focused on the masterful music.

John was tall, muscular, and had an aura that radiated power. His hair had started to gray at the temples, but, otherwise, he was a picture of virility. He kept himself in good shape, and you'd be hard-pressed to believe he had turned fifty a few days ago. Age hadn't been important to him—age, in his view, was something that one decided oneself.

He had always been aware of the importance of his physical appearance and what power a man could radiate if he wanted to dominate his surroundings. It was a lesson he had learned from his father. Today, he wore a pinstripe suit and dark Italian shoes.

He loved those shoes. Other than them, however, there wasn't much John liked about Italy, or the Italians, for that matter. But he couldn't deny that they made the best shoes in the world.

He had been to Europe several times and had once traveled through Italy. He'd hated every minute of it. *Agh,* he thought with disdain. *Those arrogant Italians who think Rome is the most beautiful city in the world.*

However, John had bought a major, Rome-based industrial company. It had been a big investment, and he had originally planned to stay there for a while to take over the company the right way. But it had been unbearable.

The company itself was healthy, and the finances were good, but the managers didn't have the same vision he did. He'd gotten rid of the entire senior management after a week and introduced his own people.

Inevitably, all his plans for the company had failed. The economic future that had at first seemed so promising had quickly turned into a nightmare of strikes, sabotage, and unexpected interruptions in production. It was clear he'd lost control of the situation; it wasn't until he'd conceded to reinstate the old management and agreed to several of their demands that the situation had been resolved—and then, only to an extent.

But his pride had suffered a blow. The project had demanded a lot of work on his side, and it had been a steep learning curve. After six months, he had sold the company, and then in the background, had launched a vicious attack.

He had used all the dirty tricks in the book to rip the company apart, and eventually, with bribes and threats, he had brought the company down to its knees. However, a small core of honest people had remained on the company's board and refused to give in.

Things came to a head when every member of that core had disappeared during a trip to one of the company's factories in northern Italy. Halfway through the flight, the plane had mysteriously banked hard and flipped upside down in the air; the pilot had increased the speed at the same time as he had pulled the stick.

During its violent descent, the plane began to tear into pieces—the speed it had been designed for was grossly exceeded. From their flight altitude of two thousand meters, it had only taken a few seconds for the plane to smash into the ground with devastating force. All seven people on board the plane had died instantly.

The subsequent investigation had been unable to determine the reason the pilot had taken all their lives.

Neither had the communication between the airplane and the control tower shed any light on the accident. What the investigation concluded was that the only viable reason was the pilot had used the plane to kill himself. However, during the investigation, they never found any motive of why the pilot would have committed suicide. The last communication air traffic control had had from the plane was that the pilot, without warning, had started screaming.

"No, no, they're coming, they're coming!" The shrieks continued for ten seconds on the recording obtained from the black box, and then stopped as abruptly as they began. The investigators never found the reason why the pilot started screaming, or what it meant.

During the investigation of the pilot, they found only typical daily problems, nothing beyond what most people struggled with, nothing that would have motivated suicidal action.

Nobody had realized that it had been John Vendrick III who had given his most trusted assassin the mission to get rid of the company's management. The man John had sent was ruthless and had never failed a mission. With a big, eagle-like nose adorning his stiff face, John thought he resembled an old Roman emperor.

The eagle-nosed man, whose real name was Jaap Winckelmann, was a wonder of efficiency. He'd been a petty thief before coming into John's employ, addicted to drugs and living a rough life in Rotterdam's underworld. He had moved between the European capitals and lived on crime and theft to pay for his next fix.

Tabula Rasa had sent out groups of men to collect guinea pigs for use in various illegal experiments. After a series of experiments in which eight subjects had died, the eagle-nosed man had survived. And after the experiment, he was a changed man.

His drug addiction was gone, he became a vegetarian, and he started an advanced training program. The change had not only been physical but also mental—the difference had been remarkable. Before the experiment, Jaap had been uncertain and evasive, with light sadistic tendencies. When he had woken up after the experiment, it had quickly become apparent that he had lost all sense of compassion and empathy, and his sadistic traits had blown into full bloom. The difference in this man between before the experiment and after had been like night and day.

Jaap had placed a small robot in the cockpit of the plane carrying the Italian management to the factory. During the flight, the eagle-nosed man had activated the robot; it had crawled out from under the pilot's seat and moved up along the side of it. When it had gotten close to the pilot's head, it had sprayed out an experimental nerve gas that quickly penetrated the pilot's lungs.

The gas had immediately provoked violent hallucinations in the pilot's mind. John's face crinkled into a cold smile when he imagined the horror the Italians must have felt when the pilot turned the nose of the plane down, trying to escape the nightmarish hallucinations he thought were attacking him. The power of the crash had been so violent that none of the debris had been larger than a meter in diameter. John enjoyed the knowledge that those who had been against him had suffered a cruel and agonizing death.

118

* * *

There was a quiet knock on the door, and John snapped his fingers to lower the music.

"Come in."

The door slid aside, and Dr. Weng-Li entered, his gaze fixed on the floor. The short, Asian doctor bowed low and then stood silently in front of John like a student in front of the principal. They were in John's office, in the top of the northern glittering glass pyramid of Tabula Rasa.

The room was magnificent, decorated with the finest pieces of art; imperial Chines vases, Etruscan handicrafts, and Asian gold masks tastefully lined the room. The walls were covered with windows from floor to ceiling. The window glass had a slight golden coating that gave the room a warm glow. Much of the furniture was ultra-modern and sleek in its design, and the contrast between old and new gave the room a special character.

John sat behind an oval marble desk that shimmered in the sunlight. On the desk, several gold coins were spread out on a soft cloth, and his hand held an ancient Egyptian knife. The knife was still sharp, and its edge glimmered. He watched a huge holoscreen that broadcasted live from Macau. The hologram generated by the screen hovered half a meter in front of it.

The smoke laid heavy over Macau. The cameraman panned over to the harbor, then swept further out toward the horizon and zoomed in on a military ship that seemed to be traveling at full speed. A thick fog of smoke slowly glided over the water.

The sleek ship came rushing straight ahead at full speed, and an unseen man began to shout and scream. John leaned forward with interest, studying the ship.

A few seconds passed as the razor-sharp bow of the ship split the water. John could see about ten men moving on the deck. Someone pushed the cameraman, and a blurry image of the ground filled the screen for a moment before he recovered his balance and returned to filming the attacking ship.

Two of the men on deck had taken hold of something that may have been a weapon, but the smoke made it hard to see the details of what was happening.

The cameraman zoomed out, and John saw that the ship's course was straight toward Flor Fria, Macau's mega-complex. The cameraman panned back to Flor Fria, where automatic defenses had been activated.

Three fifth-generation C-Ram high-speed cannons glided up from their positions around the mega-complex. The canons looked like big, white trolls, and from each of the trolls, a dark barrel slid out and took aim at the attacking ship.

Flor Fria (which in Portuguese meant Cold Flower) had been built over the course of four years in the 2030s. Macau's mega-complex was popular. It had a little more than half a million inhabitants and was at the cutting edge in many areas, but especially in the conservation and research of flowers and plants. On the other hand, Flor Fria was also controversial because of its rabid defense of nature and the fact that it was weighed down by bureaucracy.

The Chinese had four mega-complexes under various stages of development and were against Macau having its own. The Chinese thought it would be harder to recapture both Hong Kong and Macau, should they grow too strong.

The sleek ship turned sharply to port and steered to a heading that took it alongside Flor Fria. The white trolls followed the ship and prepared to open fire. Suddenly, two of them exploded at the same time. John recoiled. The third troll was still operational, and it fired. A prolonged, deep rumble ensued. The cameraman crouched instinctively but kept the focus on the ship.

The weapon on deck returned fire. A rapid-firing rail cannon spat out devastation from two long barrels, and John watched as massive explosions shook Flor Fria. The cameraman screamed, and the live broadcast went black.

A shiver went through John's spine. Damn terrorists. That was what they were. Still, the situation could be a blessing in disguise. John tapped his fingertips together as he thought. Now that Flor Fria was under attack, it's stock value would crash for sure.

John made a mental note to direct his financial analyst to begin a detailed analysis of Flor Fria and investigate whether he should begin to vacuum the stock market for Flor Fria shares. There was certainly a lot of synergies he could profit from. The anger within him was replaced by greed—one man's loss was another man's gain.

He waved his hand; the screen went dark, and he sat silently reflecting on what he'd seen. Weng-Li cleared his throat and John blinked. He had forgotten the doctor had entered the room.

Weng-Li stood before John on a hand-tied Persian rug that had cost more than a middle-class house. He rubbed his sweaty hands and bowed, if possible, even deeper than he had done a few minutes ago. His back was beginning to ache from all the bowing. John sat silently in front of the good doctor with Jackie, his Jack Russell terrier, in his lap. Jackie was one of

121

John's weaknesses, at least in his own opinion. He'd always liked dogs, ever since he was a young boy. He stroked his back gently.

John stared at the doctor, gently lifting Jackie down onto the floor. He got up from his chair and took three long steps around the desk until he stood in front of the doctor, who took a hesitant step back.

"I apologize a thousand times, Mr. Vendrick, I . . ." Weng-Li stammered before John interrupted him, anger welling up inside him again. Like red, glowing lava, it rose within him until he was ready to explode. His body was like a pressure cooker whose safety valves had been disconnected, and the pressure often built up to disastrous levels.

His head was pounding and his neck muscles were tense. John grabbed the collar of the Weng-Li's white coat and began to drag him forward. The surprised doctor stumbled. John dragged him as easily as a child dragged a doll, and he could smell the doctor's sour odor of sweat. He held him in front of the panoramic window and pointed outward.

"How do you think I created something like this?" he hissed at the other man. Naked fear shone in the doctor's eyes. Dr. Weng-Li crouched beneath John's outburst.

He stuttered, "I apologize again a thousand times, Mr. Vendrick. According to the plan, they should've been ready now. That was the idea, but unforeseen events have caused delays."

Dr. Weng-Li instantly pulled his shoulders together like an animal does when attacked. John held his collar with an iron grip, and the doctor didn't dare move a muscle.

"Look outside," John said tensely, "Look outside and see what I have created. It's my will that has done it. Mine. It's something I wanted, and it became as I wanted, do you understand?"

The doctor turned his head and looked out. The view in front of him was magnificent. Along the edges of the triangle formed by the pyramids stood buildings and houses, and beyond them, just a few kilometers away, was the outer fence. Three different access roads stretched to the west, south, and east. He looked down toward the inner area the three pyramids formed. It was so far down, he could hardly distinguish the people down below. John pulled him closer to the window and pressed his face against it.

"You see? This is what I have created. Tabula Rasa is my life's work, and even disasters like Maxim Hoy can't stop me." John's voice dripped with contempt.

Dr. Weng-Li nodded silently. John's voice softened and he released the man.

"You see, Doctor, Tabula Rasa is my legacy to humanity. For it is here that we will help humanity into the next era. For too long, mediocrity has been accepted and praised in society. For too long, humanity has been allowed to exploit nature for its own benefit. That stops here."

Outside, the sun ascended, and its rays reflected in the solar cells coating the outer sides of the pyramids. A kaleidoscope of colors painted the buildings. John leaned toward the doctor and whispered.

"It's over with that now, my dear friend. This is the last time, do you understand?"

Dr. Weng-Li shrugged and nodded quickly. "Yes, Mr. Vendrick. I understand."

"You promised they would be ready by now. It was the same thing you said two weeks ago. This is completely unacceptable. I don't understand—I give you everything you need to succeed, to become someone, so you can also take part in the success I've accomplished, but you insist on disappointing me."

John's voice dripped with sarcasm, and small splashes of spit landed on the doctor's cheek. Weng-Li didn't dare wipe them off for fear that he would have to take more scolding.

"When nobody wanted to have anything to do with you, who was it then that helped you? Who was it that believed in you when the whole world had left you to the wolves?"

Weng-Li looked up and met John's eyes—John was a full head taller than the short, stocky doctor.

"One more day. That's all I need. There were some configurations last time that failed, but now we know what went wrong. The next batch is already on its way, and I expect it to go completely according to plan." He bowed again.

John turned away from the doctor and looked out through the big window. The view was outstanding, and the sun's rays searched through the fractured cloud cover and gave the whole scene a golden tone.

"I don't know. I really don't know. I almost feel that I ought to kick you out. What would you say about that?"

Small beads of sweat broke out on Weng-Li's forehead, and he crouched even more.

"No, please," he said weakly. "I promise, I will not fail again." The silence dragged on. Tormenting seconds passed. Not a muscle moved in John Vendrick's well-trained body. He understood that Weng-Li knew a person couldn't be kicked out of Tabula Rasa. There was no way out except in a body bag. John continued as he stared out the window.

"You know I need them. Both for Tabula Rasa and to go up with the space shuttle as soon as possible. Every day of delay is another day of risking that someone else will discover what we're doing. NASA and ESA are in full swing with their landing on the moon— that will happen within a couple of days—and even though the sphere is on the backside of the moon, it's only a matter of time before they find it. They will discover the sphere, and if we don't get the exclusive rights for access to it, then everything will be in vain. Think of the possibilities that would be lost. Think of the chance we have to completely dominate the coming centuries of mankind. Think of the possibilities we have." He paused and turned to look at Weng-Li, whose eyes were glued to the ground. "Think about it being because of you that we lose that possibility."

Dr. Weng-Li rubbed his hands together and met John's stare. His eyes begged.

"I'll work as fast as I can," he said. "I'll see if there's a way to push the process even more. Yes. I promise to push harder."

John didn't answer. He turned back toward the window and looked silently out on the glimmering horizon. Weng-Li shifted uneasily behind him.

"I know I've let you down but give me one more chance. This time it will be right. I promise."

Seconds ticked by without either of them saying a word. A shadow slid across John's face, and then he turned around and smiled widely.

"Okay, my friend. You'll get one last chance. When will they be ready?"

Dr. Weng-Li blinked. "One day. No more. There will be seven of them. We're making the final adjustments as we speak."

John clapped his hands like a delighted child. "Wonderful! I'm so excited about the results. Do you have everything you need?"

The doctor twisted uncomfortably and tried to breathe deeply a few times without making it too obvious, then nodded.

"Yes, we have everything we need. We've gotten the process down to less than four weeks now, and those who come out are stronger than ever. I think the next round will be absolutely perfect."

John's face hardened instantly into a frown and he stared coldly at the doctor.

"'Think'?"

Weng-Li's heart skipped a beat. "Know. Of course, know."

John's bright smile returned. "Wonderful. Okay, then it's done. One day." He went back and sat down behind his desk. The doctor remained standing uncertainly in front of him, unsure whether he should go or stay. After a few seconds, John looked up at him with a raised eyebrow.

"Are you still here? I would hurry back to the lab if I were you."

The doctor bowed so deeply that the back of his legs strained, and then he scurried from the room like a mouse from a cat.

When he was alone, John pressed a button on the intercom. Three seconds later, a tall, slender man entered from a different, hidden door. The man's face was distorted by a long, angry scar that ran from his temple to his chin. John looked at the man.

"Make sure the good doctor has everything he needs. Make sure he focuses on this and nothing else. Report to me tomorrow morning."

The man nodded briefly and left the room.

* * *

John gazed out again over his creation. Tabula Rasa. It was here that he would create the next generation of humans who would dominate the earth. A new breed of super-humans that he would shape. By surrounding them with his own visions, they would be unquestionably loyal to him. It was outstanding that he had come so far.

There was certainly much he'd been born with—money and power were things his family had always possessed. That, and strong men who could manage and control their surroundings. But it hadn't always been like that for John. When he'd been a small boy, he had been relatively shy, content with building models and reading books. But when he was six years old, he had been given a five-week-old cocker spaniel by his mother in a rare moment of tenderness.

The puppy had been dedicated to John and had followed him everywhere. From the moment John had held him in his arms, he'd felt an overwhelming love for the little animal, and he had named him Templeton. One afternoon, they had been running around, playing in the house, and he had followed Templeton into his father's study.

John had known he wasn't allowed to be in there, but in the fun of the moment, he had forgotten. He had sat down, all sweaty, in the big leather sofa. Boy and dog had kept on playing, but in a moment when John had looked away, Templeton had jumped up on the sofa and relieved his bladder. John had noticed and tried to stop him, but the dark stain had grown slowly. Then his father's voice had come from the doorway, and John had panicked.

He still remembered the awful feeling of dread when he saw his father's eyes move from him to the stain to Templeton, who was joyfully jumping around, oblivious. Without a word, his father had started to walk toward him, and John had braced himself for the slap. But it never came. Instead, his father had bent down, grabbed the neck of the whining animal, and with extreme force had thrown him against the wall.

The little puppy had smashed into the wall with a disgustingly deep thud. John had been paralyzed, unable to breathe. His father, still silent, had turned around and left the room.

John had rushed over to Templeton and gotten down on his knees next to him. He could see that the little puppy was seriously injured. His back legs were not working, and blood slowly dribbled from his nose. John had sat there with the dying puppy, tears streaming down his cheeks. The experience had left profound scars.

Nature was like that. The strong dominated the weak. It was nature's law. That's the way it was, had always been, and would always be. There was nothing to do against the laws of nature. The best a man could do was accept how things were and go with the flow.

That was why John had dreamt the dream. He was sure of it. One night, almost a month ago, he had woken up soaked in sweat and with a single thought in his head. The Skydisc. It had called for him. It wanted to be found by him, and it had come to him in his dream to ask for help. It had been a sign, he was certain.

John had read everything about the Skydisc from Nebra and had come to understand what it was. He'd become convinced it was important. He wasn't sure why, but something inside him had convinced him. He had hired Raddick with great expectations that the man would succeed in retrieving the Skydisc for him.

But Raddick had failed.

John's internal volcano flared up now as he thought about it. With great willpower, he controlled the anger, pushing it down, and focused on what he had in front of him instead. He smiled to himself and thought about the evening ahead. There were a couple more meetings scheduled, and then he was going to have some fun.

In his extravagant apartment, there was a secret room that only he had access to. In it, he could act out his secret desires nobody else knew about. It was a side of him he knew he shared with both his father and grandfather. They had been the same—predators. He was proud to belong to a clan of such strong men who had the courage to dominate their surroundings.

That had also been the reason he'd established one of the best zoos in the world at Tabula Rasa. It was his own tribute to Templeton, whom he still remembered with warmth as an adult. But it wasn't only about Templeton. John's philosophy was that humans had a responsibility to make sure the destruction of nature around the world was stopped as quickly as possible. He wanted the people of Tabula Rasa to learn the importance of nature and to ensure that it lived and thrived. Therefore, he also knew it was his given right to fight anyone who continued the exploitation and abuse of natural resources.

A predator. That's what he was. And his prey was the dishonest, deceitful people that ruled the world.

He shook his head to clear his thoughts and grinned. In the secret part of his apartment, he had several different accessories that made pleasure possible on a new level. Applying injury and pain to another living person, in John's view, amounted to the ultimate pleasurable experience. He never felt as alive as when he saw the life leaving the eyes of somebody he strangled. Both men and women met death in his apartment. He wasn't picky or judgmental. He was the good, willing judge that helped release the weaker ones from their human shackles.

He stiffened in ecstasy at the thought.

Overall, he was satisfied with his performance.
Jonathan walked in and closed the door behind him.
In his hand, he held a paper cup filled with hot coffee.
He sipped it slowly.

He smacked his lips and enjoyed the strong, bitter
flavor. The oval-shaped room he stood in was big,
maybe ten meters across at its widest point. A dark-
gray, wall-to-wall carpet absorbed the sound of his
steps. Heavy furniture in dark oak was juxtaposed
with modern lamps, and it gave the room an inviting,
ambient atmosphere. A fire in a stone fireplace gave off
a golden glow, and shadows danced on the opposite
wall. A large, beveled holoscreen on one wall projected
a hologram of waist-up views of two newscast hosts
involved in a discussion.

Nicholas Backmann sat behind his desk. He stood
and walked, smiling, toward Jonathan. Backmann
was a diminutive man with short, gray hair. Around
fifty years old, he was in good shape, without a belly to
speak of. He ran five kilometers a day and was a
sailing enthusiast. He claimed that once he had sailed
alone from Gibraltar all the way home to Stockholm
with a thirty-footer.

Jonathan didn't know if he should believe him on
that count. Maybe it was possible to sail that far
without any help; Jonathan had no idea and had let
the matter rest. Someday, though, he would
investigate it more closely.

Backmann took Jonathan's hand. "I'm sorry. It was
terrible that Eric died. I know you two got along well."

Jonathan froze. His hand was still sore after the
fight with Raddick, and he felt guilty that it was Eric
who was dead and not him.

"Thank you."

Backmann's eyes wore a concerned expression. "Are you okay?"

"Yeah, I'm okay," Jonathan said. A picture of Eric's face as he fell flashed before his eyes. He shook his head and changed the subject. "I met an old friend of yours."

"Yes, I heard. Raddick. Mean bastard, right?"

"Very."

"Did he have his brother with him?" Nicholas asked, and pointed at a chair, indicating that Jonathan should take a seat.

"His brother?" Jonathan asked.

"Yes, he has a younger brother. It was the brother who killed the Spanish diplomat last year. They used to sell their services to the highest bidder."

Jonathan took a seat and carefully put the paper coffee cup on the table. He was quiet for a few seconds. "What does the brother look like?" he asked.

Backmann looked curiously at Jonathan. "The brother? He looks like a mean version of Laurel with abnormally long arms." Backmann was referring to the famous comedy couple, Laurel and Hardy, who had been entertainers more than a hundred years ago.

Jonathan nodded slowly. "Yes, I did meet him. I killed him." He watched Backmann with growing irritation. "He was just as dangerous as his brother. That would've been useful information to have before I went in."

The sound of a throat being cleared came from the direction of the fireplace. Jonathan turned around, surprised. There, in an overstuffed armchair, sat Marie L'angi.

"That was information we got at the very last moment," she said calmly, "and we weren't able to get in touch with you before you left for the last part of the mission."

She stood from the armchair and glared at him. Jonathan stared back at her.

"You . . . you had that information? Why didn't we get it before we went to Greenland?"

Marie's eyes were cold. She wasn't going to let anybody push her around in front of her boss, regardless whether he was a lover or not.

"I was going to tell you when I called you, but you didn't answer."

"No, okay. But you could've called back again or something. And why didn't you say anything when you came to my apartment yesterday?"

She looked at him with a mix of contempt and compassion. "Sure, I could've, but it wasn't the right moment. And before the mission started, we had no idea that the brother would be there; we actually found out pretty late." She spoke in a low voice, unsure of how far she should go.

"But both you and Eric were so focused on the mission."

They stared at each other, neither of them wanting to back down. Pride was a strong trait of them both; neither wanted to look weak in front of the boss.

Backmann coughed lightly and turned his gaze to Marie. In a cold voice, he said, "'Came to my apartment?' Did you meet Jonathan yesterday?"

Marie shifted uncomfortably. "Yes."

Backmann's look was enough. She knew she would have to explain why she had gone home to Jonathan without informing Backmann about it. He knew about Jonathan's oxycodone habit.

Backmann wasn't sure how he was going to confront Jonathan about the matter of the pills. Oxycodone, classified as a narcotic, hadn't shown up during the last three months of required drug tests at the Amber Group.

In any case, it had to wait; they had more important things ahead of them now. Backmann shook his head slowly and clapped his hands.

"The fact remains that Eric's dead and it's something we have to live with. We can blame it on each other or we can learn from it. Some things could've been done differently, that I'm sure of. But while Eric is dead, so is Raddick. His brother, too—and we retrieved the Skydisc."

Marie studied Jonathan. He made her feel a strange mix of desire and resentment. She knew it had been wrong to let their flirting go so far—they should have never ended up in bed. It was one thing when they hadn't worked together, but now, it could not continue.

It was her responsibility; it was she who was the supervisor. She comforted herself with the fact that she had never done anything like it before. She had a reputation for being a hard and demanding boss, and she demanded as much from herself as from those around her.

"You're right," she said and turned directly toward Jonathan. Better to get it over with. If it took giving him a small victory to help him bounce back, it was a small price to pay. He was, after all, one of the most promising members she had seen in a long time, and he would be a good asset to the Group.

"I should've tried again to inform you about Raddick's brother. I'll take the blame for that."

Jonathan looked at her for a moment without expression, and then his face softened. "Thank you."

He turned to Backmann. "You wanted to see me, sir?"

Marie blushed. Backmann smiled matter-of-factly.

"Yes," he said. "Since that's done and over with, we have more important things to discuss. Sit down."

He pushed a button and a screen smoothly and silently slid down from the ceiling.

"We've had sporadic contact with an individual inside the data department at Tabula Rasa over the last week. Her name is Elisabeth Snow, and she has been very helpful in getting information."

Backmann pushed a button on the computer and the form of a woman's face faded into view. Jonathan looked at the image of Elisabeth Snow, a woman of around thirty years. The readout below indicated that she was a meter and seventy centimeters tall, not married, and working as a data technician at Tabula Rasa.

"There has been a sharp increase in communication—actually, more than two hundred fifty percent—between Tabula Rasa's space station and their ground control lately. As you well know, all Tabula Rasa communication is encrypted, and we've had some problems deciphering the codes quickly enough."

Jonathan frowned. "It sounds great that this Elisabeth Snow suddenly got on track and started to send information to us, but who is she and where did she come from? Why did she start sending information to us? Was it just out of the blue?"

"No, of course not. We're actually a working organization that's been around for quite a few years, so we have some contacts around the world that you don't know about."

Jonathan turned toward Backmann. "I understand that. I was just questioning the source."

"We've had contact with Elisabeth before—before she even got to Tabula Rasa. We had her on board for a mission in Chile five years ago, but since then, we haven't had anything to do with each other."

"What was the mission in Chile about?" Marie asked.

Backmann drummed lightly on the table with a finger. "Most of it is classified. But let's say she was on board as a civilian and she did a good job. She worked to analyze several different slates of burned clay that were found in the Chilean jungle. The slates contained what looked to be an unknown language, and Elisabeth was fundamental in creating the computer program that deciphered the language. Impressive work, if I remember correctly." Backmann paused and looked from Jonathan to Marie, then said, "It was she who contacted me three days ago and asked for help."

Marie leaned forward. "Help with what?"

Backmann scratched his scruffy cheek absently. "In the beginning, it wasn't clear what it was about. She was reserved. But in the end, I figured out that it had something to do with their space station that orbits the moon. They had made a discovery, and Elisabeth was quite excited about it, but she never told me exactly what it was they had discovered. She did, however, give me a set of coordinates in space."

"What do you think it was?" asked Marie.

"I really don't know. Something big enough that she risked contacting me from within Tabula Rasa. As you know, Vendrick and I are not on particularly good terms. If they find out that she's communicating with us, she'll be in trouble."

"I have heard that." Marie got up and went over to a side table and poured some coffee. Backmann turned to the screen and continued talking, both to them and to himself.

"Vendrick's smart, calculating, and unscrupulous," he said. "When I worked at DGSE, we had an ongoing investigation on Vendrick, but every time we got close to a breakthrough, something happened. Testimonies disappeared. Phone calls got erased. The evidence went up in smoke. It was like chasing a ghost. After four years, the investigation was canceled, and I left DGSE in pure desperation."

Jonathan listened intently. "I've heard this story."

Backmann replied, "Then you've also heard that ever since I started the Amber Group, I have kept a special spot for Vendrick. Sooner or later, I will get that man." He shook his head. "He's a genuine psychopath and a sadist. And it doesn't end there. As most people know, he is also insanely rich, and that combination makes him extremely dangerous. We even believe he has a sort of . . . hobby . . . that ends in the deaths of innocent people."

Jonathan stared at the screen and narrowed his eyes. "How?"

Backmann pushed a button on the computer, and the images of two older men and a woman faded in. Across each image was a diagonal red band displaying the text *deceased*. Under each picture was another image of several gold coins in different sizes. Backmann walked up to the screen.

"Vendrick is a fanatical coin collector; he has one of the world's finest collections of gold coins. Some of his items are unique, and at one time, were in the hands of other collectors."

He pointed at the image of the older man in the middle. "This is Fjodor Patkin, a Russian oligarch who got rich from oil and mineral resources in Siberia. Patkin had a collection of American twenty-dollar Liberty Heads that were valued at more than forty million dollars. The crown jewel in his collection was a Liberty Head from 1861. There were only two known copies in the world, and Patkin owned one of them." He turned to face Jonathan and continued, "About a year ago, Patkin was found dead in his bathroom at his home in Moscow. The official cause of death was a heart attack. During the review of his assets, his gold coin collection was found, but the coin from 1861 was missing. We suspect now that the coin is in Vendrick's collection, but we're still trying to get that information confirmed."

Marie pointed at the other images on the screen.

"And these people?"

Backmann walked back to his desk and sat down. "Same thing. Both dedicated coin collectors who had unique pieces in their collections. Both of them died in the last year, and the coins they owned are now believed to be in Vendrick's possession."

Marie shook her head. "He sounds like a truly unpleasant person."

Backmann nodded thoughtfully. He pushed another button and the three images of the deceased disappeared. He changed the subject. "Elisabeth managed to contact me again yesterday."

"Yesterday?" Jonathan frowned.

Backmann nodded. "It seems she's been discovered. She sounded afraid, and the transmission was interrupted. But she did send information that we're working on confirming."

"What did she send?"

"She sent the coordinates to a point that's in orbit around the moon. Maybe they've discovered something there. We also managed to intercept communication between Elisabeth and her dad that indicates she also sent him some information. Unfortunately, what's happened with the father, we don't know." Backmann hesitated, then went on, "and there's something else, too." He glanced at Jonathan.

"We've had Paco Sanchez inside Tabula Rasa, infiltrated within the organization. He's been on site for a little more than a month now and has forwarded lots of good information, but now it seems like he's gotten himself into some problems."

Jonathan raised an eyebrow. He and Paco had met several times and Jonathan liked him.

"Paco is at Tabula Rasa now?"

Backmann nodded.

"What kind of problems is he in?" Jonathan asked.

Backmann took a deep breath and let the air out slowly. "A little more than a week ago, all contact stopped. We had contact on a regular basis before that, and everything was going according to plan, but he's missed the last two planned contacts. The situation is starting to look bleak."

Marie looked doubtfully at Backmann. "Wouldn't he have warned you if he was at risk of being caught?"

Backmann nodded. "Yes—we'd decided at the beginning that he'd send a message if he suspected someone was on to him, but that's part of the problem. He never sent anything. One day we had contact with him, and he didn't say anything about being in danger, and the next day it was like he had vanished from the face of the earth."

"Is there something we can do?" Jonathan asked.

Backmann raised his eyebrows. "That's obvious, isn't it? I want you to take a team to Tabula Rasa. We're going to try to get Paco, Elisabeth, and her dad out before they get caught. After that, we'll focus our attention on those coordinates in space."

Tabula Rasa, Madagascar
2048-12-28

At first, there was nothing, and then there was something. Nothing and something at the same time. Nothing at all. No emotions, no thoughts or problems. Nothing. There was no being. No life. No death.

Then, something, something else. He was dead, but he was not, he was there, but he was not. There was no time that he was in. There was not any now, nothing there, nothing behind, nothing ahead.

He was there, but still, he was not. A deep, pouring light embraced him. The veils in front of him danced around in big circles. He floated up through them and sank down again. He became a thought that struggled to get up out of the darkness, but he fell back down again. Fell in the dark. In the cold. The darkness embraced him, and he floated in it. He allowed it to fill him up and let it penetrate his inside. He was outside of time. It had no meaning to him. He was not in it. Did not hear its pulse, its heartbeats that slowly ate forward. All the time forward. Never backward. Always forward. He rose. Sank. Small black stars glided up in the fog and danced in front of him. A thought formed and rose to the surface. The smell of something unknown swept through him.

Am I alive?

He was this thought, and this thought was him. The black stars rose and sunk, and he looked at them. He was them too. And this thought.

Am I alive?

When he looked at the stars they dissolved in chaotic whirls, small black holes sucked them into themselves. Time was there. Ahead of him. He could feel it. Feel the taste. Feel the taste of metal. Darkness pulled him down, but he struggled to get himself up. He was there. In the middle of the darkness. Like a warrior that was fighting the monsters of the abyss. The time. Rose. Sank. Forward, always forward. Metal. More metal in his mouth. His pulse rose and fell in him. More thoughts took shape.

Do I exist?

His thoughts were shaping as a consciousness now. He could feel how he took shape. He breathed.

Where am I?

Every breath became a stroke that took him closer to the dark surface. He took another stroke. Wanted to break through the dark, hard surface. Breakthrough to the other side. The other side that he knew was there. What was behind? Behind the hard surface. There was sound. The unknown sound that meant something to him, but he did not understand what.

Swim. Come on now. Swim. You can do it. You are close now.

A voice. A voice spoke to him.

To me. It's talking to me! I understand what it is saying.

"Adam, do you hear me? Do you hear me?"

Adam answered with his thoughts.

"Yes, I hear you. Who are you? I hear you."

The voice continued its insisting question.

"Can you hear me, Adam? Are you there? Can you hear me?"

Adam shouted.

"Yes, I hear you, I'm telling you. Don't you hear what I'm saying? I'm answering you. I hear you."

The voice repeated itself.

"Answer, Adam, answer me."

Is my name Adam?

He focused all his power and stretched every thought in his consciousness and every muscle in his body and answered.

"I hear you."

He was in darkness, he opened his eyes, and he was in the light. His eyes saw for the first time. He saw, but what it was that he saw he did not know. His eyes

140

blinked and focused on the shapeless mass in front of him. Slowly the shapeless mass became sharper around the edges, and it came more and more in focus. The mass pulled together into a face. A man's face. That spoke to him. A voice spoke.

* * *

"Doctor, all the signs look good. His pulse is within limits and his vital signs are holding. I think we are ready for the last part." an anonymous technician sat hidden behind several screens.
Dr. Weng-Li nodded. He studied the clone that laid on the examining table in front of him.
"Of course, everything looks good. It is Adam that comes. Adam is my firstborn. He is the first of a whole generation of superhuman's. The ultimate man."
Pride bubbled inside him.

* * *

Dr Weng-Li had struggled for this moment for several years, endless attempts that had not yielded any results. All the different ideas that he had tried had mostly not resulted in anything except the repugnant work to clean up afterward.

In front of him stood seven large glass containers in the round room. They stood in a semi-circle, a meter apart; and in six of them, there was a clone floating. Every clone was surrounded by thousands of liters of an experimental synthetic amniotic fluid.

Dr. Weng-Li had been the one who had developed the special formula they needed for the latest generation of clones. He had created more than twenty generations since he came to Tabula Rasa, some more successful than others. Vendrick had persuaded him to come here and continue his career when the scandal had exploded in Hong-Kong where he used to live. It was in another life, almost as if it had happened to someone else.

He had been a professor at one of Hong-Kong's most prestigious universities and had a respectable career. As the university world is conservative, he was forced to keep some parts of his life in the dark. During the days he was a university professor, at nights he was Miyagi-san, a rapist that made parts of Hong-Kong unsafe. He had managed to evade the law for several years, but in the end, his luck had run out.

One of his victims had managed to get away and had alerted the police that a man had attacked her and that he had a gold tooth and a characteristic, thin scar just above his right eye. But as she had been a prostitute, the police had not believed her and dismissed her accusations. But a senior chief at the university, that for a long time had held a grudge against him, had in secret initiated an unofficial investigation. It had not resulted in any hard evidence against Weng-Li from the investigation, but his situation had still become unsustainable.

His students tattled and whispered, and different rumors circulated. In the end, during a lecture, he had been attacked by a group of women who had rushed into the lecture room, thrown eggs and screamed at him. Weng-Li had been forced to flee, and the scandal was a fact.

After a couple of terrible weeks, he had received a call from somebody with a job offer. Dr Weng-Li had been hiding in a shabby hotel room in Shanghai, and after another two conversations, he and the unknown voice made an appointment. They had met the following day, and he had gotten the surprise of his life when John Vendrick III had shown up to their meeting.

Two days later, Weng-Li had arrived at Tabula Rasa, and his gratitude had been infinite. He had been given the task to create the next generation of humans that would pick up the relay baton that seemed to have been dropped by the current mankind.

Dr. Weng-Li's work area was as a biological engineer. It was an area that had exploded in the last decade. Researchers around the world with dubious moral unofficially competed to become the first who succeeded to develop a complete human clone. The treaty from 2032 had intended to limit and regulate the research within the area, but the development progressed so fast that much of the regulation was already out of date when it came into force. This resulted in confusion and that, in turn, led to several research groups around the world continuing their experiments.

Together with his team, Dr. Weng-Li had gotten farthest. And now he had succeeded. He had created a living, breathing clone that was superior to the ordinary human in every way. They were stronger, faster, and smarter than the grey mass that humanity was made of.

Constant increasing chaos of environmental destruction, an exceptional surge of consumption of the natural resources, melting ice caps in the Arctic and Antarctica, and an ever more demanding world population had taken the earth to the edge of disaster.

It was Dr. Weng-Li's conviction that doom was approaching fast. And he had to do something. And by the grace of God, he had gotten the chance. John had taken him under his wings and given him the opportunity to create something new. A new world order. An order that was based on balance and equilibrium. An order that came from the understanding that finite resources had to be cared for, and finding a sustainable development was the most important challenge that mankind was facing. It was either that or the earth would go under within the foreseeable future. He nodded absently and signaled to the technician in the background.

"Continue with the initial configuration."

He pulled out a keyboard and entered a few commands. In front of him, Adam started to move like in a dream. The system initiated the creation of a human that the world had never seen before. Artificial intelligence configured Adams brain and mind, so it learned all the skills he was predetermined to have. Combat training, scientific knowledge, and space information was merely a fraction of the knowledge that poured into the clone's brain.

During the following hours, the remaining six brothers of Adam were born, and Dr. Weng-Li nodded contently at his days' work; he worked to confirm that all the clones had gone through genesis in a good way.

The strong smell of synthetic amniotic fluid was nothing that affected the good doctor. Extensive examinations and a whole battery of tests were conducted. There were a couple of minor adjustments of three clones, but in general, he was surprised at just how well the process had elapsed. He had been joined by Dr. Ln'geem, who acted as his right hand.

Both doctors worked quickly and efficiently. They stood at the crescent-shaped desk that was placed in the middle of the sterile room. The seven large containers were now empty. The strong rays from the ceiling lights reflected in the white tiles which the floor and walls were covered with. In front of each container stood a long, metallic examination table and on each one of the tables laid a clone. The clone's bodies shined in the sharp light, and a weak, irregular, dripping sound of synthetic amniotic fluid that hit the tiles was heard.

Dr. Ln'geem looked submissively at Dr. Weng-Li.

"It looks good, doesn't it?"

"Yes, it seems like all the subjects went through the genesis process without any bigger problems."

"On two, three, and seven we have made adjustments. Do you agree?"

"Yes. Two, three, and seven."

They continued to work in silence. They had achieved something amazing. Never in the history of mankind had anyone attempted and succeeded in creating as many as seven clones at once, where all survived, and all passed the initial configuration so well.

"Are we ready for the next phase?"

Dr. Weng-Li nodded, and together the doctors went out through a door to the adjacent room. The room was circular, and the bare walls sloped steeply upwards and outwards. About four meters up on the wall, something protruded that resembled a balcony. The two doctors went up on a staircase that led up to the balcony and they stood there and looked down with great interest.

Below them, the clones came in through the same door and walked in one after the other into the room. They walked in a line as if they were marching to an inaudible rhythm. The door slid silently back and closed. You could almost not even see where the door had been.

The clones stood evenly distributed in a circle in the room just a couple of meters apart. Each one of their bodies was a biological masterpiece. The researchers at Tabula Rasa had access to the latest synthetic drugs, and they had used these on part of the population in different experiments to continue the evolution of mankind to the next generation, who would eventually dominate the earth. Dr Ln'geem looked at Dr Weng-Li who pulled his lips back in a shark-like smile and showed his gold tooth.

Contact had been established. After such a long time it had finally been successful. Contact. It was what the spheres were meant to do. That was their goal. Contact with living organisms, with intelligent organisms.

The spheres came from another part of the universe, from another time. They were designed by an intelligent species that created them to find a way to escape their dying surroundings and preserve knowledge.

Eons of time ago, another universe had been everything, and it had been filled with living creatures that had been born, lived, and died. When it had aged, the living creatures had designed these spheres so that they could transform their physical being into radiation and back again.

It was an attempt to forward the knowledge to the next creation that would follow theirs. And now again, it had succeeded. It was the seventh time that the spheres had registered intelligent life. They had traveled through eternities of time and space, and most of them had perished in the Big Bang that created the universe as we know it.

They had come to earth hundreds of years ago because they had discovered that the planet contained intelligent life. The spheres had sent several hundreds of smaller spores that were smaller versions of the spheres, which had traveled down to the surface to establish contact. And they had succeeded. At least in the beginning. They had established contact with intelligent creatures in a couple of places on the planet's surface, and in the beginning, their mission had gone well. Just as it had done on other places in this universe.

But something had gone wrong. This time the contact had not evolved as the earlier ones. Exactly what it was that happened this time was not clear, but it had affected them so much that they were forced to call it off.

The reaction from the people that had gotten in contact with them had not been what the spores were prepared for. In the beginning, humans had reacted with joy and gratitude, but it had not taken long until those feelings had turned into hate and fear.

Instead of developing contact with the humans, the spores had been forced to flee. It was something unique, and the spores had reacted with frustration and decided to leave. The decision had been taken and was sent out to all the spores, but a few of them had gone against the decision and had hidden deep down on the planet's surface while the rest had left.

Richard Snow was tired and worried. He had spent the whole day down by the sonoluminescence reactors on the lowest level in Primus. It was physical, heavy work, and today he was more tired than usual. He was not a young man anymore, and his body ached, especially the back of his left leg.

He massaged it while he walked to get the pain to let go, and he sensed his own smell of sweat. He walked down one of the long corridors that led up from Primus to Gaudium, where his apartment was. It was not in the best part of Tabula Rasa that he lived, but that was the way it was. The color on the walls had seen better days, small paint flakes loosened and created patterns as they reached up against the ceiling. The under-dimensioned air-conditioning struggled to bring fresh air and the strained vents were loud.

A not so fresh smell filled his nose, and he moved forward. The cleaning robots that had as a task to keep the inner environment at Tabula Rasa clean and tidy did not pass by these areas as often as the nicer ones.

Even within Tabula Rasa, there were class differences. But he was used to it. One day he would manage to get away from here. He would move on. Forward. Upward. He shook his head while he stepped to the side and let two elderly ladies pass in the narrow corridor. His backpack slid off to the side, and he pulled it back.

The conversation with Elisabeth had worried him, it was not like her to call and be agitated like that. And what was that all about what she had told him to pack? That had not happened before. His thoughts kept grinding in his head, and he frantically tried to understand what had happened. He blinked in surprise and saw that he had arrived at his apartment. He had not noticed how quickly he got there.

Richard sighed and put his hand against the door. It was cold under his hand. The built-in sensor reacted to his palm print, and the door slid to the side. He was met by the voice of Barry Manilow.

The holocube was in the backpack, and he gently put it down when he closed the door. He did not know if Marina, his girlfriend, was at home. They had been arguing when he left and even if he did not remember exactly what it was they were arguing about, he knew that they would continue when he got home. He was just about to take the holocube out of the backpack when a female voice came out of the bedroom.

"Richard? Richard dear, is it you?"

He blinked, he was not expecting that kind of greeting. He thought that she would continue with the nagging she had been doing the last couple of days. His fingers dropped the holocube down into the backpack, but he changed his mind. He did not exactly know what had happened in the last weeks, but they had argued more and more.

The last couple of days he had even been glad to get away from home. His mind was racing. He moved quickly into the living room and looked for a place to hide the holocube. He did not want it in the open.

He went over to the bookshelf and put the holocube behind some books. Maybe not the best hiding place in the world but it had to do until he figured out something better. He heard Marina's voice from the bedroom.

"Richard? What are you doing?"

He went back to the hallway, towards the door where Marina's voice came from. He opened the door to the bedroom, Marina was laying on the bed. She was just over forty-seven years old. He had met her there, during the first hectic months when they arrived and started their new lives. Everybody who applied to Tabula Rasa

150

longed for something new, a new life, a new start, and Tabula Rasa gave them that opportunity.

"Come, my love. I have something for you."

Richard smiled.

"What a pleasant surprise."

He walked up to her and sat down on the edge of the bed next to her. The scent of lavender was palpable. He knew that Marina had lit scented candles to set the mood. He smiled and walked up to her. Before he could sit down, she got up and pulled him down to the bed and kissed him passionately.

It had been a long time since they had made love. The touch between them was hesitant at first, careful. As they continued, both became more and more excited. He could feel her desire under him when he penetrated her. After a couple of minutes, her fingers dug into his back while they reached climax together.

* * *

Afterward, they laid beside each other, slumbering in the soft bed. He could not say for how long they laid there, but he twitched and opened his eyes.

Richard sat up and massaged his neck. Marina lay beside him. She opened her eyes and looked at him. There was still a distance between them and he did not really know where it had come from. They were usually in a good place, but something had come between them. It was something that he could not put his finger on. Maybe it was his long working hours down at the lower levels. Maybe it was her desire to have children and his resistance to it.

At Tabula Rasa, there were various fertility programs that you could use. He had heard that the highest recommended age for women in these programs was fifty years, which meant that Marina had three years left. He knew that it was wrong, but at the same time, he did not want to spend more time changing diapers and late nights without sleep. There were no problems with having children when you were at Tabula Rasa. You would apply for permission, and for most applications, it got approved. But still. There was something that could not get him to let go.

Richard cocked his head and listened. A weak clicking sound and Barry's voice went silent. He stretched out his hand to Marina and pointed with his finger that she should be quiet. She looked surprised.

At the same moment that he realized that there was somebody in the apartment, he turned around and got out of the bed.

*   *   *

A tall, blond man slid silently through the doorway. He smiled a dazzling smile but did not speak. He and Richard stared at each other for a couple of seconds. Marina gawked shockingly at the man in the doorway. She seemed so surprised that she had lost her ability to speak. Richard took a step forward and said with a firm voice.

"Who are you? What do you want?"

The blond man's smile widened. It was a movie-star smile. Richard could see the perfect rows of white teeth shining. He seemed to be in excellent physical shape. His shoulders were wide, and his whole persona beamed a kind of brute magnetism.

"Where's the holocube?" the blond man asked, still smiling.

"What?" Richard answered, pretending to be surprised and blinked.

152

Gently, the blond man took a step forward and put his hands together.

"Don't act stupid now", he sighed, "where is it, your daughter sent it to you."

His mind was racing. He did not know how much more they knew. Maybe they did not know what the holocube contained and was only sent out to prevent an information leak. Richard knew that such leaks had happened before and at those occasions, staff from the security department had been sent out.

"I don't know what you are talking about. She hasn't sent anything."

The blond man's smile changed character. His thin lips pulled back into a thin, contemptuous smile.

"We know that you have it. You got it this afternoon. She sent it to you directly via the com-link at your work. Don't you think those kinds of things would be registered?"

Richard`s brain was working frenetically.

"It was a mistake. She sent something work-related by mistake. She called me to explain and I removed it immediately."

The blond man took a step to the side, and another man showed up behind him.

"Nice try old man, but we both know that is not the truth."

Richard stared at the two men. They looked like twins besides the obvious fact that they had different hair color. One was blond with short, crewcut hair. The other had light red curly hair that almost looked childish. There was something terrifying about the whole situation that made Richard shiver.

When one of the men moved, it seemed as the other one did as well, in a strange way they seemed almost synchronized. He glanced down at Marina who sat stiff and frozen in bed. Her eyes were wide open with fear. Richard glared at the two men and thought that even if he would have had a gun to defend himself with, he would have still been in a weak position.

"Why don't you just take it? It's in there." He pointed towards the living room.

"Yes. We know that you have it, that's true. But what we don't know is if you have made any copies and forwarded it. Have you?"

"No. How would I have had time for that? I have no idea where I should start. I don't even know what it is." His voice was an octave higher then he would have wanted it to be.

"That's true. But if you knew, what would you do then?" the blond walked back and forth with soft steps while he spoke. He moved carefully. Richard thought that he reminded him of a compressed spring that was waiting to explode.

"What kind of question is that? How can I answer about something that I don't know?"

"I really want to believe you. The problem is that I must be sure."

Marina moved silently in bed. Fear glittered in her eyes. The reddish man had moved away towards the bed and stood beside the edge. He quickly leaned over and grabbed Marina's arm. She screamed. The reddish man easily pulled her out of the bed with one arm. Her screaming intensified. Loud, sharp. The reddish man pulled her arm, and her screams tore into Richard's head when her arm was dislocated. Richard was petrified. Panic welled up in him, and he threw himself against Marina to pull her loose. The blond man moved like electricity.

His movements were so fast that it was almost over before Richard had time to register what had happened. The blond man had with a giant leap moved so that he blocked the way for Richard. Richard bumped into the blonde man's chest. It was like he had hit a living wall. Richard collapsed into a pile on the floor while Marina

154

continued her screaming. The blonde man looked down at Richard and smiled.

"Again. Tell me what you have done with it. Have you copied it?"

"No. Please stop. No more." he sobbed.

"Where is it?"

He pointed towards the shelf.

"There. Behind the books."

The blond man looked at the bookshelf and walked up to it, stopped and pulled out the holocube. Marina continued screaming. Loud. Insanely loud. The howling sound echoed in Richard's head and the soft lavender smell got mixed up with a sharp smell when Marina wet herself.

"Please, let her go." Richards's voice was weak.

"Yes. I wish that we could do that. But I think you already know what's going to happen."

"Please."

"Yes, I know, I know. Sometimes life is unfair. But that's life. Sometimes somebody dies so that others can live. Sometimes even whole generations perish, but it doesn't matter in the long run."

The reddish man still held Marina`s arm firmly while her other arm scratched at the man to release her. Blood trickled down her disabled arm in small, thin streams. Marina's eyes were wild, shocked by the pain her body was forced to endure. Richard feebly reached out for her. She stared at him, begging for help.

The reddish man stood silent, immovable, and glanced over at the blonde man. The blonde stepped forward and took an iron grip around Richard's arms, and they almost shattered when the blonde man locked them against his body. Richard screamed. The screams from both Richard and Marina were deafening in the cramped bedroom, but the blonde man seemed unaffected and smiled. He glanced at Marina and then nodded to the reddish man.

Marina yelled. The reddish man took two steps back and lifted Marina straight up in the air while he fast spun her around. Both his arms wrapped around her neck and with a snap, he broke it. Marina sank limply through his arms and slid down onto the floor. A strong metallic smell of blood reached Richard, he howled.

"No! You bastard!"

"Yes. I know. I am so sorry." the blonde man said and let go of the sobbing Richard who collapsed to the floor. The blonde man nodded to the reddish man who walked toward Richard to finish him off. Richard knew that if he did not do anything now, he would not have many seconds left to live.

His instincts took over. He did not think but went on to something animalistic inside of him that had taken over. It was now or never. He pulled himself forward, down, as if he was giving up and was going to lay flat on his stomach in front of them. His arms were pounding with pain. Both men looked at each other, unsure of the unexpected reaction.

Richard stretched out his arm under the bed and prayed a quick prayer. He had an old samurai sword wrapped in canvas under their bed, and he grabbed it.

"That's right my friend, it's time to give up." the blonde said, and he tried to show Richard that he understood that he gave up his life to the superiority in front of him. The reddish man leaned forward to grab him by the neck.

Richard moved fast. He ignored the pain in his arms and in a sweep, he grabbed the sword and at the same time as he pulled it out, he rolled around and plunged it forward. The reddish man who stood bent over him suddenly screamed but then abruptly stopped. The sword sank softly halfway in the man's body. Richard pulled the sword back and forward, and the sharp edge slashed the collapsing lung. The reddish man opened his mouth to scream but instead of sound, blood poured

156

out, his fingers grabbed after Richard's face, but Richard continued to push the sword in and out in the hole that was getting bigger in the reddish man's chest. The blonde man screamed hysterically and dropped the holocube.

Richard somehow got his leg under the reddish man and pushed with all power that he had left. The reddish man stumbled backward and fell to the floor. The blonde man ran up and took the reddish man in his arms. Richard unsteadily got up on his legs, wobbled, dropped the sword, took the holocube, and ran.

Falsterbo, Sweden
2048-12-28

Free as a bird, the white golf ball ascended the air, sailed upwards in a high arch, and landed three meters past the fairway bunker on the ninth hole on Falsterbo golf club.

A couple of curious swallows dived after it and navigated back and forth a couple of times before they disappeared out of sight.

It was just before lunch and the sun was already high in the sky. The forecast for the day was no contaminated rain, and that would not require any additional measures. The air was still cool from the morning, but the afternoon promised more sun and heat. A faint salty breeze from the southwest, which according to the forecasts would increase, caressed the yellow golf course and thin cloud veils slowly drifted by in the sky. The irregular croaking from a couple of frogs came from somewhere far away.

"How's it going with the latest flooding's?"

Erik Tuva grimaced.

"Both good and bad I guess. In the last few years, it has become better, but in the long run, we most likely have a real problem." He thought back to the big flooding of 2039 when basically the whole peninsula had been under water.

"I heard that they were upgrading the floodgate system?"

Erik nodded.

"Yes, it'll become even more powerful, but I wonder if it isn't just a band-aid on a deep wound. It won't be able to keep all the water out, especially not when it comes in a storm from the north, and all the water is pushed into Flommen. No matter how many floodgates you build, there is a limit on how much the system can handle. Sooner or later it will crumble, and when it does, we're history."

Raimondo del Louis nodded thoughtfully and looked at the beach where the big sand dunes rose like a protective wall. They were built during two years at the beginning of 2040 and went around the whole peninsula as a protective guard. Erik shrugged.

"But let us not ponder that right now. Today, we'll enjoy the day and discuss the future later. Ok?"

Raimondo smiled.

"Ok."

Raimondo had been visiting Erik in his summer house in Falsterbo for two days, and on Monday he was going home to Geneva where he lived.

Raimondo worked with work environment inspections at United Nations, more specifically at a department that went under the complicated name of the International Trade Department, shortened to ILO. He mainly worked with international labor standards and trade. His expertise was in labor law, and with the development of the so-called mega-complexes in recent years he had been very busy.

He was tasked with the coordination of work inspections at these various mega-complexes and in most cases, it often went well. One of the few exceptions was Tabula Rasa. They had time after time delayed inspections and obstructed Raimondo from carrying out his work. Controls that had been planned a long time ahead usually got canceled at the last second, and Raimondo had more and more come to suspect that they did not cooperate because they had something to hide.

All their attempts to call the responsible doctors at Tabula Rasa, Dr. Weng-Li and Dr. Ln'geem for questioning had been ignored.

They walked together out onto the elongated fairway. Erik glanced over at Raimondo.

"How's it going with your work? Is it very busy?"

Raimondo hesitated for a couple of seconds.

159

"Both yes and no."

"What do you mean?"

Raimondo looked at his friend. Erik worked with environmental issues at the Oresund's authority that had the responsibility for the strategic environmental responsibility regarding the south part of Sweden and at Zealand in Denmark. Raimondo smiled.

"Some of the information I've been able to confirm from other sources, but some I haven't been able to confirm."

"What is it that you can't confirm?"

"Well, that's the problem. Some of the things that I have found out simply sound too amazing to be true."

"Can you give me an example?"

"This information is highly confidential. What I tell you, you cannot tell anyone. Recently, we have compiled an indictment against Tabula Rasa regarding their unwillingness to cooperate with our attempts to make sure that they are really finished with their cloning experiments. Next week we'll present our material, and I am convinced that it will hold up in court." Raimondo looked at Erik that stared at him.

"You've got to be kidding."

Raimondo smiled.

"No. That's the truth. I haven't said anything to you to protect you but I'm out swimming in very dark waters here. I need somebody else in my corner. But for God's sake, keep it to yourself. If it comes out that I have leaked something, it could become very dangerous."

Erik nodded again and frowned.

"Ok, you know you can trust me."

Raimondo had come close to his ball, he let go of the handle of his golf bag that slid to a stop on the grass. He put his hand on the blade that was an iron club.

"You understand; human cloning programs were banned globally. There were some programs that were intended for animal cloning, and some of them could continue, but all human cloning programs were shut down. Nobody could continue with their attempts, and there was established a commission to monitor that the termination went as directed."

"But Vendrick didn't do it?"

Raimondo shook his head.

"What we have found out so far is that they continued. And apparently, they have come farther than before. Much farther. And the official cloning programs they have for animals are far more advanced than anyone else has access to." he said with emphasis.

"How did he manage to do that?"

"That is a good question that for the moment, we don't really have a good answer."

Erik frowned.

"I remembered I read about something, and that there were several of those dismantlement groups that traveled around the world and monitored the whole process that would terminate the cloning programs. It went on for several years. Didn't it?"

Raimondo nodded and took the five iron that the golf cart recommended.

"Yes, it did. The whole process took more than three years before it was officially finished."

Erik looked questioningly at Raimondo.

"But you mean that they didn't manage to find all the material during the dismantling? I thought those people knew what they were doing." His voice sounded sarcastic.

"Yes, they knew what they were doing. We are talking about highly-specialized men and women with a solid background and training. And some of them I had trained myself. But Vendrick obviously managed to keep parts of it hidden from the dismantlement group that was stationed there."

Erik paused. Raimondo lined up to his golf ball, swung, and sent the golf ball in a wide arch against green. It hit the edge on the left bunker at the green, bounced and then fell inside.

"Darn it," Raimondo said silently.

Erik looked after his own golf ball, saw it some twenty meters away and headed towards it. His stroke placed it on the far side of the green.

"Good swing." praised Raimondo. They continued in silence toward the green. Another two swallows shot down from the sky, turned sharply as they approached the grass and flew on.

"What does all this mean then?" Erik looked at Raimondo who was rearranging the club placement in the bag while he was walking.

"It means that Vendrick now has a pretty big head start in terms of clones and their development, and the Tabula Rasa shares continue to rise."

"What will happen?"

Raimondo grimaced.

"To be honest, I really don't know."

Survival instinct had triggered the animal inside. Richard ran aimlessly down the aisle away from his apartment. His pulse hammered in his ears and he thought he had become deaf.

He did not think, his body reacted instinctively upon being chased. Sweat poured down the sweater that clung to his back. He rushed down the stairs around the corner from his apartment. One of his knees hit the railing, and he bumped into a man who was on his way up, the man fell down screaming.

Richard rushed on, the fallen man shouted and yelled behind him. One of his arms could barely move and pain set in even harder when he tried. He did not know where he should go or who could help him.

The two men had killed Marina. That was clear. He was sure of it. She must be dead. The reddish man had lifted her up like a doll and snapped her neck as easy as a dog breaks a stick in its mouth.

Who had the men been? He did not know; he had never seen them before. They obviously knew about him and his family. They had known about Elisabeth and that she had sent a holocube that was filled to the breaking point. But it had not been enough for them to get the holocube, they had killed Marina anyway.

He knew that he would have been dead if he had not run. His heart pounded, and every beat that hammered in his chest made it feel like it would explode. Sweat poured down in his face.

He slipped, got back on his legs and ran. Every step took him farther away from his apartment, but it was as if he was running in slow-motion. His legs were sluggish and slow. The effect of the adrenaline started to wear off and subtle, grinding fatigue started to creep into his muscles. His arms still burned with pain. It felt like his feet were dipped in lead, and with each step he took, they got heavier and heavier.

At this hour, the various aisles and corridors of this part of the complex were relatively empty. Very few people walked alone, a couple of groups of older men sat and played an Asian board game. They were so engrossed in it that they barely glanced up as he ran past. He turned to his left.

It was not possible to keep running at the same pace, and his knee increasingly began to hurt. He saw a small park on one side of the hill in front of him. A couple of small houses further down, it seemed to be café, but it was closed now. He stopped and tried to orient himself. His pursuers could not be far behind.

He had not run for more than five minutes since he had left the apartment. It was hard to keep track of how much time had passed. He looked around and saw that he was at a crossroads and the traffic was light. The fiery noise of an automated billboard could be heard some distance away, and he moved away from it.

A cable car slipped by a couple of meters above his head. Silently it slid up in front of him and braked softly, stopping on the platform.

He forced himself to take a couple of deep breaths, sucking the air deeply into his lungs. He focused on the exhalation. His heart calmed down. His body tried to relax. The lactic acid in his muscles burned away the last remaining adrenaline. The muscles ached as if somebody stood and sprayed pure fire into them. He walked up to the platform, into the cable car and sat down.

The thought of Elisabeth flew into his head. Were they after her too? His thoughts moved like shadows in a storm. Flapping around, manically dancing in circles, back to the starting point. The cable car started moving.

They must be after her. They knew her name, and they knew she had sent the holocube to him. What did the damned cube contain? What was it that was so important that Marina had to pay for it with her life? He fingered his inner pocket. The hard edges of the holocube were somehow comforting.

His pulse slowed. Tiny vibrations started to creep out into his hands, out to the fingertips until it looked like he was sitting and playing air piano. He clenched his hands and pressed them down onto his lap. Tears rolled from his eyes and trickled down his cheeks.

He shook his head; he must keep a clear head. Elisabeth was still alive. Marina was not. He had to keep it together and focus on finding Elisabeth. To find her was the top priority now. Everything else had to wait, even the grief for Marina.

After a couple of minutes ride, the cable car stopped, and Richard stumbled upon his unsteady legs, walked out, and started to head towards the elevators nearby.

It was something that worked flawlessly in Tabula Rasa. There were a lot of different elevators to go around with, and you could go everywhere in the complex without any hassle. The transport system was designed to be groundbreaking in several different ways. Artificial intelligence steered the elevators and calculated how the system would be used most efficiently. Mounted cameras and sensors supplied the system continuously with information about how people moved. This gave the artificial intelligence time to send elevators and transport to where they would be most useful.

Richard moved to the elevator, and when he approached, the doors slid open. He stepped in and pushed level six, the level where Elisabeth lived. He had to find her. The men who had killed Marina had wanted to catch Elisabeth, and he had to find her first. He prayed that the red-haired man had not already found Elisabeth. His stomach turned when he thought about it, and he leaned onto one of the railings.

*   *   *

"Are you ok?" a voice asked. Richard looked up and saw a woman dressed in something that looked like a jogging outfit and running shoes. The woman stood outside the elevator and took off her headphones. Sweat shined on her forehead, and her cheeks were reddish.

Her eyes radiated warmth and Richard thought he saw real concern in them. The elevator doors were still open, and Richard wished that they would close. He mumbled.

"Oh yes, just a little sick. I'm on my way to my daughter so that she can take care of me." he crossed his fingers that the woman would be discouraged to spend time in an elevator with a sick person. The woman studied him with a puzzled look and shrugged

He froze when the woman entered the elevator, but a few seconds later he thanked his lucky stars because the woman seemed to have lost interest in him when she pulled up her headphones and put them back on her head.

Richards pulse slowed. After half a minute, the elevator doors opened, and Richard walked out of it on unsteady legs. He knew that the woman followed him with her eyes when he walked out, but he did not turn around.

He was only a few minutes away from Elisabeth's apartment, and he hoped that he had made it in time. She had said that she was going to get something, then they would meet at his place.

His beloved daughter. When she had gotten accepted into the university, he had been the proudest father in the world. Richard shook his head and tried to regain something that resembled control. He had to see her as soon as possible. His arms burned with fire. He looked

166

down. No blood. Grateful, but still with his arms filled with burning lava, he staggered towards Elisabeth's apartment.

Falsterbo, Sweden
2048-12-28

It is during the hunt that the hunter is as most alive. The tall man with the eagle nose squatted beside his control panel. He was hidden about hundred meters in the reeds, north of the eleventh tee at Falsterbo golf club.

The soft reeds slowly swayed in the wind and rustled beneath him as he moved. He was almost impossible to see where he was squatting.

The weak smell of sludge rose up from the ground around him, but it did not bother him in the slightest. The man was dressed in camouflage clothes and the contours of his body melted into his surroundings. If you did not know that he was there, he was basically invisible.

He glanced up, saw two men far away on the golf tee. A bird formation slid by in the sky.

The man focused. His breathing was soft and rhythmic. His pulse low. His mission was simple, but the work that led him to his target had been complicated. He would make sure that the man whose name was Raimondo del Louis met his maker. It was that which he would do. It was his task, to remove the threats that were deemed to be removed. He enjoyed the knowledge that he worked for the most powerful man in the world and he was proud of it.

He scratched his sharp nose, raised his binoculars and studied the two men as they moved on the golf course. A water droplet ran along his cheek, and he wiped it away. It had been hard work to get all the way into the reeds where he was located, but he was in excellent physical shape and managed that part unseen.

In front of him, on a folding table, was a black box. Next to the box was a laptop. The eagle-nosed man worked quickly and uploaded the latest DNA samples from the target. He had, several times already, been inside the house where the target lived and taken several different small DNA samples. It had been a simple job. Later he had used a portable DNA-replicator to analyze and generate Raimondo's genetic profile. In the end, he had developed a profile that he would use as target coordinates.

His fingers flew over the keyboard, and after a couple of seconds, he pushed a button on the side of the black box.

It blinked quickly, and from the control panel, a weak humming started that indicated that the dragonfly inside was ready. He aimed a sensitive microphone toward the two men who were at the eleventh tee. He put on his headphones, heard them crackle, and then fall silent. The sound quality was unbeatable. He adjusted the quality until it sounded as good as if he was standing next to them. The highly sensitive microphone picked up the conversation without any problem.

"What do you mean, alive?" a weak humming noise stopped almost instantly.

"Exactly what I'm saying." the voice crackled.

"Do you mean that the thing they found in orbit is alive? How can it be alive? What is it?" Erik's voice trembled with excitement.

"It is pretty unclear at the moment, but according to the information we've collected, it seems to be alive, this thing that they found, but what it is we don't have information about yet."

"But, oh my god. A living object in space? It sounds like pure fantasy. How can be alive in space?"

"Yes, it sounds totally incredible, but it actually seems to be true. Vendrick has been in constant contact with the space station, and they act apparently as a relay station for the communication between Tabula Rasa and the sphere."

"What are they communicating about?"

A pause as one of them leaned down to pick up something from the grass.

"That part of the communication we haven't managed to crack yet."

"So, you don't know what they are saying to the sphere?"

"No."

"It sounds like a fantasy. One of the world's most powerful men, who's the boss of one of the greatest mega-complexes on Earth has found an unknown, living object in space that they now have secret conversations with."

* * *

The eagle-nosed man had heard enough. He studied both men with his binoculars for a few more minutes. He glanced toward the tee and saw Raimondo hit his second ball, it flew in a short, sharp arch over the water and landed in the bunker.

Erik stood behind the bunkers and waved with his club to show that he had seen where Raimondo's ball had landed. Raimondo waved back and started walking up on the wooden bridge that crossed the water toward the green. The eagle-nosed man observed Erik and saw that he was busy with finding his own ball that had gone too far. He entered the commands that would activate the dragonfly.

A hatch on the control panel slid silently to the side, and after a couple of seconds an insect that resembled a dragonfly crept out. It was only a couple of centimeters long. Instead of a body of organic material, this dragonfly consisted of extremely miniaturized and efficient machinery. It folded out its wings and quickly ascended. The eagle-nosed man did not have to do anything more, the dragonfly was autonomous and would find its victim without any further involvement from him.

* * *

The dragonfly homed in on its target and smoothly flew toward it. It quickly flew under Raimondo's leg, made a sharp turn and just below the chin it released a knockout gas that acted instantaneously. The gas was a synthesized, fast-acting version of Fentanyl.

The effect was immediate. Raimondo felt like a hammer had hit his chest. He lost his orientation and fumbled wildly with his arms. His mouth opened to suck in air but instead sucked the gas deeper into his lungs. He tried to keep his balance but lost it and fell.

Erik looked up when he heard the splash, he stood next to the most remote bunker and tried to locate Raimondo. He could not see him. Nothing. Took a couple of steps to the side. Still nothing. There were at least seventy meters to the bridge. He turned around, looking after his own ball. After a couple of seconds, he again turned to the bridge and expected Raimondo to show up. Nothing.

Raimondo was nowhere to be seen. Erik grimaced. Waited. Something was wrong. An undefinable feeling of frustration and fear started to get a hold of him. He started walking towards the bridge. First slowly, then

170

faster. He threw the golf club on the ground when he started running toward the bridge. Fast steps now. Panic welled up inside him.

"Raimondo! Where are you?"

He could not move his legs fast enough. He shouted.

"Raimondo!"

He quickly ran across the green. Past the bunkers and up toward the wooden bridge. His eyes searching. There. Something glimpsed in the water. It looked like a big sack. He shouted.

"Raimondo!"

But he already knew. He knew that the thing in the water was Raimondo. He ran up on the bridge, jumped down next to his friend, stumbling when he landed in the murky water.

The brown water splashed up, and he got it in his mouth, in his eyes. It stung, and he wiped it off. Staggering now, he reached Raimondo and got a hold of his shoulder. He pulled, trying to pull Raimondo's head out of the water so that he did not drown.

It was shallow where he stood, maybe five meters from the edge. Maybe half a meter deep. The water was cold and murky. The faint stench increased when the mud swirled up in large currents when Erik struggled. He got hold of the collar of Raimondo's sweater and pulled. Raimondo's body rolled over. Dirty, stinky water washed over Raimondo's nose and mouth. His eyes were closed. Erik screamed.

"No! Raimondo!"

He struggled to keep Raimondo's head above water, but his water-soaked clothes were incredibly heavy. Erik's legs buckled as he tried to get a firm grip on his friend. He yelled.

"Help! Somebody help me!"

He gasped. The cold water quickly drained his strength. His heart was pounding like a jackhammer in his chest.

His legs sank deep into the bottom of the mud when he tore and pulled to get Raimondo's body to solid ground.

His shins throbbed with pain. He pulled and tried to drag Raimondo's body to land. A sharp pain shot through his leg and it buckled. Small, black stars began to encroach his field of vision. He stumbled, fell, got up, and fell again.

Each time, more dirty water washed over Raimondo's face. Erik could not see if Raimondo was breathing or if he was already dead. He screamed again, so loud that his voice cracked, and pain tore at his throat.

"Help me! Somebody! For god's sake, help me!"
Far away, he heard someone answer. He could not look up because he was afraid of letting go of Raimondo. He tried to answer, but only a croaking sound escaped his mouth.

Raimondo slipped out of his grip, rolled over and his face fell back under the surface. Desperately, he pulled on Raimondo's body trying to turn him around, but any strength he had, left him catastrophically fast. He yelled. With his last strength, he pushed for king and country, and finally, it slid over on its side. Dark, disgusting water drizzled out of Raimondo's lifeless body.

Erik collapsed beside Raimondo, and he sunk down to his knees in the stinking water. He turned his eyes to the sky and wondered why God had abandoned him. He was ready to give up when he heard voices getting closer. He pointed weakly at Raimondo.

"Save him. Please, save him. He cannot die like this."
Two men quickly jumped down from the bridge and with a powerful grip, they dragged Raimondo the last stretch towards the grass verge. He was not moving. They turned him over on his back and started CPR.

* * *

Further away, the tall man with the eagle nose smiled. He lowered the binoculars and nodded. Mission accomplished. The second part of the operation could now start. He knew that his brothers would take care of the lawyer who had found out too much.

Swiftly, his fingers moved over the controls and pressed a button on the side of the box. After a few seconds, he heard the extremely weak sound of the dragonfly. He saw it as it approached and slowed softly in mid-air and slid down towards the box. When it had entered the box, the hatch closed. He glanced up. A pair of swallows approached him a meter above the reeds, turning to the east when they discovered him and disappeared. He studied them for a few seconds and then returned to pack the rest of his gear and left the screaming and the uproar behind him.

It is the early bird that catches the worm. They had slept well, and both were filled with energy. Malin and Denver entered the beautiful elevator together and saw that Derek Lamm, dressed in a suit that looked like it was two sizes too small, was waiting for them.

The elevator doors closed softly behind them, and unnoticeable, they started their ascent.

Faint, instrumental music streamed from hidden speakers. Malin looked over to one of the elevator walls that were covered with floor-to-ceiling mirrors. On the opposing side, three artworks hung, and she saw that they slowly changed shape. It did not look like any elevator Malin had ever been into. She stared, fascinated, while the three abstract artworks changed appearance into something more modernistic in pace with the rhythm of the music.

Malin was dressed in a dark pantsuit. Her long hair was tied back, and her nails were perfect with a sharp French manicure. Denver had a dark blue suit with a blood-red tie. The shoes were polished, and his hair combed back. They were the quintessential picture of effectiveness. This was their specialty, a super-professional appearance that demanded respect and a little fear. They had perfected this routine in the last year and functioned almost like a single entity. One ended what the other started. They stood together in the elevator on their way up to their first meeting with Vendrick.

They had been promised two interviews during the time they would spend at Tabula Rasa and they would use the opportunity to the fullest. The set-up for the first interview was to get to know him and ask questions from a pre-approved list of questions that the press officers at Tabula Rasa had gone through with them.

If the first interview went well, and they passed through the needle's eye, they would be allowed to carry out a second, more informal interview with Vendrick. Malin's pulse increased slightly. She did not know where the longing for fame came from and it was also irrelevant, she had it, and she would act to satisfy it.

She glanced over at Denver and saw that he was equally fascinated by the beautiful, almost lifelike works of art.

"They are beautiful, aren't they?" Lamm saw their obvious fascination with the three paintings.

Malin nodded.

"Yes, they are absolutely amazing. I've never seen anything like it. It looks like they're alive."

Lamm laughed.

"Yes, they are quite fascinating. They are created by an artist named Leila Oman who lives here. We were lucky we managed to get her here, it was actually quite dramatic."

Denver turned his eyes away from the paintings.

"What happened?"

Lamm corrected his already perfect tie and told the story of how Leila had come to an application center and after dramatic events, came to Tabula Rasa. Denver sounded doubtful.

"So, she stepped straight into an application center, and just like that, she came here?"

Lamm's eyes blazed, and Malin seemed to see something furious in them.

"No, nothing like that. We have a rigorous process for investigating and interviewing all the candidates applying to Tabula Rasa. There is a whole combination of tests, interviews, and applications a person has to go through before he or she is formally allowed to apply for a place here."

Malin looked furtively over at Denver with a meaningful look. Denver apologized.

"I did not mean to offend anyone. I was not aware that you had such an extensive process for selecting candidates."

Lamm allowed himself to be appeased.

"Yes, we have. One of the toughest and most demanding selection processes among all the mega-complexes. We in Tabula only want the best. The competition for coming here is tough, so we can luckily allow ourselves to be a bit picky", he laughed, and his eyes were fixed on Malin.

Lamm smile widens just as the elevator stopped and the elevator doors quietly slid open. He gestured to Malin and Denver to step out. Malin returned the smile, and they walked out of the elevator.

"It's impressive. I have of course heard rumors like everyone else about Tabula Rasa, but once you see it, it's undoubtedly admirable."

Lamm smiled if possible even wider, so you almost saw all his shiny bright white teeth.

"Thank you, thank you, it's very kind of you. We ourselves believe that we succeeded quite well here, but it is always nice to hear it from someone from the outside."

"From the outside? Do you think of all the other people of the world who do not live here like those from the outside?"

Malin frowned, kind of jokingly.

"Well, that's not what I meant," laughed Lamm, "It was more a reflection of what you said. But, of course, I have understood that some who live here have acclimatized themselves very quickly and I have heard some talk about those from the outside when they talk to each other. I guess it is in some people's nature to divide the world into compartments."

Malin smiled and turned away and walked the narrow corridor to the vaulted exit. She knew that Derek was studying her. She had an instinctive feeling that something was wrong with him. Formally, Lamm had been very helpful. He had picked them up from their luxury suite where they had been accommodated and given them a spectacular sightseeing tour within the complex.

A lunch worthy of a king had been laid out, and Malin wondered why they received such opulent treatment. Admittedly, both she and Denver worked for an international magazine, but she still thought it seemed excessive that they would be treated like superstars. She had come to Tabula Rasa to make an honest report about how one of the most powerful men in the world had built up a vision like this. They had still not met Vendrick, and an uneasy feeling of anxiety had begun to get a hold of her. She turned toward Lamm.

"I believe we had an appointment with John Vendrick. When can we meet him?"

Lamm seemed surprised by the question but quickly found his feet.

"He is a very busy man. When he gets an opening in his schedule, I'm sure you are at the top of the list." He beamed.

Malin fixed her gaze on Lamm.

"Yes, I really hope so. I don't want to have traveled all the way here to then being cheated on the main course."

Lamm stiffened, his eyes flashed.

"No. As I said, I'm sure you're on the top of the list when he gets the time."

Lamm gestured with his arm that she should continue out through the archway. She turned around and stepped out. She gasped.

In front of her, the most beautiful scene she had ever seen presented itself. They were more than two hundred meters up and the long balcony they were on, closely weaved itself against the wall in an undulating shape.

She glanced down and saw a huge park spread out below them.

Fountains in the park below looked like small wells, and the major roads that crossed it in regular patterns resembled narrow paths. One side of the park was covered with large trees and resembled a forest area. The other had several large hills crossed by a waterfall. It was so high to the roof where they were that birds flew freely inside, and Malin stood speechless for several seconds staring at the scene in front of her.

Usually, mega-complexes had a certain crowded, claustrophobic feeling about them. Sure, there used to be open spaces where people could relax, but not in this way. Lamm saw that she was impressed.

"This is the largest of our parks. Genesis Park. It serves as a natural meeting place and is open to everyone, day and night." He smiled.

Denver pointed down to a lake where several small boats slowly slid forward.

"I see you have rowing boats you can rent too?"
Lamm snickered.

"Both yes and no. We have a variety of transports here at Tabula. Some more romantic than others. But they cost almost nothing, they are basically free."

Denver and Malin watched with fascination at the magnificent view when an open carriage quietly glided up next to them, and she saw that it was a similar carriage that the dozens of others she saw sliding around beneath her. The carriages followed what appeared to be invisible rails around the park and different trails branched out like nerve pathways in an organism.

The carriages hovered a few centimeters above the ground and were completely silent. In the larger carriages, there was space for more than ten people, in the smaller, maybe two. Malin looked amazed at the carriages slowly moving around, in what looked like a choreographed pattern. In the park, she could count eleven of them that were filled with people and slid from one destination to the other.

Lamm led the way, and they sat down in the carriage which glided down towards the park.

"How do they work, the carriages?"

"It's an invention that we developed further," Derek said proudly. "Each apartment has at least one carriage belonging to it and can be freely disposed of by the apartment owners. When not in use, it is available to transport around other people when needed. We have a sophisticated system that balances supply with demand."

"Are they powered by electricity?"

"Of course. Tabula Rasa is energy positive in the sense that we produce more energy than we spend. The surplus is sold to the continental African power grid."

"What kind of production do you have here? I know some about the fact you have research and development, but in what areas?" Denver looked out over the area.

Lamm turned to him.

"We are the world leaders in many areas, but especially in robotics and genetics, we belong to the absolute top players. Tabula Rasa has built on what generations of prominent scientists have created, and we have taken it to a new level", he paused effectively." You can almost say that it is here that the next chapter of human history will be written."

He blinked and smiled a dazzling smile.

He tried to convince himself that he was the all-seeing eye that saw everything that was going on, nothing would go undetected. John Vendrick III gazed at one of four, beveled screens in front of him while he rolled a thick gold coin between his fingers. His thoughts were interrupted when the holophone chirped.

The call was unexpected and unwelcome. He leaned forward in his chair and pushed a button. Arik Zimki's glimmering face slowly faded in on the holoscreen in front of him.

"John."

John swallowed hard and nodded.

"Arik."

Arik Zimki was one of the top leaders of another mega-complex, Helder Ster, located just outside of Johannesburg. Several different leaders of a selected group of mega-complexes around the world had secretly joined forces to expand their cooperation without the United Nations prying eyes, and Arik was one of the more prominent voices within the group.

"I have spoken with the group about the past week's turn of events, and with the United Nations increasing interest in Tabula Rasa's cloning program", he looked straight at John, "And to speak clearly, we are worried. According to our sources of information, the United Nations is preparing to press charges against you and will force you to hand over those who are responsible for the banned cloning programs."

John was speechless, he drummed nervously with his fingers on the table and damned himself the same second when he caught himself doing it. He clenched his fist and put it in his lap, out of sight of Arik. He was just about to answer when Arik continued.

"And we are all in agreement that this brings too much attention to you and indirectly to us." Arik's stone-colored gray eyes stared straight at John. John twisted.

"I know that this was not the most advantageous process, but I have put plans into action that will neutralize the threat", John smiled stiffly, "It will actually be resolved quite soon."

Arik`s face glittered when the signal for the hologram experienced interference.

"You better. We can't afford any mistakes. The group is nervous that this attention can ruin our ongoing plans."

John nodded stiffly, but inside he was raging. Arik had spoken with the group without him. It was highly irregular. When the group met, all nine members should be included, all, without exception.

Arik`s mouth pressed into a thin line.

"One more thing."

John blinked when Arik leaned forward.

"That lawyer that we have kept our eyes on. He seems to have extensive plans regarding your eventual indictment."

John felt like he was standing in front of a teacher that was lecturing him.

"Yes, I'm aware of that and also, for that problem, I'm working on a solution."

Arik glared at John.

"Just make sure your back is clear. We cannot afford any mistakes."

Before John could answer, Arik terminated the connection. John remained seated, he was still speechless. He closed his eyes and grabbed the gold coin.

* * *

John felt the hard edges of the coin and enjoyed the relief it brought him. The coin, an older American twenty-dollar coin from 1907, was worth over a million dollars and he let his fingers gently slide over it.

There was something magic about gold coins, and he smiled when he thought about the older, now deceased, former owner who had to die so that John could hold it in his hand. Normally, a coin collector would not touch the coins with his bare hands; all contact would be done gently with gloved hands, but John did not care about that. When he felt a valuable, unique coin between his fingers and let his fingertips explore every edge on the coins, he would shiver with pleasure.

He put the coin down into its holder, leaned forward, and studied the screen. It showed the two journalists walking along the aisle down to one of the research labs.

John was in his office and sat down in his handmade wooden chair. He slowly sipped at a freshly brewed cup of coffee while enjoying the smell that surrounded him. It was not just any coffee. He only drank the best. This was a type of coffee from the famous Hacienda La Esmeralda. The world's finest coffee. The coffee beans were grown only in one place throughout the world, on the famous Mount Baru in Panama.

Many coffee connoisseurs around the world could only dream of drinking a cup of coffee made from beans from Mount Baru. For John Vendrick III, it was normal. A smile spread across his lips. He was born to superiority, and it was his right to enjoy life and what it had to offer him. John enjoyed the warmth from the coffee and the divine flavor of it.

Jackie came walking up to him, and he signaled to the dog to jump up in his lap.

On the screen, the two journalists stood together and talked to Lamm. John had worked intensively with Lamm in the last few days and prepared for their visit.

This was the first time some independent journalists from outside had gained access to Tabula Rasa. It was exciting, he had always craved control, and that need had meant that the whole process that had created Tabula Rasa had in principle been done without the prying eyes of the world press.

The increase in the last years of terrorist attacks on a global level and accelerating environmental degradation had created a constant stream of requests to the mega-complexes. Admittedly, this interest had risen steadily, but Tabula Rasa application rates were still at a level far above the others.

The perception of Tabula Rasa was that it was as safe and secure as the others but also something more. Something more undefinable. A perception that life in Tabula Rasa was a part of humanity's next step. That, if a person got in there, you lived happily ever after. Tabula Rasa lived well on its legendary reputation as the elite of the mega-complexes that now grew up around the world. It was here that the next generation of humanity would arise, like an empty canvas that was filled by the creator's genius. This was his Tabula Rasa.

His eyes drifted over to another computer screen, and for the hundredth time, he saw the grainy film about how the sphere in orbit responded to their communications. The camera angle was not the best, the film came from a camera that was on the automatic relay station that was used to communicate between Tabula Rasa's space station and the ground. The space station caught sight of the sphere when it had risen from the lunar surface and placed itself in orbit around the moon.

They already had a good idea of how it behaved. They had managed to establish contact with it by chance. One of the technicians at the space station was to set up the transmitter that used laser light to communicate but had mistakenly entered the coordinates of the sphere.

The technician had quickly realized his mistake and was just about to reprogram the transmitter when the amazing happened. The sphere had responded. The film showed how the sphere had answered the communication with its own communication. John fascinatedly stared at the data stream that the sphere sent, and the relay station forwarded. The sphere had responded with a similar laser pulse that they had sent, and for John, it had decided the question of whether the sphere was intelligent or not.

But exactly what the sphere sent was not as clear. His best scientists had made progress in interpreting the information, but the code was far from broken. They needed a key in the communication with the sphere, and they were getting close to understanding what the key to knowing what the large parts were made of, but it was not all the information. But it was just a matter of time. Maybe the space station in orbit around the moon would help to solve the problem.

Dr Zoltan worked at the space station monitoring the sphere, and John had the biggest confidence in him. As John, Dr. Zoltan was a believer. He believed wholeheartedly in Tabula Rasa and would do everything to manage to uncover the secrets of the sphere.

His eyes glided over to another screen that showed the price trend of all listed mega-complexes. He nodded contently when he saw that the price for Tabula Rasa shares continued to skyrocket. The other mega-complexes were not nearly as profitable as Tabula Rasa.

He returned to the first screen. The female journalist looked good. Very good. He smiled when the familiar hunger rose within. It was always there. Sometimes it burned more intensively and sometimes it was weaker. But it never stopped burning. Never. It was a part of him. The intense fire that demanded sacrifices.

The watch on his wrist vibrated lightly. He looked down and smiled. It was time for his daily injection. It was something he enjoyed every day, the process had been going on for a couple of weeks now, and he knew that he had developed and that the process would extend his life. Ever since he was a kid, John had felt an indefinable sense of inferiority towards other people. It had been a powerful driving force for him and had motivated him to develop both physically and mentally, but it was not enough, he needed more.

As an extra bonus from the research programs his researchers were working on, John himself could enjoy the fruits of their labor. He had ordered that a specially designed cocktail of different synthetic steroids would be made unique for him. It was unique in history. Never would a man undergo such a specialized transformation as he would do.

In addition to his daily strict regime of diet and exercise, he received injections that would transform him into something like a god. It was not completely risk-free, but it was worth it. He would show both Arik and the group what potential he had.

A faint knock was heard, and the door opened, and Dr. Ln'geem entered the room.

"Good day, sir."

John nodded at the doctor.

"It's time."

* * *

The carriage arrived at the station and Lamm gestured to Malin and Denver to get out of it and move on in the long corridor to which they had arrived. The thick gold ring on Lamm's finger glimmered. The corridor was narrow, only a few meters wide, with quite a high ceiling. As she passed

186

Lamm, she again felt the weak, sour smell, she wrinkled her nose. She shook her head slowly for the smell to go away and moved on. Her eyes were drawn upwards. The ceiling arched high above them and was covered with thousands of tiny lights. Malin studied the corridor. She pointed straight up.

"What an odd design?" she said with a questioning voice.

Lamm chuckled.

"Yes, one of our research managers became over inspired and took his artistic intentions a little too far." he paused, "There is a certain artistic freedom in Tabula Rasa, but this was not entirely successful. It is scheduled to be redesigned soon though. It will get a more uniform look."

Denver took a step into the corridor.

"I don't know if it's necessary." he hesitated, "I like it."

Malin nodded behind him.

"Me too."

Lamm looked curiously at them, and a sting of doubt touched her, his gaze rested on her for a few seconds too long.

"Please continue forward. We will soon come to one of the bio-labs. It is one of those who works with our human regeneration experiments and serum."

Denver walked beside Malin.

"Isn't that dangerous, not to say illegal? I mean, human experiments? What kind of human experiments do you mean that you do here?"

Lamm seemed unconcerned.

"Not at all, this is one of our most important labs. This lab works with a lot of different antibiotics and serums. We are at the absolute cutting edge in the research both within plant and animal research, but also within human research" he paused, "Do you remember that outbreak of Tunis fever two years ago?"

Both Malin and Denver nodded.

"The outbreak lasted for five weeks. Three thousand five hundred dead, ten times the number of invalids for life. A real tragedy."

Malin remembered. The outbreak had started in Tunis, at a monastery of all places. One morning several of the monks had woken up with high fever and cramps. The sick had immediately been isolated, and help had been called for.

But the doctors had no diagnosis of what it could be, they were powerless. No medicines or treatments helped. The cramps that the patients experienced were so powerful that several of them broke bones in their bodies when the cramps struck.

After two days, seven patients were sick, after three, there were seventeen. The treatments that were given to the patients had been ineffective. All the suggestions of what it could be were wrong, and none of the treatments had worked. And the nightmare had just begun. In two weeks, the disease had spread outside the monastery, and thousands more got sick and died.

And then, like a miracle, it had stopped. The sick became healthy overnight. Just as if everyone had received the medicine at the same time, though it was impossible. People who were almost dying had miraculously sat themselves up after a day or two, without any detriment. It was unbelievable.

The researchers had analyzed all imaginable explanations, but nothing explained what happened. Broken bones usually did not just take a few days to heal, but now it did. The doctors were perplexed, and despite all analysis, it was still unknown how it had happened. In the tests that were done, they could not trace the medicine that was behind this amazing recovery. Lamm gesticulated at them to keep on walking.

"It was us. We were the ones who had the medicine available, and when we saw an imminent catastrophe, we intervened." He fell silent. Malin hastily spun around.

"Was it you?" Her voice went up an octave.

Lamm smiled at her and nodded.

"Yes, it was us. We want to help mankind, and we saw an opportunity to do it."

Hundreds of questions bubbled up in her, but she controlled herself.

"Why didn't you say anything about it?" She paused," Everyone thinks that it was a miracle. Why not take credit?"

Lamm looked straight ahead.

"At Tabula Rasa, we're not interested in getting any hero status or anything like that. There was a need for help, and I must admit that it was not just an altruistic feeling of helping that affected our actions. If the infection had spread according to our forecasts, most of Africa would have been infected within a month. And if that had happened, it would have only been a matter of time before the infection found its way over to Tabula Rasa." Lamm paused a couple of seconds and smiled, "So, you understand, it was also a part of self-preservation that was involved."

Denver looked in surprise at Lamm while they walked down the long aisle.

"But the world needs to know that it was you who helped them. Even if you don't want the attention or gratitude for it, the sick has a right to understand what helped them."

Lamm studied Denver and shrugged.

"You are probably right. But it's not my decision. The decision to not inform the world was taken far above my head."

Malin looked curiously at him.

"How did you manage to distribute the medicine to so many at once? Was it something in the water?" Lamm smirked.

"No, it wasn't." he looked at her, paused, "It was one of the easiest things. To give medicine to many people at once is not difficult. It's simple logistics."

"But how?"

Lamm arrived at the door and turned around against Malin and Denver.

"Drones. A vast number of small drones that are controlled by a distribution network. On a given command the antidote is distributed, and voilà."

Denver was just about to ask how the drones were controlled when Lamm put the hand on a sensor plate, and the door slid open with a hissing sound.

* * *

John noticed the first injection going into his body. A gentle heat began to spread throughout his limbs, and he heard his own pulse pounding in his ears. His fingers became soft and warm.

Small waves of dizziness rose up from within, and he grabbed both armrests and breathed deeply. He focused on the beautiful view from his window. The sun was high in the sky and reflected off the pyramids in front of him. A dozen flying crafts of different sizes circulated the area in front of him, some on the way up, some on the way down. He focused on a cargo plane, which after a long, slow turn went in for a landing, then he blinked.

"How are you, sir?" the doctor's voice sounded concerned, "Shall we continue?"

John struggled to control his deep breathing, and a certain amount of control returned, he nodded. The doctor studied him for a few seconds and returned the

190

nod. He reopened his medicine bag and pulled out a syringe with a reddish shimmering content. The doctor tapped the syringe with his finger and held it up against the light. John observed it. It was beautiful, like shining blood mixed with microscopic diamonds.

The sun's rays were caught in it, and John thought it had a magical look. It was in these red syringes that the real magic was contained. The treatment consisted of two injections. The first prepared the body, while the other went in and began the transformation. He nodded towards the doctor. The doctor tapped the syringe one last time, disinfected a patch of skin on Johns' arm, pushed the contents into his arm and pulled it out as he pressed a sterile bandage against the minuscule hole.

John glanced down at the bandage, bent his arm, looked out and saw the big, clumsy cargo plane come in for landing. Slow and deliberate, it turned around until it was on the right course. He stared fascinated on the four large rotating engines on the plane, slowly changing the angle, so the speed was reduced while the familiar heat rose inside.

A glowing fire radiated out from his arm, slowly at first, smoldering, and then faster. He breathed hard, erratically, and he looked up, saw the cargo plane approaching the runway and extending the landing gear.

Inside his body, the microscopically small robots rushed forth and began their work. The fire in his body grew in intensity. The heat inside him rose to an inferno, and his body became a volcano that was ready to erupt.

The large cargo plane descended towards the ground, landed, and rolled forward on the short runway.

He roared, and the volcano inside him roared as well.

* * *

John rested for an hour and then informed Derek that he should bring their guests to his office. He sat behind the desk, and the strength from the injections was rushing through him. He smiled widely when the door slid up in front of Malin and Denver, he waved for them to enter.

"Come in, dear, come in."
Malin took the lead and stepped into the room, Denver followed a step behind. John stood up and met them and took Malin's hand. She noticed his powerful yet soft handshake.

"Welcome to Tabula Rasa", John paused for a second before he continued, "I hope you have been well received here?"

Malin looked up at John Vendrick III, who was a head taller than she was. His sharp features and strong chin were as chiseled stone. The head was covered with dark hair with flecks of white-greyish strands, and his eyes were pale gray. His well-defined muscles moved beneath the expensive shirt, and she got the impression that he was in excellent physical shape.

His skin glowed, and Malin could not see any wrinkles at all in his face. She had expected a middle-aged man, and she had to try not to stare when she saw the youthful man in front of her. John nodded at Lamm who remained standing outside the open door. Lamm took a step forward and closed the door. Malin looked at Lamm when he closed the door, turned to John and nodded.

"Thank you, it's very kind of you. And yes, we have been well treated." She studied his eyes, tried to penetrate them, "It's really kind to let us come here."
John's eyes sparkled.

"That's good but call me John. I have given Derek strict orders to take good care of you, and it is nice to hear that my instructions have been performed as instructed." he turned to Denver, "and you must be the famous Denver Mikkelsen."

Denver was as tall as John. He met John's eyes and smiled.

"Thank you, John. It was kind of you to meet us."

John took a step back and gestured at them to follow him.

"Let us sit down and talk." He walked over to a sofa set along the edge of the large room. John's scent reached her when she followed him, it was magnetic, intoxicating. She shook her head to clear her mind and looked around. Everywhere she looked, she saw precious art on the walls and beautiful sculptures placed around the room. She glanced over one of the paintings as she passed by and for a moment lost her breath, she could barely believe her eyes. The painting she saw on the wall could not be original, it was impossible.

On the wall hung one of the world's most famous theft items in the art world. More than sixty years ago, a spectacular theft had taken place at the Gardner Museum in Boston. One night, two men had dressed as police officers and had gained access to the museum. Once inside, they had overpowered the guards, and in less than an hour, they had stolen some of the world's most famous paintings, including the one Malin looked at in front of her.

She did not remember the name of it, but she knew that it was painted by Rembrandt. The painting depicted a small boat filled with people who struggled on a stormy sea. Malin remembered that she read an article about the theft several years ago. John's voice was behind her.

"Is everything ok?"

Malin spun around and damned herself. She had been in the room for less than a minute, but she had already made a fool of herself, she nodded and forced a smile.

"Yes, everything is fine." She paused for a couple of seconds before she continued, "It's the painting, it really caught my interest."

John looked at the ship that was seconds from capsizing. He smiled.

"My Rembrandt? Yes, it really is a real gold nugget I have there." He took a few steps toward it, "and the story behind it is almost as amazing as the painting itself."

Malin kept silent and hoped it would entice John to share more information. She held her breath. John studied her carefully.

"The story is actually pretty interesting, if I may say so myself."

She frowned in response to his indirect question whether he should continue.

"As you know, there was a famous burglary in 1973 at the Gardner Museum in Boston. The paintings were gone for over 40 years. But seventeen years ago, Interpol made a breakthrough. Eleven of the paintings were found after an anonymous tip, hidden in a warehouse in Milan that belonged to a local art dealer who had died three years earlier."

Malin looked doubtfully at John.

"Eleven?"

John smiled.

"Yes, eleven. One had been destroyed during the escape. And the last one had disappeared. It was not found together with the other eleven."

She was dry in her mouth. John saw her reaction and chuckled.

"Yes, guilty. It should be returned, I know, but it speaks to me. A friend of a friend managed to save the painting from the fate of being wrapped in a warehouse for decades and not having someone who could enjoy it."

Denver stood silently behind Malin and John, they seemed to have forgotten that he was there. Denver walked up beside Malin and looked at the painting but saw nothing special. John pointed.

"There. Do you see?" His finger pointed toward the boat. Denver followed his pointing finger and looked. He saw some of the men in the boat sitting together in what seemed to be a discussion while others fought so that the boat would not capsize. Denver shook his head.

"What am I looking for?"

John's smile grew wider.

"There", he went closer and pointed at a specific figure that sat in the middle of the group of men.

"It's Jesus."

Denver gasped. Now he saw it. The man had long curly hair, and he saw that the man resembled how Jesus used to be depicted on paintings and pictures.

"What is he doing? Does he hold a sermon while the storm is sinking them?"

John Vendrick III laughed, and Malin felt his scent, but she could not take her eyes of Rembrandt's *The Storm on the Sea of Galilee.*

Fear had granted her additional power, but now she started to whittle. Elisabeth's heart pounded in her chest, sweat poured down into her eyes and stung. She wiped her eyes and blinked to focus. Her mouth was dry and sandy, and she struggled to generate saliva in her mouth.

She rushed on into the park and past a couple of futuristic fountains; the pouring, splashing sound calmed her down when she passed them. At this time of the day, the park was deserted, not many people were on their way to their work or doing errands.

There was something desolated about the surroundings. Elisabeth had reflected about it before when she sometimes had worked through the whole night and got home early in the morning, but she never paid much attention to it. But now, as her senses were working overtime and she registered every impression as a potential threat, it was like every shadow contained something that could jump out and attack her.

She forced herself to slow down, she tripped and nearly fell. In front of her, the area opened up. Large holosigns showed the way to different places and were deployed at strategic points around the area. Stone covered walkways that cut through the park were sparkling clean, and she saw the small automated cleaning robots slide around.

An elderly lady walked past and raised her eyebrows. Elisabeth forced herself to walk and fixed her eyes to the ground. She followed a path that went to some service elevators that she knew were a bit further ahead. While she tried to move on as fast and unnoticed as possible, she saw a couple of guards on the left that was approaching.

Usually, you rarely saw any guards at Tabula Rasa, and when you did see them, they used to be at a distance. Praxis within Tabula Rasa was that the guards kept their distance at all times, except for when it came to an emergency. Elisabeth forced herself to walk even slower, but she saw the guards in the corner of her eye getting closer. An icy feeling rose in her chest. She could run, but it would have been useless. The guards were well trained and would catch up to her in no time. One of the guards spoke to her and stepped in front of her. She was forced to meet his eyes

"Hold on there, miss." His mouth made a thin smile. She tried to say something, but her voice did not obey. Fear tore inside her like a hurricane. Sweat poured down her back and spread cold chills through her body. The guard studied her thoroughly and stretched out his hand to indicate that she should remain where she was.

"One moment." she heard steps running behind her, and instinctively she tensed her back muscles and pulled up her shoulders and expected to be tackled. But the impact never came. Instead, the other guard jogged up to her, and while he smiled, he pulled out a scarf. She looked in astonishment around to the place where the other guard had come from.

"Here Miss, you dropped your scarf." the smiling guard nodded at her while Elisabeth mumbled.

"Thank you."

She damned herself for being so reckless and tried her best to behave normally and smiled to the guards while she turned around and walked away. She glanced discreetly at them to see if they were following her, but they had turned around and now walked back to the elevators.

A stone fell from her chest when she saw that. She took a couple of deep breaths, tried to get her heart under control and sat down on a bench to get her thoughts together.

It was not her father who had convinced her to come here, but he had spoken very highly of Tabula Rasa to her for a long time. He had searched for something new, and he had found it here at Tabula Rasa.

Elisabeth lived, during that time, with her husband in Madrid, but her husband had died in a car accident when he was on his way home from work, and she had become a widow.

She looked up, and the artificial sun warmed her face. A couple of service carriages further down along one side of the park cleaned the streets and a couple of sanitation workers walked with small, mobile cleaning units. A faint smell of cleaning detergents reached her. Elisabeth looked at them, but everything was different, what was normal yesterday was now the opposite.

A violent, dark shadow had taken over inside of her, and at once the world had become hostile. Some service technicians were walking together and talked about a reparation assignment they were doing. An elderly lady was out walking her cat on a leash.

She hoped intensely that her father had managed to get out of the apartment and brought the holocube with him. Her mind raced.

She arrived at one of the elevators that would take her to her apartment and stepped in. She touched her pocket, the holocube was still there. Safe. As something steady to hold onto when her surroundings had started to crumble. A few minutes passed. She stepped out of the elevator. Glanced up and down the long aisle. Nobody there. Slowly, she walked up to her door, entered the code on the lock when a voice whispered behind her.

"Elisabeth!"

She jumped and spun around at the same time. It was her father, and she exhaled explosively.

"Dad! What are you doing here?" she threw herself forward and gave him a big hug.

Richard held his daughter hard and tears ran down his face.

"Marina is dead. I can't go home, they know. They know everything."

Elisabeth gasped.

"What are you saying? How?"

Richard shook his head while he told her of what had happened in the apartment. He told her about the men that had come for the holocube and how the red-haired man had picked up Marina as if she was a doll and how he had broken her neck. Elisabeth saw the terror in her father's face, and tears started to run down her cheeks.

"Dad, I'm so sorry. I didn't know that they would come so fast."

Her voice choked, and when he saw how she suffered, he took her in his arms and held her tight.

"It's not your fault. You couldn't possibly have known that those men would come." he calmed his voice while he tried to find strength, "it's not your fault."

They stood a couple of minutes and tried to digest the terrible thing that had happened to Marina. Richards's voice was low.

"They'll be coming after us too you know. Those men won't quit. I saw that in them. They will keep on coming until they get want they want. We must escape, immediately. You can't go to your apartment. We have to leave right away."

Elisabeth nodded thoughtfully.

"Yes, they will probably do that. They want what is on the holocube. It is information that we have to get out from here."

Richard looked at her.

"What does the holocube contain? What is it that is so important in it?"

Elisabeth swallowed.

"Do you have it? Did you bring it when you fled?"

Richard dug his hand into a pocket and pulled it out. She took it and turned it over in her hand. She nodded solemnly.

"It contains information that will change the world. Forever."

Richard stared blankly at his daughter.

"What do you mean change the world?"

Elisabeth took up her own holocube and kept both together in her open hand while a sweat drop ran down toward her eye. She wiped it off.

"We are not alone. We are not alone in the universe and here's the proof."

Jonathan was slowly closing in on his destination. The boat bobbed forward while he stretched out on the hard bed below deck, the rhythm of the waves lapped softly against the hull.

He tried to enjoy the salty smell of the sea that surrounded him. The metallic taste of blood had come and gone in the recent hours, and he took a couple of deep breaths to clear the taste and focused on feeling the air flowing in and out of his body instead.

It had been a long trip, but it had gone well. He had gotten to Africa's east coast with the private jet that the Amber Group had access to and there he had gone on board Teis, an eight-meter-long boat that would take him further toward his destination.

He rolled over to his side and pulled out his phone. It was a high-tech model that contained some extra features that the Amber Group's technology department had added. He looked at the screen and read the message from Marie for the tenth time.

"I love you. I'm sorry. I shouldn't have given up on us."

He knew that Marie had real doubts regarding their relationship, but they had something good going on. That was what he thought anyway. And he thought she felt the same thing. But it had been her who had broken off their relationship.

He stared at the phone and sighed. It was not the best moment to have love troubles when you were going out on a mission. But maybe that's just how it was. To try to balance a professional career as an agent with a love life was doomed to become complicated.

What should he answer? He was not sure, he gazed at the message a long time before he sighed, shrugged, and closed the phone.

He pulled the Oxycodone jar out of his baggage, opened it, took two pills, and put it back. The small pink colored pills looked innocent in his hand. A couple more days. Yes, just a couple more days and he would quit.

With that thought in his head, he took a sip from a water bottle and swallowed the pills. He sat for a couple of minutes, then pulled a thick sweater over his head and went up through the floorboard.

"Good morning, Jonathan, sleep well?" a warm voice said.

He turned around. A short, slender man was standing ahead by the edge of the boat and smiled widely at him. It was Jann Edel, the Captain. Jann and Jonathan had met once before, but this was their first mission together. Jann was a few years past fifty and had a face and a head that was covered with white hair and beard. Jonathan thought that he looked like Santa Claus with his extravagant hairy coat. He chuckled.

"Good morning, Jann. How's it going up here?"
Jann bent down and pulled up a rope.

"It's going great. We have kept good speed during the night, and I estimate that we haven't more than a couple of hours left."

Jonathan had counted on that Tabula Rasa would not discover their small vessel. Tabula Rasa had, without a doubt, access to a huge arsenal of weapons to keep both curious guests and more determined intruders away. But there was also a limit on how much control they could have on their surroundings, they could not control all small ports along the coast of Madagascar. There were too many. That was what Jonathan had counted on. They had planned to dock at a small fishing port on the western side, five kilometers south of Tabula Rasa. Backmann had arranged that one of their men would be waiting in the village that was next to the fishing port.

The boat was designed so that the radar would deflect off it and not back to the transmitter as much as possible. It would help them not to be detected. Besides that, there was also the fact that the boat was made of carbon nanotubes that absorbed radar waves that would further help them avoid being detected.

The nanotubes were built in a honeycomb shape structure, its comprehensive properties meant that when a radar wave hit, it absorbed the radar waves energy inside the complex structure that the material was made from.

Besides the stealth features, it also had a mini-submarine attached under the keel. Jann nodded at Jonathan.

"Not much time left now. I think you should get ready."

Their plan was as simple as easy. Jonathan had never liked plans with many complicated moves. The more moves there were, the bigger the risk it would fail. Keep it simple had been his motto as far back as he could remember. He nodded.

"Good, I think this is close enough. Give me two minutes to prepare and get ready. When you give the green light, I'll go."

Jann glanced toward Tabula Rasa that silhouetted against the horizon. Its structures reached up against the sky like a modern artwork that had grown into gigantic proportions. He pointed.

"Have you been there before?"

Jonathan stared at the pyramids far away on the horizon while he shook his head.

"No, never. Have you?"

Jann laughed.

"Yes, of course. I have been there many times. Many of those who live at Tabula Rasa usually go out around Madagascar to explore the surroundings here. You know, it's a pretty dramatic landscape here."

Jonathan's cheeks blushed.

"I apologize; I didn't mean it like that."

"No worries," Jann said, patting Jonathan on the shoulder and pointing at the gear that Jonathan was busy with,

"What you got there?"

Jonathan opened two big bags made of cloth that was in front of him and lifted something that looked like a heavy tube with a small propeller attached on the side of it. Jann frowned while he helped Jonathan take out the heavy equipment. When they were done unpacking, Jonathan smiled contently and pointed down at what they had unpacked.

"That will get me close to Tabula Rasa without detection."

Jann scratched his chin.

"And what exactly is that thing that will do that then?"

"This is an underwater scooter." Jonathan replied smilingly, "A compact unit that can produce a cruising speed of almost fifteen knots and have a range of almost an hour."

The underwater scooter in front of them was a powerful, compact model and could basically soundlessly tow a person over twenty kilometers under water. Jonathan pointed at his wetsuit and air tubes.

"And with those, I can also keep warm without any problem. It will be great, I will arrive at the shore dry and rested." He laughed, "Any contaminations in the water that I should worry about?"

Jann shook his head and gave him a thumbs up.

"No, the levels are not harmful, and your wetsuit will give you enough protection. Just make sure you don't swallow too much water."

* * *

Jonathan held the handles hard and tried to relax while the water closed in around him. The current was relatively strong, and Jonathan had to struggle to keep his balance while he slid forward under the water. His arms were stretched out, and his body slid behind the scooter. The strong engine rushed forward through the water, and the equipage quickly reached its cruising speed of about fifteen knots.

The range was a little more than twenty kilometers, but it would be enough. The speed increased slowly in the beginning, but after not more than thirty seconds it was going at full speed. Jonathan used his body to steer, and he slid through the water. The relatively warm water ensured that his wetsuit did not have any problems to keep him warm. He was basically completely covered in the rubber suit that went all the way down to his ankles.

He slid through a weightless universe where the sun glittering rays penetrated down through the water, but instead of shoals of fish in all their colors that glided past him and corals below him, an underwater desert spread out in all directions.

A couple of stingrays slid into his field of vision from the left, and he changed the course until he slid softly by them, the animals majestically turned to the right and continued their soundless journey under the water. It was something magical but at the same time frightening to be under water.

He had always been fascinated by the sea and the animals that lived there. In his youth, he had often dived with his friends and when he had been eighteen he and a friend had traveled to Thailand where they both had taken a diving certification and worked for a summer to receive tourists that came there to dive in the beautiful, lost underwater world.

But the destruction of the sea that had started a long time ago started to reach its way here too. A cold chill went through his spine when he saw the grey, lifeless bottom slide past him.

He adjusted a couple of relays on the scooter and noticed that the battery drained faster than he had expected. Before he had departed, he had calculated on a downstream of a little more than two knots but now that he was in the water, the downstream not been as strong as he had expected.

He made a couple of quick calculations in his head. It would suffice, but he would have a smaller margin than he had counted on. He adjusted the course further to be sure he took the shortest route to the beach a couple of kilometers from Tabula Rasa that was his target.

After barely forty minutes, a warning light started to blink on the main display on the scooter. It was the battery. Jonathan's stomach clenched involuntarily.

He pushed the scooter as much as he could, and every meter he continued was a victory for him. After a further minute or so he could feel how the speed decreased, and he tried to make his body as streamlined as possible. He turned off the scooter, let go of it, and let it sink to the bottom and confirmed his position.

* * *

From the beach below the fishing port, there were no more than fifty meters to the village. The Amber Group had quite reliable information about Tabula Rasa's safety perimeter, and Jonathan hoped that it would be enough.

The contact who Backmann had spoken about seemed to be aware of the problem. The contact would have an access card that gave the holder and four guests' access to Tabula Rasa. Once inside, he would locate Paco, Elisabeth, her father, and his girlfriend, and smuggle them out safely. That was the plan, roughly.

Jonathan moved fast. He got out of the water, pulled off the wetsuit and dug a hole in the soft, wet sand and pressed the wetsuit into it and covered it. The moon was low, the warm wind breezed through the area. He ran crouching in the wet sand, took cover behind a rock and was just about to move on when there was something in his consciousness that warned him.

It was a clock inside of him that started ringing. He heard the lonely sound from a cicada and smelled the weak smell of tobacco. Carefully, he peeked from behind the stone and investigated the darkness. He could not distinguish anything, but after less than thirty seconds he saw a flame that quickly went out.

It must be a guard. The guard was about twenty meters away from him in open terrain. It was too far away for him to make it there and overpower the guard before he would pull out his weapon and he did not want to kill the man.

Jonathan suspected that if the guard disappeared and did not answer his normal radio calls, it would soon be discovered. He had to find a way around the guard without being detected. His mind raced, he had to do something that distracted the guard enough for him to pass unnoticed.

From his backpack, he pulled out a black capsule, barely ten centimeters long. It was coded to his fingerprint and could only be opened by him. He placed his right thumb on the edge, the casing slid to the side and a buzzing sounded for a couple of seconds before going silent again. His fingers pushed on the control screen that covered one side of it and then held it out straight in front of him.

After a few seconds, a robot slipped out of a side. The robot was barely a centimeter long and resembled a larger mosquito. Basically, it was almost completely invisible. Slowly it moved up and forward. Jonathan put the capsule back in the backpack and got ready. He looked tensely into the darkness and waited.

Earlier he had programmed the mosquito to act as bait. It would go to a defined point and from there send out sounds that mimicked human voices. After a defined command, it would return to the casing.

The guard had put out his cigarette but had not moved. About ten seconds passed. Jonathan could faintly hear something that sounded like a conversation. The sound seemed to come from the edge of the forest that was just behind the shore.

He carefully peeked up behind the rock again, and he saw the guard moving along the edge with his weapon pointing forward. Jonathan smiled to himself.

Jonathan took himself in a wide arch past the guard and continued inland towards the village. After a few minutes, he heard a weak click from his backpack telling him that the mosquito had returned to the nest. He took a couple of deep breaths, focused, and ran.

Sydney, Australia
2048-12-29

The chain of events was inevitably moving forward. Below Dennis Topps apartment, a dark van stopped down the street where it been staying every night for the past week. The rain poured down, and everything it came in contact with was made wet and shiny.

The streetlights threw long shadows over the wealthy street as the branches of the big trees swayed in the wind. A weak scent of jasmine slid through the air.

The van had no windows in the back, and the windows in the front were toned so that you could not see in. The driver of the car pushed a button on the dashboard, and in the back of the van two men who sat on metal-chairs started to work. The smell of old coffee was strong inside the van, and the inside echoed of the drumming sound of the rain on the roof. One of the men had a long scar that ran diagonally across his forehead.

"Jaap did well on the golf course in Sweden. It seems like the mission went well."
The other man nodded.

"Yes, our brother is talented", he paused, "Have we gotten the death confirmed?"

"No, not yet, but it must just be a matter of time."
The man nodded thoughtfully.

"How does it look with our mission?"

"Looking good. Our robot friend is ready to go and do some work."
They worked quickly and silently. Large screens inside the car gave the space a surreal feeling, but they were professionals and were wholly focused on the mission. They had done this before, and they knew what was expected of them. Up on top of the van's roof, a valve opened soundlessly, and after a few seconds an artificial machine crawled out from the valve. Gently the dragonfly ascended from the roof of the van flew up to

Topps's apartment and entered through the ventilation system.

* * *

Once inside the apartment, it navigated into the living room and flew up to the ceiling, placed itself upside down. Straight underneath, the target sat. Dennis was sitting below, unaware that he was being monitored. After a couple of minutes, the phone rang, and he answered.

"Yes?" he was silent for a couple of seconds.

The dragonfly could, without a problem, forward what the target said to the van down the street, but it could barely register what the voice in the phone said. It turned up its sensors to the max. Topp continued his conversation.

"What do you mean, onto it? You have been so careful; how could've somebody has discovered it?"

The dragonfly had increased the sensitivity on its sensors, but there was a limit though where even it came short. Below, Topp had started walking around in an inpatient circle while he was talking.

"Ok, I will do that, you be careful too. See you on Saturday. Good luck." he hung up.

* * *

Below, in the van, the men at the control table worked efficiently. One of them cleaned the signal from the noise from the rain, impurities and other interferences on the recording that the dragonfly had forwarded from the apartment and opened a special computer program

210

that started to process and enhance the voice from the phone.

* * *

Up in the apartment, Dennis sat and watched the live broadcasts from Hong Kong. The situation there was of increasing chaos. The journalist walked on the deserted, blocked-off streets in the city that was home to over a million people.

In recent weeks, the authorities had imposed curfews to curb the increasing disturbances. Dennis thought back to the time when he had been a boy and lived with his father, Dennis Topp Senior, in Hong Kong.

His father had been working in a bank, and when Dennis' mother had died in a car accident when he was just was six years old, his father had been offered an overseas stationing, and he had said yes and brought his son to Hong Kong.

Dennis had lived there for eight years, Hong Kong had shaped much of his upbringing, and he still had a deep bond to it, despite not having visited it for over twenty years. He listened to the journalist who summed up the situation.

"Here we now see the effects of the curfew imposed by the authorities. Street after street is completely abandoned."

At the end of the twentieth century, China had partially regained governance over Hong Kong who had been under British rule since the Opium Wars in the 1840s. In 1997, Hong Kong had transitioned from the British to the Chinese, but Hong Kong had been promised 50 years of its own governing, free from Chinese involvement, under the slogan *One Kingdom, two systems.*

A surprisingly similar process had taken place with Macau. Macau was a former Portuguese colony which was the last European colony to be returned. In 1999, Macau was returned to Chinese rule with the similar 50-year promise given to Hong Kong, but as they approached the end of the fifty years, the unrest had grown.

Violent factions had emerged and fought increasingly desperately for freedom. The Chinese, who eagerly saw that both Macau and Hong Kong was returned to Chinese hands, became increasingly annoyed. In the end, the powder keg had exploded. Dennis shook his head. That they never learned. He turned off the screen and stood up.

Dennis downed another whiskey, prepared himself for bed, and walked into the bedroom. He took off his clothes, folded them neatly, and put them in place on the chair next to his side of the bed; he looked at his wife's peaceful face as she slept and smiled. Carefully he laid down in the soft bed, and the warmth from his wife's body welcomed him.

Eleven minutes later, the dragonfly registered the regular breathing of the couple in bed. It flew softly into the bedroom and hovered half a meter above Dennis's head. Kathy laid beside in a deep sleep. The dragonfly hung in the air. Immobile. As a small black hole that magically floated weightlessly above the unexpected couple. A minute passed. One more.

Dennis turned and rolled over on his back. He stretched in his sleep. Another minute passed. Dennis snored in his sleep and opened his mouth; the dragonfly saw the opening.

While Dennis yawned, the dragonfly saw its chance and quickly collapsed into a hard ball and fell silently through the air into his mouth. The hard ball continued rapidly down the throat. Dennis coughed a couple of times and fell back to sleep. The ball continued all the way down to the stomach where it started to unfold itself again.

Once inside his stomach, the dragonfly started to excrete an artificial chemical that was designed to seek its way deep into the arteries where it started to reshape itself until it looked like the plaque that naturally is built up in every person's veins throughout the years. The process went fast. Way faster than the natural route that took many years. Instead, this only took a couple of minutes.

Dennis kept sleeping for a while but woke up with a twitch. He rubbed his chest. His heart pounded, and panic crept up over him. He sat up and looked around, saw Kathy next to him, and swung his legs down on the floor. A slight pinch crawled in his left arm, and he stretched it instinctively. Thousands of tiny needles stung it, and he massaged it gently.

He stood up and slipped his feet into his slippers next to the bed. Unsteadily, he went out to the living room, around the couch, and out to the kitchen to get some water. He took two steps when his chest tightened, he stopped, gasping, and had to lean onto the edge of the couch. The pain in his chest tore as hot as flaming fire and with his right arm, he tried to massage away the cramp. It tasted like metal in his mouth, and he saw that there were small drops of blood on his hand.

"No, no. Not now, not now." He gasped.
Wheezing, he leaned forward while the cramp spread in his chest. His right leg buckled, and he went down on his knees. Inside his body, his heart was fighting to maintain the pressure in his veins, but the artificial plaque grew bigger with every heartbeat.

He tried to call for his wife, but only croaking sounds left his lips. Staggering, he stumbled into the bedroom against the bed where Kathy still was sleeping. Before he made it to the edge of the bed, his legs collapsed beneath him.

When he pulled the cover, Kathy started to wake up. The croaking sound escaped from his mouth, higher this time. The pain in his body was excruciating. Each time, blood rushed past the artificial plug in the veins, it further increased by some micro centimeters and now blocked almost the entire passage. The pain he experienced was different from all he had previously experienced, he opened his mouth and tried to breathe but no air entered his lungs.

Kathy drowsily sat up and a split-second later stared in horror at the distorted person who sat crouched by the side of the bed. A few seconds passed before she recognized her husband and her horror was mixed with panic. She shouted and threw herself forward.

"What's happening? Dennis!" she took his face in her hands and looked at him in despair.

Dennis tried to talk but instead of the croaking came now a deep hissing instead. His head felt like it would explode, it was like molten steel pouring through his body.

"Tell me! What I should do? Please, Dennis! What's happening?" Kathy continued to hold his face with her hands as if she could cure her husband's terrible illness with her hands.

Dennis' body was paralyzed, and his limbs did not obey him. He kneeled, struggling to stay upright with both hands convulsively pushing against his chest as if he was trying to push the evil out from his body.

Pain poured over him again, and he fell on the side with a dull thud. Blood splashed from his mouth when his chewed-up tongue hit his teeth. He lost control of his bowel and the sharp smell hit him hard. Kathy screamed. The last thing he saw before darkness took him, was Kathy's terrified, screaming face.

The one who seeks shall find. Silas Bommer sat on the hard chair in the fish shack and looked out through the dirty window for the hundredth time. He looked over the port at Madagascar's west coast while his fingers tapped the table.

The sky was covered with cumulus clouds, and the sunlight struggled to penetrate the cloud's cover. Inside, the fishy smell was heavy, but it did not bother him. His father had been a fisherman and his grandfather too.

Silas had grown up with the expectation that he would follow in their footsteps. But he had already at an early age realized that he would never follow his relative's career choices because of the simple reason that he became seasick.

He had, on several occasions, tried to go with his father when he was working, but instead of being of any help, he had constantly been vomiting over the railing. And as the pollution of the oceans increased, the fish disappeared more and more.

In the end, his father had been forced to throw in the towel and abandon his profession as each catch got smaller and smaller. He remembered with bitterness the sorrow his father had experienced and how he became a broken man after that.

Silas hardened fingers continued drumming, now against the book that laid in front of him on the table. Silas had brought the book just because he knew it could become more stressful to sit and look out after the man. Therefore, he had brought his favorite book. Journey to the Center of the Earth by Jules Verne. He loved that book and had read it tens of times throughout the years.

But today, he did not have peace of mind to read, he looked again at the watch and started to have second thoughts. The man might not come. Backmann had said that the one Silas would help into Tabula Rasa would arrive around dinnertime.

Backmann and Silas had known each other for many years. Backmann had been in South Africa on a stationing many years ago. He had met Silas during a period that Silas had worked as a liaison officer for the South African army during the construction of the mega-complex Helder Ster outside Johannesburg, and they had become good friends.

Much later, when Silas wife had got sick and needed medical assistance that was only available at two specialist hospitals in Europe, Backmann had helped him, for which Silas was forever grateful. His wife had gotten help and had lived for three more years but when she was on her way home from the last follow-up visit she had been stopped by robbers that wanted her car. She had not given it to them quickly enough, and the robbers had shot her. She had bled to death in a ditch in western France. That was seven years ago.

Silas looked out again but saw only a weak reflection of his weathered face in the window. Backmann had called him the night before and unexpectedly asked for a favor. Silas had promised to help Backmann with whatever he wanted.

He and Backmann had agreed that Silas would help a man called Jonathan from their organization into Tabula Rasa, and then help him to get out again when his mission was done. Backmann had also told him that Jonathan needed an access card that gave passage for Jonathan and four guests and Silas had promised Backmann that he would do his best to arrange it.

Immediately after their conversation, Silas had called an old friend that he had in Tabula Rasa who would send the codes that Silas needed to update one

217

of the many fake access cards he had. The problem was that Silas was still waiting for his friend to send the codes, without them it was impossible to get in. A cold sweat made his back moist.

Backmann had said that the man named Jonathan would wear a green cap. But now Silas doubted that their plan would succeed. He had been waiting for more than ninety minutes, still no Jonathan, and no codes. Doubtfully, he stared out again over the port, and a shiver slid over the cold back.

*   *   *

Jonathan's heart was pounding, and he took a few deep breaths to calm down. He stood behind a tree looking down at the small village. A group of small wooden houses with worn walls and windows was in a crescent around the port.

Beyond the village was the edge of the forest boundary. Tall palm-trees stretched upward and slowly swayed in the warm wind. From a couple of the small wooden-house, chimneys rose slow plumes of smoke.

The houses looked worn, the wood that the houses were made of was old and tired and the color flaked from the walls. Here and there were sporadic fishnets strung up for repairs on high poles, but most of the poles were empty. The village looked relatively abandoned.

The port consisted of two breakwaters that stretched out into the sea like the arms in an incomplete hug. Inside the port were perhaps a dozen small, rickety fishing boats scattered, some of them looked barely seaworthy.

The damp heat was like a warm breath against him; Jonathan wiped his forehead and squinted. He saw a few people moving in and around the village. A couple of children ran and played with a dog, a woman seemed to carry something against one of the houses.

*   *   *

Silas went despondently out of the fishing hut and closed the old wooden door behind him. He laid his hand on the red pennant that was attached to a string outside his door when he looked up.

Completely by chance. There. Over by the tree line. There was something that looked like a man's shape. A man stood there. Partially hidden behind a tree, but Silas could clearly see the man's green cap. Silas's heart skipped a beat. The man did not move. It must be him.

*   *   *

Jonathan stood by the tree line. The soft sand was warm, and his feet sank down into it. He looked down at the eastern cottages, looking for the red flag that was the sign.

There. The hut farthest away. A man came out and laid his hand on the line that hung a red pennant. The man looked up and froze. With a blank face, he released the line and walked back into the house. Seconds dragged on. The adrenaline flowed through Jonathan's veins, and he took a couple of deep breaths to calm down. He started moving towards the fishing hut.

*   *   *

Silas gently closed the door and rushed to the window. He pulled the old curtain to the side and looked out. At first, he did not see anything, but after a few seconds, he saw the man with the green cap moving down towards the village. He ran quickly. Silas saw how the man approached and disappeared out of sight behind a couple of houses, his pulse increased.

Thirty nervous seconds passed when it knocked weakly on the door. Silas let go of the curtain, left the window, and went up to the door. He took a deep breath and opened, let in the man with the green cap and then closed the door. The men looked at each other in silence. Silas opened his mouth first.

"Hey, I'm Silas." He offered his hand. Jonathan shook it.

"Hey, my name is Jonathan."

Silas nervousness subsided slowly.

"That was close, we nearly missed each other. I was just above to leave."

Jonathan nodded.

"Yes, it was close, wasn't it? I got delayed down by the beach. Nothing serious, but it took a little time."

Nervousness rose in him again.

"Delayed? Were you discovered?"

Jonathan smiled in the weak light.

"No. I lured away a guard, nobody knows that I'm here."

Relief slid over Silas' eyes, and he exhaled.

"Good, good. That's good."

Jonathan looked around in the room, a small work desk was filled with different knives, nets, and lines that were used by the few fishermen who still struggled on. He turned to Silas.

"And now what? What's the plan?"

"The plan?" Silas laughed unsurely, "I will help you into Tabula Rasa. You will do what it is that you should do, and then I will help you out again."

Jonathan noticed Silas insecurity.

"Is there a problem?"

Silas did not answer directly.

"For the access card to work, the codes must be updated." His unsure eyes glanced at Jonathan, "But the problem is that my contact inside Tabula Rasa has not yet sent them. The access card doesn't work."

Jonathan nodded bitterly. Time for plan B. There had not been time for longer planning with Backmann before he had to leave. He touched his ribs and rubbed them gently. They hurt when his fingers touched them, but he was still fascinated by how well those injections Marie had given him had been.

He had broken a couple of ribs once before during a soccer game, and they had hurt for several days before the worst had passed, but this had gone much faster. It was less than twelve hours ago that he had got the injections and already, his ribs felt a lot better than he had expected. Jonathan pulled out his phone and sent a message to Elisabeth. He crossed his fingers and hoped that she would receive it.

"Ok, no problem. In that case, I must improvise. I will get myself in there as soon as possible and then find the people that need my help."

Silas nodded and showed Jonathan a worn table along one of the corners in the fishing shack.

"Here. Look here." Silas unfolded a large map, put it on the table and pointed at a point on the coast.

"We're here. A little less than five kilometers from the west entrance. From this village, a small gravel road will take you north. The road connects to one of the main roads leading into Tabula Rasa and that makes the traffic denser the closer you get to Tabula Rasa."

Jonathan leaned forward and studied the map.

"Why are there so few people in this village? Shouldn't it be crowded with people if there is so much traffic around Tabula Rasa?"

221

Silas shook his head.

"No, this village is a good distance away from the main ports. There are two major ports to Tabula Rasa and traffic flows almost exclusively through them." Silas smiled broadly, revealing two teeth missing in his mouth, "The village is fortunately too far away to be noticed by them."

Jonathan nodded.

"Ok, sounds good." he mumbled, "We'll sure need some luck on this one to pull it off."

Malin was glad that Denver was with her and could share her joy. The interview with John Vendrick III had gone surprisingly well. John had been both open and inviting, and Malin had received lots of information.

It would be a magnificent piece of work that she would write. She smiled. And as if that was not enough, John had promised them that the second interview was going to happen. She was thrilled, now she would have time to prepare follow-up questions on everything she had found out today.

They were with Lamm, and the elevator slowly ascended. The floor was soft, and the sounds inside were muted. It did not go straight up like a normal elevator but more obliquely along with the ceiling, diagonally upward.

Below them, the main area spread out. An oval-shaped park was in an arc along the western edge, and a couple of smaller lakes lay next to each other. The sun rays shimmered in the blue water. Small asphalt and gravel paths crossed the park in an irregular pattern.

Outside the park, the green surroundings changed to more modern settings. An oval road surrounded it, and the road was filled with various vehicles on their way to their destinations.

Smaller vehicles, which accommodated one or two people, moved softly in and out of the regular traffic rhythm. Larger vehicles, which resembled busses, moved more slowly, and Malin absorbed the scene in front of her.

The vehicles were moving rhythmically in and out of traffic like a beating heart. When she stood still and took everything in, it seemed as if some invisible power played the role of conductor and helped the vehicles in traffic to find their natural placements. She smiled.

After the interview with Vendrick, Malin and Denver had spent the afternoon together with Lamm, who gave them a tour of Tabula Rasa's world-famous Zoo. All citizens had free access to it, and after a few hours there, they were now heading back to their apartment to rest.

Malin looked over at Lamm who stood beside her looking at his cell phone. She shook her head when she smelled the faintly sour smell that constantly seemed to emanate from him and shivered. In three hours, they would be picked up for dinner.

During the afternoon, in addition to the Zoo, Lamm had shown them both the giant greenhouses that were in Cibus and produced the grain that was consumed at Tabula Rasa and the power stations that were in Primus and generated power from the earth's interior. Both Malin and Denver were impressed with the efficiency by which Tabula Rasa had arranged everything. Her mind was filled with impressions of everything she experienced during the afternoon.

She glanced over at Lamm who had been an excellent host, but somewhere inside her a warning bell still rang faintly. There was something that was not quite right with him, but she still could not quite put her finger on it. It was not only the smell but something else. Something undefined.

His smile seemed to be natural, but she still felt something that lurked beneath the surface. She shook her head to clear her thoughts. Perhaps she was being hypersensitive and was just a little worn-out, and that made her see ghosts everywhere. She heard a sound and was yanked from her thoughts.

Small drones ascended and headed for their destinations while others came in for landing. A couple of larger vehicles resembling small helicopters slipped by as if they glided on water.

Malin was riveted by the scene. She had never seen any society that seemed so calm and controlled, but at the same time so alive. She had come to Tabula Rasa and did not really know what to expect. What she had heard and what she had learned was that Tabula Rasa was at the forefront in many scientific areas and that in recent decades they had pushed on even more.

Metropolitan cities like New York, London and Tokyo had all introduced strict exhaust requirements, and the air quality had improved the last decade, but here, it did not seem to be a problem at all.

At the beginning of 2030, the smog in the largest cities on earth had been so bad that hundreds of people had died every day. The conversion to green energy had accelerated after 2021, but the development had not gone fast enough. In the major cities, both petrol and diesel cars had been banned, and a ban on certain types of aviation fuel had been introduced, but it had not been enough. During certain periods, pollution along with certain special weather conditions had caused the thick smog to settle like a suffocating blanket over the cities.

People had been forced to remain indoors, and mobile air purifiers for home use had sold out immediately. People had hoarded dust protection and gas masks to the point that they were almost worth their weight in gold.

The crisis had meant that authorities around the world had been forced to draconian measures for both transport and heating transgressions, and the climate issue had in just a few years emerged as the most important issue facing humanity.

The measures that were introduced helped somewhat, and slowly the environment improved in the big cities, but there were also other downsides that now made themselves felt. The economy quickly slid into a downward spiral when transports stopped, and deliveries failed to arrive, many companies quickly went bankrupt, and millions of people became unemployed.

Malin glanced over at Denver. His forehead was wrinkled, and she saw that he was deep in thought. She looked out through the panoramic window in the elevator where they stood. They stood together, close to the edge, and watched the view. She glanced furtively over at Lamm. He spoke in his phone with a low voice. Malin leaned closer to Denver.

"It's impressive, right? One million high-performing people in a high-tech environment with all possible resources. That is something of a breeding ground for amazing results or what?"

Malin followed his glance down to the crowd of people.

"Yes, it certainly seems so. The potential here seems to be almost limitless."

"But what do you think the downside is?"

"What are you thinking about?"

"I really don't know, but I have a feeling that everything may not be as rosy as our guide, dear Mr. Lamm, wants us to believe. Not to mention the boss himself." He said and winked.

"Yes, there's something with Derek I cannot put my finger on. He does nothing wrong and says all the right things, but there is still a small alarm clock in me that keeps going off."

Malin looked up, Lamm left his assistant and took a few steps toward them. He smiled widely.

"Well, my friends. How are you doing? Are you satisfied with the day?"

Denver nodded and returned the smile.

"Absolutely. The whole afternoon has been both informative and productive."

Lamm laughed.

"Excellent" he turned to Malin, "And you are also pleased, Malin?"

Malin smiled.

"Yes, we are very pleased. We have got a lot of material to go through for our story."

Lamm beamed.

"That sounds great." He looked at the clock on his bracelet, "The time is now a little after five. You will be picked up at around eight o'clock, and we will meet for dinner. Would that be ok?"

Malin looked towards Denver who nodded.

"That'll be perfect. Then we can manage to do some work before we get ready for dinner."

Lamm shone even more.

"Fantastic." He smiled at them, "I'll make sure that you really have a wonderful evening ahead of you. You go on to your floor, and when you get there, you will find your way." Lamm winked, "And if you get lost, just ask anyone, and you will get help. We are nothing if not helpful here in Tabula Rasa."

Malin smiled at Derek. The elevator stopped softly, as on command. Lamm bowed deeply and walked out of the elevator, followed by his assistant.

ESA, seventy kilometers south of Paris, France
2048-12-29

He loved surprises. Louis Timmo worked as an operator at ESA, the European Space Agency, which was located south of Paris.

He was standing at the coffee machine, waiting for a cup of steaming hot coffee to get made. He liked the smell of freshly ground beans. Almost everyone else in his department thought that the coffee from the machine tasted like something the cat dragged in, but Louis liked it.

He gently picked up the cup with the steaming hot liquid and sipped it. He was barely thirty years old, tall, thin, and most of the time wearing a black polo shirt and a pair of worn jeans.

He walked the long, narrow, passage whose tiled floor echoed slightly when he walked. The passage led to the big control room, and he sat down at his desk and his monitors.

ESA had the task of controlling and coordinating European cooperation regarding space. Over the past decade, ESA had more than seven launches of astronauts and two missions to the moon. ESA had gained more and more influence the last years when it was clear that the next big race with the other superpowers would be in space.

The resources of Earth had begun to deplete, and with the last few decades' population growth, it became increasingly clear that sooner or later humanity would have to start colonization of the moon. Shortly after 2040, the global population had been estimated at more than eleven billion.

The thought was staggering. So many people strained the available resources and forced new, radical solutions. He would sometimes fantasize that the Spanish and Portuguese explorers must have felt the same way many hundreds of years ago when they were about to leave to discover new, unknown lands.

ESA was one of the key players in space research, and Louis was proud to be a part of it. He looked around the room and saw his early-bird colleagues sitting next to him in long lines at identical desks just like him.

It was early in the morning, and there was already quite a crowd in place with all the operators who sat at their workstations and who now stood in groups talking. A dozen sat and controlled their experiments. Gigantic holoscreens were placed on the walls around them and this gave the room an appearance similar to a digital version of an auditorium.

Louis had been there for almost four years and still had that tingling feeling when he was on his way to work. He had the task of analyzing data from different, active experiments, and he also oversaw data that streamed down from a telescope that was in stationary orbit around Earth.

Normally it was quite a lot of routine work, but Louis still thought every day was an exciting challenge. A couple of minor crises, like failing solar panels on a space probe, the past year had been averted, but nothing serious.

Louis carefully put his coffee on the shelf next to his terminal and sat down. He took a sip and looked at the screen in front of him. It showed an area around the moon and the two rockets that were heading for it. It was a mission that was jointly administered by ESA and NASA and was tasked with preparing that people finally be sent to the moon within the next two years.

It was the most ambitious project they had undertaken, and it consisted of several major expeditions where the former expedition laid the foundation for the next and so on. The task of the present mission was to send the housing modules to the moon and make them land safely. It was a mission that included thousands of researchers, engineers, vast sums of money, and lots of hard work, but it should finally give them their reward.

Louis pressed a couple of buttons and adjusted the resolution and saw how the two unmanned, automatic rockets approached the moon and made the necessary adjustments. They were fascinating. Instead of human pilots, they were equipped with advanced intelligence in the form of an electronic brain that controlled everything on board. The AI should, in principle, handle the entire mission without any requirement for human intervention.

Everything in Louis's responsibility had gone smoothly, he took another sip of coffee and looked forward to when the two rockets landed so he could relax. He was on station for almost eight hours at a time, and he would be there a little more than two hours more until his part would be over.

Satisfied, he leaned back in his chair, relaxed, while the two rockets hurled towards their destination. The screen was filled with its dusty surface.

He watched them for several minutes, pondering the next step in the process. In a little less than an hour and a half, both rockets would begin to prepare for landing and Louis tried to imagine what it would really look like on the moon when the two rockets landed.

He imagined the big dust clouds that would be created by the powerful rocket engines, the clouds would rise high above the surface until it reached the top of the thin atmosphere.

Louis sat deep in thought for a long time while his eyes automatically followed what was unfolding on the screen and he did not understand what he saw at first. He blinked. It must be something wrong with the screen.

Along the edge of the screen, a dot slowly grew. Louis sat up with a jolt and spilled hot coffee over his shirt.

He swore and leaned closer to the screen to see while he rubbed a hand over the hot coffee stain on his shirt which quickly cooled. Louis' fingers flew over the keyboard, and he adjusted the screen to get that strange dot to disappear, but nothing helped.

The dot stubbornly remained and had now grown to the size of a grape. His mouth became dry as sand. Stunned, he looked at how the big rockets appeared to approach whatever it was. His hands were sweaty, and alarm bells began to sound in his head. The control room was usually airy, now it was as if the walls were closing in to crush him.

The image in front of him was as steady as before, and whatever he did, data showed that there was nothing wrong with his system. He stared at the screen in front of him but could not believe his eyes.

Quickly he adjusted the settings, perhaps it was some interference? No, it wasn't. He ran a diagnostic program that can up clean. That didn't work either.

His mind raced. ESA had access to more than four different telescopes in orbit around the world, and he quickly sent the coordinates of the object to a colleague who had access to another telescope. He put on the headset and pressed a button.

"Johnnie." a voice answered.

"It's Louis."

"Hey Louis, how's it going today? What..."

Before Johnnie could continue, Louis interrupted him.

"Listen, it's important. I have sent coordinates, and you must align Pegasus VII to them. "

The headset was quiet for a few seconds.

"Pegasus VII? You know that I can't do that. The boss will be furious."

Louis continued to look at his screen.

"It doesn't matter. You must do it right away," he was silent for a couple of seconds, then continued, "I have a stationary level seven object on the screen."

It took a few seconds before Johnnie understood what Louis said.

"A stationary level seven object?" He hesitated. "But that's not possible."

Louis nodded.

"I know. The problem is that I'm looking at it right now. It looks like it's in orbit around the moon. You must immediately interrupt what Pegasus VII is doing and target the telescope to the coordinates I just sent to you."

Louis listened while he heard Johnnie click furiously on his keyboard.

"Okay, interrupting now. The boss can kick me later. "He laughed nervously, "Programming the coordinates you sent."

Relief rolled through Louis, at least he would get confirmation if his system was broken or if it was true.

The dot in front of him did not move. It showed a glowing sphere that could impossibly be above the lunar surface but did it anyway. He had never seen anything like it. Louis continued to adjust his controls while calling his boss, Magdalena Ribovitz. Her voice was sharp.

"What?"

"It's Louis, we've got something here. Something you've to see."

A few minutes later, Louis sat and adjusted his controls when steps behind him came closer.

"What is it? I was in the middle of my workout." the voice sounded slightly annoyed.

"Excuse me, Magdalena, but I have a surprise for you,"

Louis replied, rubbing the now cool, wet spot on his chest.

The soft, vaulted walls dampened the sounds when the elevator doors closed. Malin glanced at Denver.

"We're allowed to move on our own?"

He went to the window and looked down.

"Yes, it certainly seems so."

They approached their floor, and the elevator came to a halt. Denver was just about to ask Malin if she wanted to rest for a while when they got back to their apartment when a faint, rasping sound started.

She froze. Denver moved instinctively from the window towards the center of the elevator. They looked at each other, both on edge. Several seconds passed. Then another sound. Same rasping, a bit lighter this time.

The doors opened with a hissing sound. Malin and Denver looked straight at a blonde woman and an older man that held an arm around her. The woman's gaze was haunted and at the same time exhausted. None of them said anything.

It was Malin   who broke the tense   moment. She gesticulated to Denver and both rushed out of the elevator to help the woman and the older man. The woman smiled gratefully when Denver took over the weight. Malin rushed to help the woman, and they sank down on the ground in front of the elevator.

"What's happened?" Malin asked while she put her arms around the terrified woman.

The woman trembled.

"It's a long story."

Malin gently cleared away a couple of curls that had fallen in the woman's face and clutched her hands. She could see that the woman seemed to be at a breaking point. Tears rolled down her cheeks, and her hands were cold.

Malin looked tenderly at the woman.

"No problem. We'll not hurt you. What happened?"
The man Denver held in his arms groaned, and his eyes fluttered. He seemed to be dazed. The woman turned to Malin.

"Who are you?"

"My name is Malin Persson, and this is my colleague, Denver Mikkelsen," she said, nodding over at Denver who held the older man's shoulders, "We're journalists, and we are here to do a story on the Tabula Rasa and life here."
The woman seemed exhausted and her eyes welled up with tears.

"Good god, thank you. Thank you." As a hissing balloon, the woman collapsed on the floor next to her father and leaned against him. She put her hand gently on the older man's legs and looked up at the Malin.

"My name is Elisabeth Snow, and this is my father, Richard." Her voice was weak.
Malin squatted in front of Elisabeth.

"What happened?" Her eyes were troubled, and Elisabeth studied Malin's to see if she was honest. She could not flee anymore without getting help. Especially not now, when her father was about to collapse. Elisabeth was afraid that it was his heart that was on the brink of stopping.

She knew that her father had been at the doctor a couple of times in the last six months. Her father had not said anything because he did not want her to worry, but she had found out about it anyway. Elisabeth shook her head.

"It's a long story. I work at a computer lab here at Tabula Rasa, and we must get help to get out from here."
Denver looked over at Elisabeth.

"Out of here? What do you mean?"

Elisabeth did not look up when she wiped away some droplets of sweat from her father's forehead.

"Exactly what I'm saying. Away from here. My father and I must leave Tabula Rasa. We have to get out of here, and we have to hurry."

Malin looked in surprise at Elisabeth.

"Why do you want to get away from here? Is there someone who is chasing you?"

Elisabeth looked up against Malin.

"We must get away from this elevator. Those that are chasing us are still on their way. They've not stopped. They are coming."

Denver interrupted.

"Why?"

Elisabeth's eyes flashed.

"Don't you hear what I'm saying? Im telling you that there's somebody after us."

Malin decided not to push Elisabeth as she was dangerously close to breaking point. She studied Elisabeth, there was something about her eyes that reminded her of her best friend, Grace. She nodded softly and stood up.

"Ok, we'll help you."

Denver flinched and glanced at Malin but said nothing. Elisabeth's eyes blinked with gratitude.

"Thank God. Thank God that we met you."

Malin helped Elisabeth up to her feet.

"It is ok." she paused, "We'll take you to our apartment, and we'll figure out the next step there, ok?"

Elisabeth was surprised.

"Do you have an apartment here? Weren't you journalists?"

Malin smiled at her.

"Yes, we are. But we have an apartment here while we carry out our work and interviews."

A touch of suspiciousness slipped into Elisabeth's voice.

"Who is it you will interview here on Tabula Rasa?"

Malin hesitated a second before she replied.

"John Vendrick III."

Elisabeth gasped.

ESA, seventy kilometers south of Paris, France
2048-12-29

When you are the least prepared, the biggest surprises will come, and Magdalena hated surprises. She grunted. She was an older woman with a quick temper. Her body revealed that she liked good food and that she willingly took both a second and third time down in the restaurant. To keep her weight in check, Magdalena had started spinning in the past few weeks and was now in front of Louis in very small gym clothes and with a damp forehead. She sank down in the padded chair next to him and said challengingly,

"Well, what's so important that I have to leave my work out?"
A strange mixed scent of different foods emanated from Magdalena, but he ignored it and pointed at the center screen at his control while his fingers quickly flew over the keys.

"I was supervising the last part of the Lynx mission and analyzed data when I discovered an unknown object in orbit around the moon. I'm going to get the sphere's position confirmed by Pegasus VII, it seems that the sphere is directly above Mons La Hire."
Magdalena looked in surprise at him.

"What? Sphere? What on earth are you talking about? Is there an object above Mons La Hire? Why is it positioned there?"
Louis listened to the flow of questions but could only shrug as an answer.

"No idea."
Mons La Hire was a major mountain on the lunar surface, and it stretched about a kilometer and a half up. The mountain was named after Philippe La Hire, a French mathematician. Magdalena looked over Louis's shoulder on the screen in front of them.

"How could we miss that there is a sphere in orbit around the moon? Haven't we been observing the moon closely the last few months in connection with Lynx?"

Before Louis could answer, the alarm sounded from the D-Sub system. A small red light on the side of the screen started flashing rhythmically, and a sharp sound rang through the room. Louis blurted out.

"What?"

Magdalena leaned forward, turned off the sound and pushed a button on the keyboard.

"Start scanning."

The automatic scanning program started to identify what the D-sub system responded to. The D-sub system was a monitoring system which had the task of monitoring space around Earth for any comets, meteorites, and asteroids that might collide with Earth.

During the twenty years, it had been active, the system had detected a handful of potential objects, but none of the objects had required any further actions. Normally, all the objects passed at a safe distance from Earth. The comet last year had passed closer than seven hundred thousand kilometers had gotten the entire journalist assembly excited.

For ten intense days, they had besieged ESA and demanded interviews with everyone who might have something intelligent to say about the matter.

Louis blinked and tapped on the screen in front of him.

"Here, look." he indicated with the finger on the screen what he meant.

"It was just detected; the position is being confirmed now."

Magdalena did not seem to hear him.

"What kind of warning did you say?" She leaned forward, her bad mood blown away.

"A level four."

"In orbit around the moon? Why does D-sub react to it?" She asked although she knew the answer.

Louis knew that D-sub would not react to stationary objects. The system would certainly detect it, but if it was not on a course that potentially brought it close to Earth, it would not do anything. Louis shivered. If D-sub indicated alarm, it must mean that the sphere was not stationary. It must mean that it is moving towards Earth.

Louis grimaced.

"It actually looks like the sphere is heading towards us."

Magdalena did not reply. Louis looked at the screen.

"I have asked Johnnie to realign Pegasus VII, so we can confirm."

Magdalena stared at Louis, the screen and then back at Louis. She hastily pulled up her cell phone. While Louis watched, his system worked furiously to get different monitoring systems targeted at the sphere. ESA's monitoring systems were among the best in the world. There were several different monitoring systems that were active.

* * *

High above the Earth, the ESA flagship, the expensive Pegasus VII telescope, aligned itself towards the newly discovered sphere. The powerful cameras and sensors targeted the sphere and sent data down to Earth for analysis. On Pegasus VII, a radio transmitter extended itself and prepared to send down large amounts of data.

Pegasus VII was more than fifteen meters long and contained a powerful telescope that was more than four meters in diameter. The telescope consisted of a main mirror that collected light from the universe and through an ingenious system of mirrors concentrated the small amount of light. Data that was collected from the main mirror was processed through the telescope's sensors and equipment and sent it down toward the ground-based station that was in control. The telescope was equipped with large solar panels that turned toward the sun to generate maximum power, they started a slow turn and placed the large telescope so that the mirror pointed straight towards the new, unknown discovered sphere.

* * *

During the fifteen minutes that Louis had first seen the sphere, more and more operators had taken their places. Now, a crowd of them stood behind Louis and watched with rising excitement how the sphere clearly appeared on Louis' screen. Louis cried out with an excited voice into the now overcrowded control room.

"We have confirmation! The sphere is confirmed by two more sources. Data shows that the object is a sphere and is between twenty-five and fifty meters in diameter. More analysis will give us a better indication. We have also contacted NASA and the other authorities."

From the crowd of people who had now occupied the before calm control room, a voice shouted.

"Do we have a chemical composition of it? What is it made of?"

Louis surveyed the group staring fascinated alternatively on him and the screen.

"The initial scan is indefinite on that point. It seems to consist of several different materials. And because of that, it takes time to break down the chemical composition." He hesitated for a couple of seconds.

"Yes, I know it sounds far-fetched, but the analysis seems correct so far, and it seems to be confirmed that it contains at least seven percent organic matter."

The group in the room fell silent, and all eyes were directed at him, he swallowed hard, as on a given command the group roared.

"What? That can't be correct? It can impossibly contain something organic."

A faint feeling of panic grew within. He held up his hands.

"I know, I know. We are waiting for confirmation from several sources before we can say for sure precisely how it is formed."

The atmosphere in the room was electric. It was so tense that the hairs on his arms stood up. He did not know how to say the last bit of information he had at this time. When he said it, he did not know how they would react. He took a deep breath, motioned for silence in the excited group.

"The sphere was not there a week ago. It seems that sometime during the past seven days it has placed itself in the position it is now, and it seems to come from the backside of the moon where the Tabula Rasa had its satellite. That area has been off-limits for us in the past month due to suspicion of espionage, that must be the reason we haven't discovered it before. And one more thing" he took a deep breath, "It looks like the sphere is heading towards earth."

The room exploded into frantic activity. Magdalena looked despairingly at the chaos that now controlled the room and frowned, she really hated surprises.

Fear can bring a human to her knees. Malin could feel the smell of fear oozing from Elisabeth and spoke to her with a soft voice; she could see a faint spark of hope being lit in Elisabeth.

"Thank god."

"Let's call the police here at Tabula Rasa, they have to help us," Malin said to Denver, "We have to call the police and get help."

Elisabeth started violently waving her arms.

"No! No! They'll come after us!" Malin jerked with surprise and lifted her hands as protection against her attack. Elisabeth's hands slapped at her, but the feeble blows did not do any harm. Malin firmly grabbed Elisabeth's wrists.

"Calm down. Calm down." Malin held her arms, "We won't call the police. Don't worry. Take it easy, we are friends."

Malin nodded at Denver.

"Come. Let's bring them to our apartment."

Elisabeth stared at Malin.

"Why are we going there?" Elisabeth pulled up her shoulders and started to pull away from Malin. Denver interrupted.

"We have to get out of here. We can't stay here; somebody will find us."

Before Elisabeth could say anything, Denver had picked up Richard. Malin looked around, they were still alone in the aisle. She grabbed Elisabeth's shoulders and helped her up. Elisabeth trembled under her touch and sobbed silently.

Malin looked down the long aisle, which led away from the elevator and began to walk to their apartment. They reached the door and were almost inside it when

242

an older couple walked by and saw how Denver carried Richard into the apartment.

* * *

Malin cursed silently when she saw the couple following them with their eyes as they entered. She smiled at them, shrugged, and went in. The door closed automatically behind her. Denver brought Richard into one of the bedrooms and gently placed him on the bed.

Malin placed Elisabeth on the couch, got a blanket for her, and sat down next to her. She stroked Elisabeth over the forehead while her eyes started to flutter. Elisabeth tried to say something, but Malin put a hand on her mouth.

"Get some rest now. You are safe here."

Elisabeth struggled to keep her eyes open, but a compelling force closed them. Malin looked tenderly at her, then stood up and went over to Denver in the bedroom where Richard laid on the bed asleep. A lamp was lit and spread a faint light in the room.

"How's he doing?"

Denver looked over at Richard and saw how sweat glistened on his forehead.

"It looks like his arm is broken. How serious it is, I don't know, but he should probably go to a doctor who can look at it."

Malin nodded.

"I think it's probably going to be difficult to find a doctor who can help us."

Denver did not answer. Malin looked at Richard who was twisting in his sleep as if he was beset by nightmares.

Denver frowned.

"It's a bit strange, he must have experienced something highly traumatic that must've strained him completely. The broken arm shouldn't make him collapse like this."

Both Malin and Denver stood in silence for a few minutes and discussed the elderly couple who had seen them entering the apartment. Malin looked up at the door to the living room where Elisabeth was.

"Ok, I have to go out to Elisabeth and see how she is doing."

Denver nodded. Malin turned around when Richard violently threw off the blanket and sat up.

"The red one is coming! The red-haired monster is coming!"

* * *

A couple of hours later, a light knock on the door was heard, and Malin froze. It must be Lamm who had come to pick them up for dinner. Her eyes drifted toward the closed bedroom door. Behind it was the sleeping Richard and the awake Elisabeth.

She had explained to Elisabeth what would happen, and it seemed that she had understood that they must be dead silent while she and Denver were away for dinner. She looked at Denver, who was standing next to the bedroom door, wearing a suit and nodded.

"Ready?"

She glanced over at the beautiful hallway mirror.

"Ready."

She swept her hand in the air, and the door slid open. Outside, Lamm beamed at her, and before she could object, he stepped into the hallway. Malin smiled automatically and tried to control her breathing. Lamm looked appreciatively at her.

"You look particularly lovely today, my dear."
She blushed, and she became annoyed with herself for reacting like that.

"Thank you, that's nice of you", she continued, "Shall we go?"
Lamm raised an eyebrow.

"Are we hungry today?"
Before she could answer, a moaning sound came from the bedroom. Malin stiffened, and her stomach froze when Lamm spun around.

At the same second Denver grabbed his stomach and moaned theatrically.
"Yes, god yes, I'm really hungry."
Malin held her breath. A couple of seconds dragged by.

"Yes, me too, let's enjoy the exquisite dinner that is being prepared for you."

Lamm smiled, spun around, and walked out. Relived, they followed, and the door closed behind them.

*   *   *

It was early in the morning, and they had tried to get some sleep during the night, but it had not worked out very well. Malin and Denver had come back around midnight after the dinner with Lamm, and by then fatigue had begun to set in. But she did not think Lamm suspected anything. At least not yet.

When they came home, Malin had been sitting with Elisabeth, who was asleep on the couch in the bedroom. Malin had put a blanket over her and wondered what kind of a nightmare she had gotten herself in to.

Their mission to interview one of the world's most powerful men had switched to a rescue operation for a couple of people she only had known a few hours. Malin shook her head and tried to bring some order to her thoughts.

They had placed Richard in bed and given him painkillers to help him get some sleep, but it had not worked. His broken arm became worse, and if he did not get to a doctor to put the broken arm right, the wound would soon develop into blood poisoning, and he would end up in shock.

Malin looked at Richard where he lay in bed. He looked pale and smelled of sour sweat. His arm had swollen up to double its normal size, and small black lines had spread like a spider web over his forearm.

Denver entered the bedroom and walked around the bed to Malin where she sat next to Richard. Richard's forehead was wet with moisture and the pillow he laid on was dark and wet. His eyes were closed, but his eyelids flickered. He moaned, and it sounded like he was dreaming. Denver stood next to Malin, and her hand reached up to him. He took it tenderly in his own.

"How's he doing?"

"Not very well. He's in enormous pain, and that arm doesn't look good."

"No. It looks like he needs to see a doctor right away to get help."

"Yes."

They were both silent. Richard continued to twist in his nightmare.

"What do we do now?"

"I'm working on it. We need a way out of here."

Malin looked at him.

"Out from the apartment?"

"No. Out from Tabula Rasa."

"But that's impossible. They know that we are here."

"I don't think that they know that we have both Elisabeth and her father here. In that case, they would've already been banging on the door."

Denver stood up and started pacing back and forth in the bedroom.

"Somehow, we have to get out of here. We must find a way out that doesn't bring any suspicion. What do you think, can we keep them hidden here until we go home the day after tomorrow?"

Malin shook her head.

"It's too long. We managed dinner, and I don't think Lamm is suspecting anything, but we can't leave them here much longer while we go around here sightseeing and interviewing John Vendrick III again." She smiled.

They sat silently for a few minutes when a woman's weak voice was heard.

"We can get out of here. Help is on its way."

They spun around and saw Elisabeth, who looked at them from the couch with her phone in her hand.

*   *   *

Malin stood up and walked over to her. She looked dazed but seemed better.

Malin took her hand.

"How do you feel?"

Elisabeth smiled weakly.

"A little better now, thanks. I probably needed sleep."

"Good." said Malin, "it's always impressive how different something can feel when you have slept."

Elisabeth returned the smile. The two women saw something in the other that made them trust one another. They quickly found each other's rhythm. Elisabeth picked up her phone.

"Backmann has sent help to get us out of Tabula Rasa. A man named Jonathan is on his way, and he has been sent from the Amber Group to help us."

Elisabeth told her about her contact with Backmann and how she had previously worked with the Amber Group. Her eyes looked past Malin, toward her father, who was tucked up in the bed. Without a word she walked past Malin and went around the bed until she stood beside Denver who sat on the edge of the bed.

"How's my father?" asked Elisabeth.

Denver glanced over at Richard.

"Not too good. He has broken one arm and has scrapes and bruises. The scrapes and the bruises are not that bad, but it's worse with his arm."

"How much worse?"

Denver looked straight at her.

"He needs to see a doctor as soon as possible. The arm will be infected, and he'll risk blood poisoning or blood clots if he is not operated on."

Malin swallowed hard.

"Blood poisoning or blood clot?"

Denver had a sister who was a nurse, and he had learned some about the human body throughout the years, he nodded thoughtfully.

"Yes, it depends on how the fracture is. There is a risk that fat leaks out from within the bone marrow and that it can cause blood clots, or gangrene may set in. Or a thousand other things. He must get to a doctor as soon as possible."

Elisabeth stood as still as a statue. Malin studied her carefully and thought she could see how the gears in her brain spinning. Malin led her to an armchair in the corner of the room. She sat on the bedside to face her. Elisabeth pulled the blanket around her until she was completely wrapped up.

She smiled weakly.

"I have completely forgotten to say thank you." She paused for a moment, met Malin's eyes, "So, thank you. Thanks for all the help."

"No problem. We are glad to be able to help."

Malin was quiet. Waited. She did not want to push Elisabeth as she still seemed fragile. For some reason, Elisabeth had been almost completely panicked when Malin had wanted to call the local police in Tabula Rasa for help.

Elisabeth struggled with whether she should tell Denver and Malin what happened. Perhaps it was best to keep it a secret, but on the other hand, both risked their lives for her and her father. They deserved to know. She began to speak without warning, slowly, quietly.

"They discovered something in space that should not be there. A living sphere. They wanted to keep the discovery a secret and exploit it for their own purposes, and not share it with the world. That's not right. The discovery is not theirs, it doesn't belong to them. The discovery belongs to everyone."

Her voice was silent, Malin looked at her.

"What was it that they discovered?"

Elisabeth looked straight at Malin.

"That we are not alone in the universe."

Go with the flow; that was the thought he had. Jonathan looked down at the western checkpoint at Tabula Rasa's border, and he could hear the activity there before seeing it.

The cool, salty sea air mixed with the warm, lush scent of the jungle around them. He got closer and carefully studied the passage. It might be possible to get in that way, but he was not sure. It was a gamble, but they had to do something. Staying here was not an option. He continued to study the surroundings.

The checkpoint was buzzing with activity. Two large passages were built in concrete, one led traffic in, and the other out from Tabula Rasa. Each of the passages was as big as a four-lane highway. Small dunes of sand lay rolled along the edges, and thin veils of dust drifted irregularly through the passages.

Jonathan shook his head. You could probably fit an ocean liner in one of those passages. A control room was located high up in the middle of the two passages and had a birds-eye view of the entire area.

He knew that a passenger ship a day came to the harbor and thousands of people flocked to Tabula Rasa to try to get permission to pass. The chances for them to get in were slim, but there were many desperate people.

Trucks with both two and three trailers drove rhythmically out through the passage. Small trucks and cars seemed to gather in groups and drove out together when there was a hole in the rhythm of the big trucks. It was a fascinating sight. Pulsating, vehicles and people flowed in and out of the area.

Jonathan glanced up. Tabula Rasa's pyramids loomed in the background. They were so tall that the sun haze obscured the view of the top when looking up at them from the ground. He had managed to establish contact with Elisabeth inside Tabula Rasa, she had responded to his message, and for that he was grateful.

But Elisabeth had texted that there were two extra persons with her, two journalists. Jonathan was not sure how to deal with that. Maybe it was a trap? He was not sure. And anyway, he had come this far, and it was not really an option to turn back now.

And he had not managed to establish any contact with the agent, Paco, who had disappeared the last week. He did not answer any of the messages that Jonathan had sent. But all was in any case not completely pitch black. Only the fact that he had managed to contact Elisabeth was positive. It was one thing that had gone right on the mission. In all plans, there was an element of uncertainty. And when the plan that you laid for yourself met reality, reality usually won.

What was more worrying, was that Elisabeth had written that Richard had a broken arm and that he had to get to a doctor as soon as possible. They did not have much time and there was no possibility to visit a doctor. His mind was frantically trying to come up with a solution.

Slowly he walked down the hill he stood on, and then back to the old, rusty truck where Silas waited. Jonathan walked around, opened the door to the passenger seat, and jumped in.

Silas sat silently and smoked a cigarette. A long soft wreath of smoke rose up toward the ceiling and swirled around. He looked at Jonathan and raised an eyebrow.

"And now what? Did you find any way in?"
Jonathan frowned.

"No, not really. It was like you said, there seems to be a lot of traffic there with many vehicles going in and out."

His hope shrank. The planning of this mission had been fast, maybe too fast. There were some holes in the plan and here was one of them.

His mind was racing to find a solution. Silas broke the silence.

"Yes, every vehicle that goes in and out must have approved permission to pass", he continued, "Each passage is approved by a small transponder sitting on the car or whatever it is. And all passages must be approved in advance."

Hope fell further.

"Does that mean all the vehicles, you say? Isn't there any exception?"

Silas shook his head.

"No, I don't think so. I've seen those transponders, and they seem like they have very strict control over every one of them. The codes that the transponders work with are updated every day", he paused, "to be honest with you, I think it will be difficult to get in using a vehicle. I actually think you have a better chance on foot."

Jonathan nodded thoughtfully.

"Yes, you're probably right about that. If there isn't any way in with the truck, then I have to figure another way out."

It was a setback, but Jonathan clenched his teeth. He would have liked to get in there with the truck, it easily had enough room for two more passengers. Now he would have to figure out something else. He sat deep in thought and did not hear the phone that beeped. Silas pulled it out from his inside pocket and read the message. A smile spread on his face, and he pulled out an access card from his pocket and inserted it on the side of the phone, pushed a button and waited. He cleared his throat and smiled at Jonathan.

"But fortunately, I can actually help you there." He smiled even wider and held up a small access card.

*　*　*

Jonathan left the truck and set off on foot towards the western checkpoint. He had received the updated access card from Silas and walked towards that part of the checkpoint where people were moving ahead with bikes, small scooters, and other similar vehicles. It was a mishmash of people.

He tried taking it all in, but the sheer number of people was so great that it was difficult. He estimated that at least several hundred people were moving there. He slowly moved forward to give himself time to study the surroundings.

To the side of the left passage for the vehicles was a similar but smaller passage. Jonathan estimated the length to just over fifty meters. Two control towers were built at the beginning and the end of it and had a clear view of the people moving in the middle. Several armed guards moved in the crowd. Jonathan assumed they were there as a deterrent.

Terrorism had also reached Tabula Rasa. On at least two occasions, terrorists had blown up car bombs inside the area of Tabula Rasa with several hundred dead. But in reality, it had probably happened many more times. Tabula Rasa had control over which news that was released and had, for sure, access to completely different information.

He had heard rumors that there had been at least five separate attacks during the last three years alone. Jonathan joined the human mass that moved forward.

*　*　*

Jonathan's pulse pounded in his chest, and his mouth was dry. It was a gamble, he knew that, but he had to try. There were no other options. He got into the area and saw that the concrete floor was covered by a thin layer of sand.

He looked to the left and saw what looked like a group of red-dressed monks with gold colored belts that were walking together, most of them with their arms reached out. A woman in front of the group seemed to be the leader. She had a long pennant with a red and white flag which she constantly brought back and forth like a metronome as she continually spoke into a microphone that reproduced the sound of the group behind her.

Jonathan looked fascinated at the strange group when it moved forward. He did not know what religious belief they followed. In recent decades, a myriad of new religious views had emerged. Crises tended to accelerate people's inclination to believe in something.

The crisis of faith that mankind had experienced at the beginning of the century, in some parts of the world, had been transformed into a violent religious awakening thirty years later. A combination of human disasters had acted as a catalyst for a revolutionary change in how people handled their faith.

He looked up and his pulse increased. It was barely ten meters left to where they scanned the access card, he straightened up and tried to look forward. It looked like the people held up their cards against a scanner which then shone green, beeped and a boom gate opened. Armed guards stayed in the background, looking suspiciously toward the people moving forward into the Tabula Rasa.

The group of monks approached the checkpoint in front of him, and he saw them slowly moving forward. A couple of people passed, and Jonathan reached the scanner and started raising his access card when he looked up. One of the guards pointed at him and Jonathan's heart rate increased. The guard turned to a colleague, said something and together the two guards moved towards him. Sweat broke out on his forehead, and he had to force himself not to start running. He looked straight at the scanner. The guards had nearly reached him when a violent roar was heard to his left.

Jonathan could not understand what was happening, for chaos around him exploded with furious force. He threw himself down to the ground and took cover. In the air, he turned his head, and in that fraction of a second, he saw two stragglers of the group of monks had pulled out machine guns hidden under their clothes. The two monks cocked their weapons, knelt, and opened fire.

The shots sounded so loud that Jonathan thought that he had become deaf. As an oversized zipper that was being closed, the sound of the machine guns roared over the area.

He looked up and saw how both guards that had been coming towards him were lifted as by an invisible hand and thrown backward. Small red spots exploded on their clothes when the bullets smashed into their bodies.

People screamed in panic and struggled to escape. An alarm went off, and the entire area was overshadowed by flashing red lights and howling sirens. The noise was deafening, and the sound tore through him. He felt with his hands at his chest and stomach. No injuries. None he could feel anyway. He spat out sand he had gotten in his mouth when he hit the ground.

Jonathan peeked up and saw the two guards on the ground, shot to pieces. They laid beside each other. One could almost think that they were laying on a beach sleeping if it weren't for the angry red spots.

On his left, he heard how the two monks talked Malagasy with each other. Jonathan understood some words but before he fully could fully understand what they were talking about he saw how both ripped off their hoods, and he gasped when he saw their black military uniforms under.

The other monks laid down on the ground, petrified. The woman with the pennant lay a little to the side and touched her body where blood was oozing out. She made small whining sounds.

A couple of seconds passed while the two people dressed in all black spoke to each other. Jonathan heard several voices shouting from within Tabula Rasa coming closer. He looked up at the control tower and saw several people with binoculars pointing at them, he looked over at the black-dressed people who seemed confused over what they should now do.

They had nowhere to go. They could not go backward, they were almost at the entrance and fifty meters back they were surrounded by concrete walls. Forward was the only way to go, but there were guards in their way.

Jonathan saw that the black-dressed persons were a man and a woman. They did not seem to be old, no more than twenty-five years. The woman was the youngest and had a beautiful face but now was it sandy and dirty and a trickle of blood ran down her right cheek. Her eyes radiated determination.

The man resembled the woman, and Jonathan realized that they must be siblings. The man was taller than the woman, and his sad eyes looked tenderly at her. While Jonathan watched, they hugged each other. The sound of the guards came closer, and in slow motion, Jonathan saw how the siblings released one another and went down on one knee and turned their weapons against the oncoming guards. They carefully aimed and opened fire.

The guards were more prepared now and fired back. The sound thundered through the concrete passage. Jonathan had earlier thought that the passage was big, but now when the violent roaring pulsing through, the passage was too small to fit everything that was happening.

Jonathan lifted his eyes again and saw how the bullets hit the sibling's bodies. The woman got a shot in the head and was thrown back to the ground. The man screamed and stood up in rage and emptied his clip against the guards. People that still laid pressed to the ground screamed in terror.

The man's body was torn to pieces in the guards' hail of bullets and fell backward and lay motionless on the ground. The guards shouted to the people to remain where they were while they were moving cautiously forward.

Jonathan looked hypnotized at the shot terrorist and, to his surprise, he saw that the man was not dead. Slowly he moved his hand down to the side and pulled something out. Jonathan could not see what it was. He heard the guards shouting and saw another salvo penetrate the man and how he died.

As in a dream, he saw the man's arm fall and a hand grenade rolled out. Before he could think, there was a blinding flash and his body lifted and then nothing. Only darkness.

They were obsessed with her story. In the living room, Malin and Denver sat and listened to Elisabeth. She had spoken how she and her father had come to Tabula Rasa a couple of years ago to build a new life. She had explained about her work in the research department, her desire to make a name for herself in the world of research and of how happy she had been in the beginning; but also how it had dawned on her that John Vendrick III had wanted to keep one of the greatest discoveries in human history hidden and use it for his own personal gain.

Malin had not believed her ears and had at first wondered if Elisabeth had imagined it all, but as Elisabeth spoke, Malin believed her more and more. Malin studied her carefully while she spoke. Elisabeth's eyes were firm and clear, and nothing in her body language indicated that she was lying.

"In recent days, contact with the sphere has increased. What the communication has contained I don't know, but it looks like there seems to be communication with other spheres that seem to be on Earth. For some reason, they have now somehow become activated. How or why they have been activated, I have no idea."

Elisabeth paused and carefully looked at Malin and Denver to see how they reacted. They were both silent for a couple of moments. It was Denver who spoke first.

"That sounds completely unimaginable. That there would be living spheres around in the planetary system" Denver's thoughts raced," Why right now? What is it that is so special right now? Why not a hundred years ago, or a thousand?"

Malin tried to gather her thoughts.

258

"And what is equally important, what are they? Are they alive? Alive like us?" Her voice was doubtful. Elisabeth shook her shoulders.

"There are a million things we do not know about them. But if this is correct and is true, it's the biggest discovery in our history. It would prove that we are not alone in the universe once and for all."
Denver thought out loud.

"Yes, it's nice all of this. But it doesn't answer the question of what has happened with you two? You still haven't said what has happened to you and your dad." Elisabeth sat down on the couch.

"Vendrick. John Vendrick III wants to keep the discovery of the sphere to himself, if possible, and without the involvement of others to get as much communication with it as possible. That is why he sent his assassins after me and my father. When I realized what was happening, I downloaded as much as I could on a holocube. But the download was interrupted, and then I knew that I had been discovered."

"And your father? How does he fit into the picture?"

"I sent a lot of data to him at work via a com-link. And dad copied all the data into a cube, so he has the only complete copy of the data I had access to."

"Which you had access to? Do you mean there is more data somewhere?"
Elisabeth nodded.

"Yes, there are at least two other labs that are working on this. Vendrick is obsessed with the number three. Most things in Tabula Rasa is based on three. He's got it from the ancient Mayan empire, they also had a craze for the number three. Three pyramids, three labs and so on."
Malin looked at Denver who shook his head.

"But just before I was discovered, I got in contact with a friend who promised to help me. He promised he was going to help me." Elisabeth pulled her hand over her face. Her fatigue began to show.

"Why did Backmann contact you?"

Elisabeth thought for a couple of seconds.

"From what I have understood, Backmann's organization is working to retrieve different archaeological objects from around the world. Exactly how many or who they are, I do not know exactly." She paused, "Backmann contacted me because he thought Vendrick had stolen the Skydisc from Nebra."

Denver cut in.

"I think I've read about it. It was found during the nineties by a couple of private treasure hunters in Germany. They found it and then sold it on the black market or something like that."

Elisabeth nodded.

"Yes, that's the same story I heard. But Vendrick is convinced it's genuine. And he is convinced that it has a hidden functionality that is unknown. Somehow, it would have something to do with all of these objects."

Denver frowned.

"How?"

Elisabeth shrugged.

"I don't know, but he thinks that the Skydisc has some influence or is some kind of key to these objects. That's at least what I've heard through the grapevine."

"How does Backmann come into the picture?"

"A couple of years ago, the Skydisc was stolen, and some time ago they tracked it down. Backmann thought it was Vendrick who had stolen it and sent someone who took it back from Vendricks men."

Malin looked curiously at Elisabeth.

"And why are you doing all this? Now, when they know you've stolen their discovery, you're done here, they will not stop chasing you."

Elisabeth shrugged.

"I know. But it was the right thing to do. The spheres belong to the whole world, not just John Vendrick III. It may be that my career is over, but if that's the price, I'll be happy to pay for it."

The darkness that surrounded him lost intensity, and he slowly regained consciousness. Jonathan was somewhere where nothing existed but, in some strange way, he woke up and rose up from the mists.

The light became stronger and he opened his eyes, blinked several times and looked around in the room. It seemed to be a hospital room.

A faint smell of disinfectant danced in the air. He was in a bed in the middle of the room, and a small holoscreen hung on the wall in front of him. Several different machines surrounded him, and he heard the weak beeping from the different instruments. A grinding headache gnawed in the back of his head, and his body was heavy.

He moved his arms and legs and felt relief when he noted that he was not paralyzed. His head spun, and he closed his eyes. Small fragments of memories flashed before his eyes. He remembered the long passage and how he had almost entered Tabula Rasa, and he remembered how the whole world had shattered in a chaos of explosions and gunshots when the terrorists had attacked.

A few minutes passed while he recovered his orientation. Slowly, he pulled himself up using his hands and managed to get up to a half-sitting position in bed. A feeling of uneasiness spread through his body.

With the vague hope that his jar of Oxycodone would stand on the side table, he turned glanced to his side but was disappointed. The grinding pain inside him grew.

The door clicked open, a man dressed in a white coat came in. The man looked serious. He was tall and had an elongated, thin face and a pair of horn-rimmed glasses. In his hand, he held something looking like a diagnostic plate. With a concerned face, he typed on it while he read what it said.

Jonathan was silent and tried to force the headache out of his head. The doctor looked at him, winked with one eye.

"And how does this gentleman feel then?"
Jonathan opened the mouth to answer, but no sound came out. His mouth was full of sand. He swallowed hard and nodded.

"I think I feel fine. Somewhat tired perhaps."
The doctor laughed so that his glasses almost slid off his nose.

"Yes, I can believe that. It was something of a beating you got down there. I'm surprised you're not more hurt. There were many others who were not as lucky as you."
Jonathan blinked.

"Many others?"
The doctor nodded.

"Yes, there are four dead and fourteen injured, seven of them seriously." He was silent, let the words sink in. "Both the terrorists died from their injuries."
Jonathan moaned quietly.

"My God." his mind was racing, "Who were they?"
The doctor walked around the bed, checked a couple of instruments and the drip that went into Jonathan's arm, nodded with satisfaction before answering.

"Madmen. Madmen who only try and destroy", he paused, "never mind that now. You were incredibly lucky to survive without any serious injuries. We'll do like this, you remain here for now and try to rest as much as possible. It's important that after a violent experience like this you have to give the body a chance to recover."

Jonathan nodded and noted that the headache had finally started to relinquish its grip. His sense of taste seemed to come back and reminded him that he needed to brush his teeth.

The doctor went around to the other side where a machine had started with a soft beeping, and he pressed a few buttons, so it fell silent. He turned to Jonathan.

"What's your business in Tabula Rasa by the way?" Jonathan looked blankly at the doctor. The doctor was not smiling now but stared rigidly at him, and the discomfort grew within him. A few seconds later, the doctor's facial expression changed when he realized that he was staring. The doctor's stiff mouth opened in a big smile and exposed a perfect white line of teeth that dazzled Jonathan. Jonathan mumbled.

"I was on my way to visit Tabula Rasa as a tourist. I had gotten permission to spend two nights here in the related festivities of the moon landing."

The doctor seemed to tower over Jonathan who was wondering if he was believing a word of what he said. The doctor's smile did not budge.

"Yes, of course. We will have many guests and visitors the next 24 hours who will join and celebrate this wonderful, global event."

The doctor stood a few seconds too long by the bed and without a word checked a couple more things on his diagnostic pad before he winked at Jonathan and walked over to the door and opened it. Just before he disappeared through it, he turned to Jonathan.

"Make sure that you get some rest. There is somebody who really wants to meet you."

Before Jonathan could answer, the doctor vanished through the door and closed it behind him.

Did they know that he had come to Tabula Rasa to save Paco and the woman who was called Elisabeth and her father? He did not know that and had no way to determine how much they knew.

Slowly, he sat up and tried to control his racing pulse. The blood in his veins seemed to be made of acid when he tried, and his body ached. The headache increased once more, and he saw stars before his eyes as he swung his legs out and over the bedside. He took hold with his arms and was about to stand up on the floor when darkness came rushing in on him like a train. It reached after him. He fainted and fell back down on the bed.

Slowly, Jonathan woke up again. Infinite darkness held him down under the surface and his own mind in a dreamlike state. Shadows slipped in and out in his vision, and he glided through the abyss.

He opened his eyes and stared at the ceiling. He had not got out of there, he was still in the same room. His eyes were hurting, and he tried to focus. It did not go quickly, but eventually, he regained control of his body. He sat up, looked down at the floor and smiled to himself. Had he fainted and fallen forward, it could have been bad. Jonathan leaned on his hands and pushed off.

He swung his legs over the edge and stood up and walked over to the chair and to his clothes that were folded there. While holding his breath, he put his hand into the inner pocket of his jacket, pulled out his phone and opened the localization program and blinked.

The program was the Amber Groups own and could track through a variety of ways. He went over his mission, it was to save both the captured Paco and Elisabeth and her father, but he could not clone himself, he had to choose. He thought for a short second, Paco had a greater chance of surviving without assistance than Elisabeth and her father did, so the choice was in fact quite simple.

He chose the DNA profile that was in the database for Elisabeth Snow. The program began to search, and after seven seconds it vibrated in his hand. He smiled. According to it, Elisabeth was only a few hundred meters from him. That was fabulously lucky he thought, he threw a quick glance at the clock, quarter past three.

He had to go all-in now, he was already several hours late for his meeting with Elisabeth, and if he was unlucky, she would not be there when he arrived, and he had no way to contact her. He pulled off the electrical electrodes attached to his body, gently pulled out the needle that went into his arm, and quickly put on his clothes and disappeared out through the door.

* * *

He moved fast through the hospital area. He was careful to try to stay in the shadows when he met someone in the corridors. The briefing he had with Marie about the layout inside the Tabula Rasa helped, and he remembered Elisabeth's apartment on the map. He knew roughly where he was in the hospital area and it was quite close to her apartment.

It was the afternoon, and quite a lot of people were in motion. He was grateful for that; it would make his escape so much easier. He reached the exit of the hospital area and looked around for an elevator that he could take up to the floor indicated by the tracking program.

There. Further away. There seemed to be some sort of elevators, for the murmuring crowd in that direction became bigger and louder, the closer he came.

Slowly, he followed the human mass into one of the elevators, looking furtively down at his phone. He was going up three floors and then fifty meters to the west. He tried to move as normally as he could, but he wobbled a few times and had to concentrate not to fall.

Inside the elevator, a holoscreen was showing an extraordinary news story, reporting of the discovery of what appeared to be an unknown object in orbit around the moon. The news host was visibly excited and spoke quickly with several space experts from ESA and NASA.

Jonathan listened curiously with the rest of the people in the elevator. He smiled weakly to himself. Now the discovery was at least out in the open, with all what that meant.

When he came out of the elevator, he came out into something that seemed to be a long aisle that took him away from the main area.

Carefully, he opened the phone and checked that he was on the right track toward Elisabeth's location. After a couple of minutes, he stood in front of a door. He hesitated, knocked gently. Silence. No answer. He waited a couple of seconds and knocked again. Behind the door came a faint answer.

"Yes?"

Jonathan's heart skipped a beat.

"Backmann sent me from the Amber Group to help."

A few more seconds passed. The door opened. A young woman stood inside the door and watched him cautiously. Jonathan did not hesitate but went straight in and closed the door behind him. He looked around the room, a weak, confined smell of sweat and something else was noticeable.

A heavily built man stood to the left, tense like a steel spring. The woman who opened took a few steps back to put some distance between herself and the man who entered the room.

Jonathan glanced to the right and could see what appeared to be another young woman in the bedroom, and he saw something that looked like a man on the bed. Before he could say anything, the woman who was sitting on the bed jumped up, rushed to the bedroom door and slammed it shut.

Jonathan cleared his throat.

"I'm Jonathan, from the Amber Group." He tried to seem calm despite his pounding head and nausea that grew in his stomach. He smiled at the woman who had opened the door.

"But it seems that you have other plans?"

The woman had not spoken yet, but now she took a step forward and smiled.

"There has probably been some misunderstanding. I have not called for any help. I and my colleague are journalists and are here to conduct an interview."

Jonathan listened to what the woman said and cocked his head to the side.

"Ah, it's not you that I'm supposed to help. It must be the woman in the bedroom?"

The woman who opened the door took another step forward but did not reach out. She looked with suspicious eyes against Jonathan.

"Who are you?"

Her scrutinizing gaze analyzed Jonathan.

"Backmann and the Amber Group sent me."

Malin looked doubtfully at him.

"Are you alone? How can you help us if you are alone?"

Jonathan smiled at Malin.

"I suppose Backmann could've sent more but it would've been harder to keep it a secret and would increase the risk of detection", he paused, "considering the short planning time, this was the best solution."

Malin did not seem convinced. She stood silent for several seconds while she finally decided.

"Malin Person."

Jonathan automatically reached out his hand.

"Jonathan Jarl." He turned to the heavily built man and repeated his name.

Denver relaxed, and after shaking hands with Jonathan, Denver pointed at an armchair and sat down on the bed. Malin stood beside Denver and looked quizzically at Jonathan. Jonathan sat down in the armchair. The atmosphere in the room was tense, so thick that you could cut it with a knife. Malin smiled at him and then nodded toward the closed bedroom door.

The group consisted of Jonathan, the two journalists Malin, and Denver, Elisabeth, and her father. They had left Malin and Denver's apartment and were now heading down to the lower freight levels in Cibus. They could not use the access card that Jonathan had brought with him because it would not allow passage for all of them.

Not many people were out and about at this hour, and the aisles were relatively empty. A slight scent of greenery surrounded them. It was at the lower levels of Cibus that all shipments and deliveries took place.

Normally, hundreds of deliveries were done each day of a variety of products, goods, and merchandise; and Jonathan hoped they would be able to find a less guarded transport of some sort that they could steal. He glanced at Malin who walked next to him.

"What do you think?"

"If we are lucky maybe we can find something, but I don't really know how big our chances are."

He would have preferred to get in with the older truck that Silas had access to, but it had not worked because they would certainly have gotten stuck in the controls during the passage into Tabula Rasa. If you did not have the correct passcodes, you would be taken aside for a more thorough check, and then it would be game over.

Denver's strong arms supported Richard when they walked, and Richard's arm had become worse during the night. Elisabeth had gotten hold of some painkillers and had given two tablets to Richard that had taken the edge off the worst pain, but Richard was still in bad shape. Jonathan saw the pills and had to muster all his willpower not to ask for one.

Elisabeth walked in silence and seemed to be lost in her own thoughts when she heard Jonathan and Malin's discussion. She looked up.

"The usual deliveries are handled by two large companies that are stationed on the east coast of Africa. The safety measures in their trucks and transport are at the top-notch, so we'll not have an opportunity to steal any. The vehicles are equipped with both hand scanners and DNA scanning. Without the proper preprogrammed combination, they will not start."

As Elisabeth shared this information, Jonathan's hopes fell.

"So, there is no chance?"

She shook her head.

"Well, most likely not."

His shoulders sank, she gave him a crooked smile.

"But."

Both Jonathan and Malin stared at Elisabeth.

"Sometimes there are deliveries of food from distant villages with local delicacies. Not so often, not daily, but sometimes. And those transports don't have as much security. Some of them are even so old that they only need a key." She winked at them, "But the downside is that there are not many of them, and they do not come daily."

Malin looked thoughtfully at Jonathan.

"We have no choice, we must get to the transport area and keep your fingers crossed that there is transport from the villages."

Jonathan nodded.

"Yes, and with Richard in such a bad condition, we don't have time for any advanced plans."

They looked affirmatively at each other and went silently to a conveyor car that would take them down.

*　*　*

They squatted behind a meter-high wall that went along a slope down toward the huge loading docks. They had managed to get down to a service area, and while they were sitting there, three big trucks rolled in and started unloading goods. Malin sat next to Jonathan, and they both gazed down towards the open area.

She surveyed the area and formed an idea of how many guards were there. She could see a couple of them standing at the western entrance, but no one at the actual loading docks. Powerful lights around it were lit, and the boom gate at the entrance rhythmically went up and down on a regular basis.

As she watched, a larger truck drove out through the boom gate and turned up on the western road that led out of the harbor and headed down south. The whistling sound when the battery-powered truck drove away from them died down.

"What do you think?"

Elisabeth shook her head.

"Those trucks are too modern to be coming from some local village. Not a chance."

He nodded.

"Yes, you're probably right about that."

Jonathan sat down with his back against the wall next to where Denver and Richard sat together, and Elisabeth helped his father in correcting the improvised sling they had made for him. Her kind touch made it bearable for Richard, and he smiled at her. Jonathan glanced over to Elisabeth and her attempts to help her father. He saw the obvious love between them.

"I think we have to try to have some patience and hope that somebody else will come." Malin looked at Jonathan.

"Yes, it looks like we don't have a choice."

For the next three hours, they sat there and looked hopefully over the wall every time they heard a vehicle approaching; and each time they were disappointed when they saw big, modern transports approaching. Jonathan did not know for how long they could be sitting there without anyone noting their presence. Automatic robots took care of the unloading and transporting the goods.

Occasionally, Jonathan perceived a faint, sour smell in the air, but he could not place what it was that smelled or where the smell came from, he turned to Elisabeth and Malin.

"Do you also smell that?"

Malin nodded.

"You smell it too?" she looked relieved at Jonathan, "I thought that I was the only one who smelled it, I thought I was getting sick."

Elisabeth leaned forward and frowned.

"The smell is coming from the Tabula Rasa itself."

Jonathan looked quizzically at her.

"What do you mean?"

She smiled.

"The smell started last year. The first time it was noted, it was on Cibus, but in the last six months, it has spread to all parts of the complex. It is not entirely understood what it is, but there is a suspicion that something unknown is happening to the food or the air in the closed ecological system that makes up Tabula Rasa, and it affects people in a greater or lesser degree.

The researchers are in full swing trying to investigate what it means. If there is only a minor inconvenience or a sign of something that is fundamentally wrong", she stretched her back while she continued, "Some people are more vulnerable to the smell affecting them."

Jonathan stared incredulously at her.

"Oh, my God."

Elisabeth nodded and glanced over the wall. Still no trucks. A half-hour passed, and Richard slid in and out of consciousness and Jonathan was near breaking point when a faint, hacking sound was heard. It was different than the other sounds, and Jonathan glanced over the wall. There. An old, small, diesel-powered truck driving slowly up the ramp that would take it to the unloading ramps. Hope within him flared up.

"What about that one?"

Malin and Elisabeth looked over the wall and did not have to say anything. Jonathan understood from their body language that this was what they were waiting for. Elisabeth nodded.

"Yes, it's for sure a local supplier. If we should take a chance on any transport, then it should be this one." Jonathan looked intently at the two women in front of him.

"We'll do it like this. Elisabeth gets to the truck and tries to get the driver's attention. If you come alone, I don't think he will see you as a threat. The rest of us will take ourselves to the truck on the other side. There are no guards, nor any security. That should work."

They nodded, and hope grew stronger in the small group.

* * *

They saw the driver leave the old truck and walk toward the back of it. While Jonathan and Malin watched, Elisabeth walked up to the truck. It was barely thirty meters away. The driver had not come back when she arrived at one of the fenders. She hesitated for a second and then went around to the other side.

Jonathan held his breath and nodded to the others.

"Now, move!"

Together they moved forward, and Denver was soaked with sweat when they reached the point where Elisabeth had walked around the truck. He was just about to open the truck door when a surprised voice called out.

"What are you doing here?"
He froze but realized that the voice had not spoken to him. It had spoken to Elisabeth and Jonathan heard her voice answer something he could not make out. The other voice, a man, sounded angry.

"What? That's not right. Stay here while I call the guard."

Ice spread in his stomach, and he got ready to run around the truck and hit the driver when he heard the sound of a blow and then a muted thud. Unsure what to do, they stood still when Elisabeth came walking back from the other side of the truck. She smiled sheepishly and rubbed her hand. Jonathan looked surprised at her.

"What happened?"
Elisabeth looked at her father and then at Jonathan.

"My father taught me self-defense when I was younger. He thought that it was something that all women should learn."

Before Jonathan or Malin could answer, Elisabeth and Denver helped Richard get up into the truck and then jumped in after him.

Denver sat down in the driver's seat. He had driven rally cars in his youth and did not intend to let this opportunity pass him by.

The small diesel engine responded to Denver's throttle and the truck accelerated. Elisabeth had said that the service roads to the Tabula Rasa had little traffic early in the morning and they had managed to get out on that road and headed straight to the harbor. A few minutes later they saw their destination.

The harbor was shaped like a horseshoe with two sides that reached out in the water a couple of hundred meters. In the middle part of the harbor, several large houses and warehouses were located. A pair of giant loading docks and several smaller ones were scattered in the harbor. On a couple of them, cargo boats were in various stages of loading and unloading. A light rain had begun to fall, and they slipped out into the roadside, bounced when they drove over a pothole in the road. Behind them, Richard moaned and slipped in and out of consciousness.

*   *   *

Two clones followed the image on the screen in front of them. They sat in the cockpit of a small, agile reconnaissance craft. The vehicle looked like a small helicopter without rotor blades. Three very small yet highly efficient motors gave the craft unsurpassed maneuverability.

It was its agility in the air that had given it its nickname, the hummingbird. It could hover and spin around on a dime.

The two clones had tracked them after they had managed to get out of Tabula Rasa. One of them, Fredric, shook his head. A light rain had begun to fall, and the sun was rapidly on its way down, dusk came fast in these areas.

Fredric maneuvered the smooth hummingbird and put it in a parallel course with the truck that was heading down to the harbor. The hummingbird came in fast at an altitude of not more than twenty meters.

He smiled to himself. It was just for this kind of mission that the handy craft really excelled. He glanced over at his brother, Gerard, who sat next to him and felt the deep connection they shared.

*   *   *

Denver looked out through the front window of the truck and tried to keep an even, steady speed. They hit another pothole and the truck bounced and bumped, and Richard moaned from the back seat.

"Sorry," Denver said over his shoulder.

Malin laid a hand on his shoulder and squeezed.

"He still looks pale."

Denver looked in the rearview mirror, saw Malin and Elisabeth sitting on the floor of the truck and gave a thumbs up. Jonathan sat in the passenger seat next to Denver and watched the screen he had in his lap.

"We have about three kilometers left. When we come down to the harbor, Silas will help us."

Denver nodded and looked at Jonathan.

"I don't know if I had time to say it, but thanks for the help."

Jonathan winked at him, shrugged, and smiled.

"No problem you know. Just doing my job."

It was not far now. The plan was that they would go down to the harbor, and there they would meet Silas. Exactly what Silas had planned, he did not know, but he would worry about that later.

Now, it was all about getting down to the harbor in one piece. He glanced out the side window and saw a flash of light. Before he could shout a warning, everything exploded around him.

Denver did not see the rocket as it approached. The hummingbird had risen to forty meters and sent off a missile at them. It was not a direct hit. The rocket hit the ground three meters to the side of the truck, and instead of wiping the truck out, the explosion lifted it up and threw it like a glove. The explosion blasted through the evening and rolled the truck on its side.

An overheated gas cloud exploded and sucked in all the air within a ten-meter radius. Glass shattered in thousands of pieces, metal distorted, and a deafening rumbled roared through the evening.

The truck continued forward in the air and twisted while it fell back to the ground. It landed hard and slid a dozen meters before it glided with a screeching sound over the ground until it finally stopped against a palm tree.

*   *   *

Denver got up on shaky legs on the wet, muddy ground. He had been thrown out of his seat when the truck tipped over on the side. His ears rang as if a siren was blasting in his head.

He looked around and saw their demolished truck. Small flames burned behind it where it had slid down the edge of the road. He could not see any of the others. Frantically now, he looked around. There. A man's body laid bent against a palm tree.

It must be Richard or Jonathan. He shouted but there was no answer, he started to stumble towards the body, but his legs did not obey him. His right leg wobbled, and he looked down. His pant leg was torn to piece and he saw blood on his thigh.

He stared at his own body. There was no pain. Nothing. It was as if it was somebody else's leg that was attached to his body. While he looked at the leg, it buckled, and he fell to the ground. He screamed.

*   *   *

Fredric saw a man stand up. The truck had fared surprisingly well considering that half a kilo of explosives had gone off almost directly on it. But it had not been a direct hit.

Fredric made a mental note that he should report it to the weapons department so they could investigate exactly what had happened. Usually, the small helix rockets were almost a hundred percent accurate.

The man who had got up looked dazed. He turned his eyes down to his leg and seemed to freeze. Fredric leaned towards the screen and studied him. He seemed to be in shock. Gerard sat motionless next to him and looked at a screen.

"He's injured," Gerard continued, "But I cannot see the others. Start scanning."

The hummingbird slipped around in a circle while scanning the area.

*　*　*

"Elisabeth!" Malin waited a couple of seconds, "Richard!" No answer. She tried to move, tried to turn around to see how it was with Elisabeth and Richard that had been in the backseat. Malin saw the rearview mirror close to her. She reached out, grabbed it, and managed to twist it. There. Elisabeth was stuck under the seat belt. A trickle of blood ran down her forehead.

"Elisabeth!"

Malin fought and got up to a seated position. Her ears still rang after the explosion, and she was disoriented. She heard faint crying, but she could not identify what the voice said or where it came from.

She turned around, trying to look out the front window but saw nothing because the window was covered by thousands of small cracks.

* * *

Gerard studied the screen intently and tapped his finger on it. He used the DNA scanner because all the small fires that the explosion had caused disrupted the thermal scanner.

"There. There are three DNA signatures in the car. Two women and one man. And the man outside of course." His voice sounded astonished, "They all survived. What lucky bastards."

Gerard maneuvered the hummingbird as it hovered about forty meters away from the wreck. They were still at about ten meters in height, surveying the chaos in front of them. He scanned for a good place to land. Fredric pointed at a place maybe twenty meters away from the burning wreck. There was a clearing some distance away from where their targets were.

"Put me down there. Then lift and take a position above me."

Gerard followed Fredric's pointing finger and nodded again. That was how it was. It was Fredric who was the stronger of the two. Gerard wondered to himself if all twins had it that way. That one of them was stronger, more dominant.

He suppressed his thoughts and focused on the mission. Easy on the hand, he softly brought the craft into the clearing that Fredric had pointed towards. The thick palm leaves on the trees around them swayed violently as they approached. They took no more than a few seconds before they had reached the clearing and Gerard expertly steered the flying craft.

"Five seconds."

Fredric kept his eyes on the burning car wreck in front of them and nodded. One of their targets was still in front of the wreckage, and the other three did not seem to have come out of the truck.

He smiled, it would be a simple match. His father would be proud of him. The helicopter smoothly descended until it barely touched the ground. Fredric quickly unfastened his seat belt and jumped out. He landed, rolled on the ground, and stood up.

He breathed hard. It had not been necessary to make a roll when he came down, it was not a high jump, but the adrenaline was pumping in him.

He looked up and saw his brother control the helicopter back in the air and take a position some distance away to protect him if something unexpected occurred.

*   *   *

Denver was still lying on the ground, and his legs burned like fire. He had to get up. Now. Immediately. Slowly and with the help of a thick piece of wood that lay next to him, he managed to get up. He looked over at the burning wreck. It did not burn so violently, which meant that the tank had not exploded. But the danger was far from over.

"Malin!" a couple of seconds of silence, "Elisabeth!"

At first, he heard nothing, then Malin's weak voice.

"Denver! We're in the car, Elisabeth and Richard are alive, but we have to get out of here!"

Somehow, Malin's response renewed his powers. The pounding pain in his leg slipped back in his consciousness, and his body was empowered by a strange force. With one leg dragging behind him, he managed to cover the distance to the car. He banged on the passenger door. Elisabeth banged back.

"Watch out, I'll try and open the door."

He took a steady grip and pulled, the door did not budge even a millimeter. The handle was slippery and covered with mud. He wiped his hands and grabbed it again. Just when he was going to pull, he saw in the corner of his eye how something big came closer.

He quickly looked up and saw a rotor-less helicopter approaching. The powerful engines whipped the big palm leaves with their airflow. Denver became increasingly frightened when a black-dressed man jumped out of the craft and smoothly rolled when he landed. A sense of panic grew in him when he saw the man.

"They're coming!"

Malin's voice sounded muted through the metal.

"Open the door! We have to get out from here!"

Denver saw the man approaching; maybe ten meters. His fingers slipped over the handle once more, and he had to struggle to hold onto it. The taste of blood penetrated his mouth.

His body went on pure adrenaline. His heart was pumping like a jackhammer; he gripped and pulled so much so that the tendons in his fingers almost snapped. He pulled, and the door flew open with a loud bang and fell to the ground.

He saw a glimpse of Malin sitting next to a lifeless body who must be Elisabeth. Richard was not to be seen anywhere. He stood up to locate the man who had jumped out of the helicopter but did not see him.

He spun around and was just getting around the corner of the wreck when a hand grabbed his collar and violently pulled him backward. Denver tried to stay on his feet, but his injured leg buckled under him and he was thrown headlong from the car, and he landed hard.

Air was knocked from his lungs, and he gasped for breath as he rolled around like a rag doll. As through in a haze, he saw the man lean down toward the open passenger door lying on the ground and reach into the cabin.

Malin screamed, and with a superhuman effort, Denver managed to get up on his feet once more and heard Malin's panicked voice again. The man's torso was halfway into the car, and while Denver watched, he violently pulled out Malin from the cabin.

She screamed and fought, but the man seemed almost untouched by the effort. Without any apparent discomfort, he held Malin hard by the collar and with one hand lifted her up in front of him. With the other hand, he went through the pockets of her jacket and pants. He was obviously searching for something.

When he found nothing of interest, he lowered her down to his face while saying something Denver did not perceive. Malin glared at the man and shook her head. Denver watched the man shrug lightly and with one hand, throw the screaming Malin more than five meters away, where she collapsed in a heap.

Rage stormed up from within. He looked around on the ground and saw a long piece of metal torn from the truck. It was barely half a meter long, and one of the ends narrowed to a jagged, sharp tip. He snatched from the ground and ran. Denver threw himself forward, infused by adrenaline and drove the long metal piece into the man's back.

The man's body tensed like a spring, and he staggered forward, then backward. Small droplets of blood sprinkled from his mouth and colored one trim on the car in a red-spotted pattern. He opened his mouth to say something, but no sound came out of his mouth. He swung around, and Denver saw blood flowing out of the man's mouth, over his teeth and down his chin.

*   *   *

Gerard saw how the man quickly approached Fredric from behind. Before he could warn Fredric, the man had driven a sharp piece of metal into Fredric's back.

"Brother!"

Powerlessness washed over Gerard like a giant wave. While he struggled to keep the hummingbird stable, he saw how his brother turned to the man who attacked him, and blood gushed down his mouth.

"Fredric! Brother!"

As in a dream, Gerard saw Fredric falling backward against the car. Gerard shouted repeatedly in the cockpit.

"Brother! No! No!"

Something inside him snapped. Like a rubber band that broke. A violent bang, a hard flick, and pain. Infinite and endless pain.

He turned to the man who killed his brother. Focused on him. The world around him moved out of focus until only that man filled his whole mind. The powerful engines worked under him. The wind moved the helicopter, and he automatically adjusted the controls.

He became the craft, and the craft became him. Gerard looked at the man and knew that he would die. It was the only thing that was important to him now that his brother was gone.

Gerard took a tighter grip on the control stick and steered resolutely toward the man below.

*   *   *

Denver stared at the man at his feet. He did not move. Blood still pulsed from the man's chest, so the heart must still be beating. But that would not do any difference. He would be dead within a few minutes. Denver almost jumped on one leg over to Malin where she laid in an abnormal pile. She did not move.

"Malin!"

He came up to her and gently turned her over on her back. He stroked her hair that clung to her forehead and his fingers became sticky with blood. Gently, he talked to her, and she began to move. Slowly she sat up.

"What happened?" her voice was unsteady and dazed.

Denver pointed toward the bloody man.

"He seemed to be angry with you." He hesitated, "what did he say to you?"

Malin rubbed her eyes and tried to remember.

"Don't really remember, he talked about where it was or something."

Denver nodded. Malin looked past him at the truck.

"Elisabeth and Richard. They are alive, you have to get them out of there right now!"

Denver looked over at the truck and saw Elisabeth's body slumped in the passenger seat. He got up again and jumped over to the car and reached in. Elisabeth was moving under his hand.

" Come on, come on!"

Elisabeth did not answer, but she raised her torso by using her elbows and crawled out.

Denver heard the sound the helicopter growing in strength. He turned around, looked up and saw the helicopter coming straight at him. In a few seconds, it would arrive at the car. He got up and looked at Malin still lying on the ground with the blood flowing from a gash in the forehead. He looked at her and knew what he had to do.

*   *   *

Gerard lowered the nose of the hummingbird straight toward the wreck and the man who killed his brother. Slowly he increased speed. He did not think. His whole body reacted like a robot and as if someone else had control over it.

The man in front of the car wreck began to quickly jump from the car, toward two big palm trees which stood by the side. Gerard adjusted his course and increased the speed further.

*   *   *

Malin barely had time to react. She saw Denver jumping over the road, and she saw how the man in the helicopter changing the course and following Denver. She realized in horror that the man in the helicopter would not stop but instead use the helicopter as a big missile.

"Denver! Watch out!"

But it was too late. As she watched, the helicopter crashed into Denver. Both Denver and the helicopter disappeared in the huge fireball while Malin screamed his name.

*   *   *

Denver was gone, but she was still alive. She stared at the burning wreck and sobbed. She did not realize how long she had been standing there when she heard something. A faint voice brought her back, and Malin ran up behind Jonathan where he was sitting next to the van.

"I thought you were dead?"

Jonathan turned to Malin and smiled weakly.

"I thought so too. I must have been ejected from the wreck. I passed out when I was thrown out and woke up over there." He pointed to a palm tree by the roadside.

"Where is Denver?"

Tears welled up in Malin's eyes again.

"Dead. The helicopter flew straight into him. He's gone."

Jonathan saw the pain in her eyes.

"I'm sorry."

She nodded quickly and wiped away the tears.

"Let's get away from here before they come back."

The wait had been nerve-racking. Silas Boomer opened the deckhouse and stuck his head out. The tepid wind ruffled his hair, and he glanced up against the road that went from the harbor up toward the forest.

The soft waves gently hit the hull. The road disappeared into the dense forest, and the thick, small palm trees waved in the wind. The sun was still low in the sky. It was early in the morning, and the real heat had not set in yet.

He put on some clothes and walked over to the portable radio that was on a table inside the cabin. It was on. He had not heard anything from Jonathan yet. They had agreed that Jonathan would try to notify Silas when he had found the people he was taking out from Tabula Rasa.

But if he could not contact him while he was inside Tabula Rasa, he would try to do it during the way down to the harbor. It would give Silas some time to prepare and get the boat ready for departure.

He checked the radio again. It was working as it should. His eyes were dry, and he rubbed them. He had barely got any sleep last night when he had tried to find the reason why the engine did not start. His boat was old and worn but he had maintained it throughout the years, so it used to work as it should.

But just yesterday, the engine had died when he was to take it out for a reconnaissance tour. He had spent several hours looking after oil leaks and other things, but he had not found anything. While he stood there wondering what to do, he heard a faint sound of a vehicle that was getting closer from the forest.

Silas looked up against the forest and heard the sound increase. A flock of birds took off from the edge of the forest.

Silas was just about to turn around when he heard an explosion. The shockwaves rippled out from the forest, and he instinctively recoiled. He stretched to see what it was that was happening, but he could not see anything. After a couple of seconds, a black cloud of smoke rose from the forest. Silas stared in horror at the rising cloud.

He spun around, and a freezing cold feeling spread in his stomach. He ran down the ladder and looked at the powerful engine in the boat and all small parts and tubes that were scattered around it.

During the entire night's work, he had not managed to find out why the damn engine did not start, so he had, in desperation dismantled all circuits, tubes, and other things that he could reach.

It was a desperate act, he knew that, but maybe water had got in or there was something else in the engine that made it unable to start.

The smell of smoke drifted down to the boat and stung his nose. He stared at all the small parts that laid scattered before him. He squatted down and started to reassemble the parts he had taken off the engine. He slipped several times and had almost mounted the last water hose when he dropped it.

He cursed, reached down after the hose that had fallen next to the engine, down on the floor. When his fingers touched it, he heard another deep rumble from the forest, and he froze.

The deep rumble grew in strength and then slowly resided again. He rose and looked sideways out through the deckhouse and saw a glimpse of another smoke cloud, closer this time, rising from the forest.

Quickly, he sat down and fished up the hose from the floor.

*   *   *

Silas hurried and tightened the last part that he mounted, he closed his eyes while he tried the ignition. The engine coughed a couple of times, but then it started. He breathed out, and the relief washed over him.

A couple of minutes later a battered group came staggering out from the jungle and approached the boat on foot. Silas squinted and tried to determine how many it was that came, but it was too hard to see for all the smoke.

He definitively saw Jonathan who seemed to support an older man whose arm seemed to be broken. He also saw what seemed to be two women following closely after the men. All seemed dazed and ran with staggering steps towards the harbor. He ran up to the edge of the boat and waived at Jonathan.

"Here! Over here!"

The small group of people staggered ahead on the dock and Silas helped them down into the boat. Malin exhaustedly sank down on a bench and looked blankly up towards the gravel road they had come from. Two large, military vehicles drove out from the clearing and large dust clouds whirled as they got closer. She saw to her despair how Jonathan took a big leap back up on the dock.

"What are you doing? They are coming!"

Jonathan looked down at her.

"My mission isn't over. There is another one inside Tabula Rasa that needs help."

Elisabeth was dumbfounded.

"But they will kill you!"

Jonathan smiled at her and gave her the thumbs up.

"Not if you're asking me." he turned to Silas, "Take them and leave, get out of here."

Silas put the pedal to the metal, the boat shot off, and Elisabeth saw how Jonathan set off toward the jungle. He moved fast, and weak hope returned to Elisabeth, but with horror, she saw how another helicopter silently rose up from behind the tree line and fired a football-looking projectile against Jonathan.

She did not react fast enough to shout out a warning before the football had unfolded itself to a big net that hit Jonathan in the back and instantly wrapped itself around him and she saw him fall.

Despair swallowed her when they quickly accelerated away from their fallen savior.

Paris, France
2048-12-31

Back in safety, their closeness to death seemed to be far away. Twelve hours later, they were in the group's headquarters outside of Paris.

After they had managed to escape, they arrived at a village on the east coast of Africa. There, Backmann had arranged for a plane to be waiting for them, and it had taken them to Paris.

They had received medical help, and Richard's arm had been bandaged. They had been received by Backmann and had gone through what had happened. Elisabeth sat and sipped a cup of tea. The soft chamomile scent calmed her, she was still upset that Jonathan had been captured.

She found herself in what she thought was a gathering room and stared at the holoscreen. On the screen, three people sat and discussed the developments in the last hours in Hong Kong and Macau. At the bottom of the screen, an update rolled of the recent clashes that had resulted in more than a hundred deaths.

* * *

Richard was down in the lab with Malin and Elisabeth. They stood in front of a metal table and looked at each other. It was hot and humid in the room.

Beads of sweat broke out on his forehead and ran down his temples. Small, weak electronic humming permeated the round room.

It was hard to locate where the sound was coming from as there was no visible electronic equipment anywhere. The walls were covered with what looked like large beveled mirrors, and Richard saw infinite copies of themselves that glided in and out of each other in a surrealistic dance.

The floor was made of white metal material that gave a mute, muffled sound when you walked on it. All the round ceiling was covered by what looked like an oversized lamp and gave a constant, cold light. From the floor arose a massive metal pillar straight up a meter.

The surface on the metal pillar shined as it was so polished that Elisabeth could see every detail in her face.

A weak, clicking sound was heard, and one of the wall mirrors fell in and then slid behind the other. In the opening, Julius Dann stepped in.

The long white coat softly caressed his body. He was tall and thin, verging on the limit of skinny. But behind his fragile appearance, there was a razor-sharp mind. Julius had studied space technology in Lulea, and he had one year left of his education when he dropped out. After he dropped out, he was recruited by Backmann to come and work for the Amber Group. He looked at Elisabeth.

"What's this you have found?" and held up the holocube. His eyes shined with expectation, and he could barely contain his enthusiasm.

Elisabeth saw Julius put it on the table and he pushed on a screen on a control panel.

Elisabeth looked intently at the surface of the holocube but could not see what it was made of. The surface had an opaque, silvery appearance, but it had, at the same time, what seemed like small whirls drawn on the surface.

After several seconds, she saw that they were not drawn nor static. They seemed to move around on its surface. She gasped. They glided against the edges of the holocube and without being affected, they glided over the edge and continued as if nothing happened.

The holocube looked like it was alive. Julius raised his hand.

"Wait, watch this."

They watched when Julius walked over to a cabinet, opened a box and pulled out something wrapped in soft velvet. Without a word, he walked back to the table and gently put down the wrapped object he was holding in his hand. They gasped when Julius pulled out the Skydisc from Nebra from its velvet wrapping.

Julius carefully lifted the Skydisc and laid it on the table next to the holocube. They stared bewitched on the beautiful green-golden bronze disc and the small holocube. At first, nothing happened, and Richard was just about to ask Julius what he meant when something changed.

They stared at the holocube that slowly rose up over the Skydisc. It seemed like gravitation had decided that just now, just there, for the holocube in front of them, gravity would no longer be in effect. It was free to do what it wanted. Her finger trembled as she pointed at it.

"It's floating. But, how can it float?" Like her finger would remind gravitation that it had an object here that did not obey orders. Julius smiled.

"This is something outstanding we are dealing with here; it's completely unique." Julius sounded thrilled. Elisabeth stared at him.

"What do you mean?"

"It's absolutely amazing, I hardly understand it myself. It seems that the information stored in it has somehow changed it and the Skydisc seems to be a key to the information", he paused, "it's like the information in the holocube has affected it physically." He shook his head. Elisabeth looked at the holocube in front of her.

"What is it that you're saying?" her eyes narrowed. "Is it some kind of trick?"

Julius laughed.

"No, no. This is something wonderful, I've never seen anything like it. What was previously a common holocube is now something more." He cleared his throat and continued, "It seems that it contains information. A lot of information apparently."

"Information about what?"

"Yes, that's a good question. According to what I have been able to decipher so far, it contains information about space."

"Space?"

"Yes, it describes what seems to be several million different star systems. This is something quite exceptional. This is information that we don't have available on Earth."

"How do you mean?"

"I mean whatever this is, it is not coming from us."

"Are you saying its extraterrestrial?"

"Yes, that's exactly what I'm saying."

Malin was silent and observed the holocube while it rotated in front of them. As Elisabeth watched, Malin reached out her hand toward it. Before Elisabeth managed to say anything, Malin touched it with her index finger. Elisabeth gasped, and Malin quickly pulled her hand back. She blinked rapidly.

"What happened? What did I do?"

"Why did you do it?"

"I don't know. It wasn't me." she fell silent.

"Whatever you did it seems to react to it." Julius pointed.

The holocube had started spinning faster and faster. Along the sides, it began to glow faintly, then more and more intense. It was like a light inside had been turned on. The glow increased in intensity until they began to squint.

"What's happening?"

Before anyone could answer, the glow changed character. From being completely white, the light began to change to bluish tones. The whole room was increasingly colored with the bluish shades as the holocube transformed. In Richards's voice, a hint of worry could be noticed.

"What does this mean?"

"I have no idea. Can we stop it?"

Elisabeth somehow knew that the holocube was not dangerous. She did not know how she knew. It was something primitive inside her that spoke to her. The group stood around the blue shimmering sphere and stared at it. The rotating light cast long shadows on the wall behind them and the shadows slowly danced around.

Elisabeth was about to speak when the holocube changed yet again. This time, it was not the light inside of it that changed but the holocube itself. Elisabeth fell silent when she saw that one of the edges of it seemed to soften, and after a couple of seconds, it sank into the middle.

They stared at what was taking place in front of them. The holocube accelerated and at the same time started the other edges to dissolve. It started to lose its cube-like shape. The edges sank into the middle, and it had started more and more to look like a ball.

* * *

Richard stared at the holocube, which floated no more than fifty centimeters above the Skydisc. Elisabeth held her breath. Faster and faster, it accelerated around its axis. Both Malin and Julius instinctively took a step back. But Elisabeth was not afraid.

296

It changed its appearance again, and the soft form assumed the appearance of a pyramid. It became more and more pronounced when the holocube edges sank into the middle. Small, fixed edges appeared on other parts of the sphere and rose to the surface.

"I would not be surprised if you measured it, it would appear that it was a perfectly shaped pyramid," Julius said quietly.

The others looked at him.

"What do you mean?"

"I mean, that if it by itself, it can reshape into a perfect geometrical shape; it is an expression for something intelligent. Neither you or me or anybody else would be able to create a perfect shape of something using our hands."

Malin stared at the pyramid that spun around in the air in front of them.

"You're saying that we wouldn't be able to make a perfect shape?"

"No"

"I don't believe that. I wouldn't need help from a computer. I could do it using paper and a pencil."

"You're not listening to what I'm saying."

"Yes, I do, right?"

"No, I mean without any tools at all. To create something perfect without having any tools or something else. That is something completely different than what you are talking about."

"Is it really that difficult?"

"Yes, it's actually impossible. It depends on which scale you have when you measure it, but if you go closer and closer it becomes harder and harder to reach perfection. Every surface that you create contains small variations that disturb the perfection."

"Yes, of course. When you get closer and closer, it always shows that the smoothest surface looks like a moons landscape in miniature."

"And if you continue measuring, then you see that the landscape of the moon starts to look more like the Grand Canyon. And, if one goes even further down in the resolution, you'll see that Grand Canyon looks like Mount Everest. And so, on and on."

Elisabeth, who had been silently standing next to them now seemed hypnotized, staring at the sphere that floated in front of them, opened her mouth.

"Look, it's changing again!"

The edges of the Pyramid started to soften up again. The sharp edges seemed to get softer and softer, like butter getting heated up in a microwave oven. The edges started to get more and more rounded until you could barely see that it was a pyramid anymore. Now, it looked more like an uneven ball. The surface of it started to shift from silver-grey to a more bronze-like color. Small ripples of different colors rose up from inside and spread out over the surface.

It was as if the pyramid had realized that it was dealing with an intelligent species. As if the thing that spun around in the air in front of them did something with it to not scare them.

They stood silently in a circle around the table for what seemed to be an eternity. Slowly, without a word, Elisabeth started to reach out for her father and Julius. Rows of text started to roll down the big screens that surrounded them.

Elisabeth stood petrified and awed at the same time. The screens in front of her were filled with row after row of text that quickly scrolled down. The characters came first slowly, then faster and faster until they held a steady high speed. No one could write that fast, Elisabeth thought it resembled a core dump from a computer. The green light from the screens was unusually bright and she squinted to not be dazzled.

"What's happening?" Julius whispered quietly.

Richard shook his head. This was something he had never seen before. The text in front of him rushed forward at a rapid pace. Every second more than ten lines of text rolled on the screens, and according to what he could see, it was not the same text on the screens.

"Look, the text on them is different."

Richard looked around at the other screens. There were five of them, and he let his eyes glide over all. He gasped.

"Yes, you are right." he pointed at two of the screens, "You see that?"

Elisabeth leaned forward and looked back and forth at the two screens.

"What am I supposed to see?"

Richard tapped his finger on one of them and at the same time pointed at the other one.

"It is not the same signs on the screens. It is not the same signs on any of the other screens. They are all different."

Elisabeth carefully studied all the screens and gasped.

"You're right. They are different." she was quiet for a couple of seconds before she said hesitatingly, "What does that mean?"

Before anyone could answer, the information on the screens changed again.

Paris, France
2048-12-31

The insight that something extraordinary was going on had become increasingly clear to him over the past day. It was late in the evening, and Backmann stood beside his desk, his hand trembling.

A bead of sweat trickled down his neck, and he shivered when it ran inside his shirt. He had just finished a video conference with seven employees placed around the world and what they had told him was upsetting.

Normally, he was not a man who was easily affected, he was known for his stoic calm and had an eerie ability to control his feelings. For some, he appeared more like a robot than a human being. It had always been like that, he had always had it in him. Usually, he was a rock, but now he was shaken. He looked over at the holoscreen that hung on the wall.

The extraordinary newscast had spoken about the discovery of a large glowing sphere that been found in orbit around the moon in the previous days, but which now seemed to be moving toward Earth.

The news anchor was significantly affected by the seriousness of the matter. The initial analysis had claimed that at this moment there was no further information about the sphere, but they worked hard to gather more information.

He blinked and wiped a drop of sweat from his lip. Now that the discovery of the sphere was public, the circumstances had changed. If it were so that the sphere was no longer in a stationary orbit around the moon, it would change everything.

The question was whether he should also contact the authorities to inform them about the Amber Group's work. But what authorities? The Americans, the English, the Chinese? He hesitated. At the same moment, as the authorities were informed, he would lose control.

At the same time, he had received alarming reports from his colleagues. The conversation with the seven had made a deep impression on him, and he struggled to regain his bearings. They worked in an industry that, to a great extent, was hidden from the eyes of the public.

People usually had an idea of the historical treasures and works of art that were found during archeological expeditions; which would then naturally come in the hands of various museums which then gave the public access to view them.

Nothing could be farther from the truth. The fact was, that the archeological industry was an industry that balanced on the edge of a knife. Daily struggles of life and death arose when ownership of different artifacts was argued.

Fantastic discoveries were made and failed to be reported. Fanatic collectors who acted in a twilight world went above and beyond to expand their collection of unique artifacts. Both men and women fought and died anonymously to continue to fuel the insatiable black market that constantly demanded the latest discoveries and the most amazing treasures.

It was within this dramatic scene that the Amber Group acted. It was here, in the shadowy side of society, that they offered a service to reclaim artifacts that had gone astray for a variety of reasons. The Amber Group was not cheap, but the service they provided was of high quality. Discretion was their trademark.

He shook his head while he walked around the desk and sat down in his leather chair. The seven colleagues around the world had said the same thing. Three of them worked together on a mission that involved two Chinese bronze dragons.

The others worked alone on their missions, but their feedback had been eerily similar. Everyone had reported on exceptional events in the last few days. Normally, extraordinary events occurred occasionally, but what happened now seemed to be something completely different.

One of his colleagues, Julia, told that she had been in an excavation in Chile and two glowing spheres had been found within less than three days. The excavation had been focused on an ancient Aztec sculpture, but everything had stopped when they had come into what looked like a small cave during the excavation work.

In the cave, a shining sphere had been found along with a disc, which according to the description, was similar to the Skydisc from Nebra. Three days later, the incident had repeated itself when another cave had been discovered.

Another colleague, Thomas, had recounted the recent events he had experienced at the border between Mongolia and China. Thomas worked together with a Chinese archaeological group to dig out a temple found last year, and they had managed to keep the work secret. Two days ago, the group had entered the temple and did their first initial investigations.

Exceptional paintings and statues had been discovered, and Thomas had been completely captivated by the secrets that the temple seemed to hold. Further inside the temple, Thomas and the group had discovered something that seemed to put the rest of the discovery in the dark. In a room, by itself, a bright sphere had been discovered. And that was not the most amazing thing.

What really impressed them was that the sphere was not on the ground or in any container. Instead, it seemed that the sphere, by its own force, floated in the air in the middle of the room above a disc of gold. Backmann had asked about the details and Thomas had answered the best he could, and by all accounts, the discovery seemed identical to the others.

The others had recounted similar stories, and even Lisa King who worked in Costa Rica had reported that she had found one of the mystical objects. The glowing spheres started to appear around the world at an astonishing rate. According to Backmann's calculations, at least nine spheres had appeared in the last few days. It must mean something, perhaps was there a pattern in it all, and what did it mean in that case? The spheres had been found on almost every continent. And that was only part of the problem.

The information about the spheres on Earth had previously only been available to a handful of people, but now the amount increased exponentially. The more people gained access to the information, the faster the stories would arrive. It was inevitable. And now that the sphere in space was all over the news, it could not be stopped.

He sat down at his desk and sat in silence for a couple of minutes while pondering his next move. He thought of Marie that had been silent as a clam the last days. He knew that it had to do with Jonathan, and he knew that he had to deal with that sooner or later, but not now.

Now there were more important issues on the agenda. He took out the latest report from one of his agents, Paco, that had managed to infiltrate Tabula Rasa but had not been heard from for a while. Backmann had tried to contact him but had not been successful.

Paco had been a reliable source that had forwarded lots of useful information, but now, it was as if he had vanished from the face of the earth. Backmann sat preoccupied while he read through the report. After a while, he pushed a button on the intercom.

"Please send in Marie, Richard, and Elisabeth." He knew that Malin was busy with her own work.

A metallic voice answered.

"Yes, sir."

A couple of minutes passed in silence as Backmann went through the last day's events to himself. There had been so many extraordinary things happen that it was hard to keep track. A short knock on the door.

"Come in."

The door opened, Richard and Elisabeth Snow entered the room and closed the door behind them. Backmann gestured for them to sit down.

"How's it going with you?"

Elisabeth smiled.

"Well, it's going fine, thank you. Much better now that we have got out from Tabula and away from the assassins that were after us." Backmann smiled at his comments. He nodded thoughtfully and pressed the intercom again.

"Where's Marie?"

The metallic voice sounded stressed.

"I can't find her, sir. She doesn't answer my call."

Backmann looked over at Richard.

"Yes, it seems that it was a dramatic rescue?" he paused, "and you look pretty tired Richard?" and raised one eyebrow. Before Richard could answer, Elisabeth nodded.

"Yes, it really was. It was a close call. For a while there I thought that we wouldn't make it" she paused, "But I'm so sorry for what happened to Jonathan. I couldn't believe that he jumped out from the boat just when we were getting out of there."

Backmann smiled grimly.

"No, I don't know if he told you, but his mission wasn't only to rescue you."

Both Elisabeth and Richard stared blankly at him.

"What?"

Backmann shrugged.

"I suppose it doesn't matter now, but he was also going to get in contact with one of our agents that we have lost contact with. Apparently, Jonathan thought that he had a chance to do that after you were rescued."

Elisabeth slowly shook her head.

"What a fool. To get back in there after all that happened and so close to dying that we were."

Richard leaned forward while choking a yawn and put a hand on her arm.

"But we didn't. We made it, and we can only pray that Jonathan will also make it."

Elisabeth smiled at Backmann.

"Yes, thank you again for all help. I don't know what to say. I am forever grateful for your help. Without it, both I and my father would be dead for sure."

Backmann pushed back the chair and rose.

"We are working with the United Nations and some hidden diplomacy about how we will get Jonathan out of there, but it will probably take a little time before the planning is done." He paused, "But there are more things happening now that make us have to gather our forces and think how to handle the immediate future." He paused, "Specifically, that holocube you brought out of Tabula Rasa. How is it going with that?"

"There is something happening that we don't understand. The data on it was supposed to be only that. Data. Nothing else." she paused, unsure of how she should continue. Backmann looked at her, waiting for her to continue. When she did not do it, Richard helped.

"What's happening to the holocube sounds impossible, but it seems that the information stored on the holocube alters it."

Backmann stared blankly at both Elisabeth and Richard.

"What do you mean, it alters it?"

Richard shrugged.

"Exactly what I'm saying. When Julius used the Skydisc, it was like a key inserted in a lock. They fit together, and it seems that the information itself that is stored on the holocube gives it the possibility to change the physical composition of it. Usually, a holocube is just a holocube. Or in any case, it usually is. In our case, it is not like that though. It seemed that it changes into something that we don't understand. We can't connect it to a computer and read the information." He paused, "It changes constantly."

Backmann stared at them.

"You can't be serious."

*No, no, no. No more. No more. I can't. Please. I promise.
I'm sorry. I can't, no more. She is dead. There is nothing
more I can do. Yes, I know, I held her when she died. I
held her body when she took her last breath. I know how
it feels. I know how it feels and I can't, no more. Please.
Please stop. She is gone. Chantelle too. I lost them both.
I know. Both of them. First one of them, and then the
other. I know. I should've done something, but I couldn't
do anymore. I didn't know what to do or how I could save
her. I couldn't. Couldn't. All the toxins they pumped her
full of and said that it was her only chance. Her begging
eyes that looked at me. Praying for something. Do you
understand? She asked me for something. I could see it
in her eyes. The pain was too strong. She couldn't
anymore. She knew. She knew already you see. That it
was meaningless, that it wouldn't help. But I couldn't. I
had to. Chantelle forced me. It was her fault. She made
me do it. Forced me to agree to give Kristina more toxins.
Even if we all knew it was pointless. Do you understand?
Do you understand how it feels to be forced to give your
child poison? Do you understand how it feels when I nod
to the doctor who stands outside the room to come in with
a syringe with toxins for your child and injects it into her
when you hold her in your arms? When her eyes ask you,
no, not ask you, beg you, yes that's the right word, begs
you not to do it. When Chantelle is sitting beside and
nodding and crying at the same time. I don't want to. But
I must. I must, for Chantelle says that's the only chance
Kristina has. I know. I should have said no. Should have
stopped it. But I was weak. Couldn't resist. No more. No
more! I'm sorry!*

Jonathan twitched and sat up. He gasped. His pulse
was racing, and he raised his trembling hands to his

face. Sharp blasts that sounded like gunshots echoed in his head.

Violent nausea rushed up inside him, and he was close to vomiting. His eyes were moist, and his forehead was wet. With shaky fingers, he rubbed his face and tried to collect himself. The memories of him running on the beach rushed back, and his confusion slowly passed.

One of the guards had a black container that Jonathan faintly remembered as the guard had held it up against him, after that incident he remembered nothing. He must have been transported to Tabula Rasa and was somewhere in its dark depth. He surveyed the room where he was. It was small and circular, barely three meters in diameter.

The windowless walls seemed to be of smooth, black metal and without any joints except where a thin, faint line marked the door. The walls tilted inward and joined together at the top like a pointed igloo. Near the top of the igloo, a small but strong string of lights spread a sharp, clinical light in the strange room.

He was on a narrow bed that was placed in front of the door, and he swung his legs down to the ground. His body ached, partly because of the harsh treatment the guards had given him and partly from the lack of Oxycodone.

He cursed himself that he had been so arrogant that he thought he could escape the pursuers. Slowly, he took a few deep breaths and tried to focus on the air that moved in and out of his body.

Slowly, he calmed down and regained some control. He sat silent for a while. He glanced up at the clock on the wall, a few minutes over two. He stood, walked to the door, and felt the handle. Locked. He tested his mobile phone lying on the nightstand. Only a local network from Tabula Rasa.

Jonathan sat down on the floor with his legs crossed. He focused. Focused on his breathing. The meditation helped, and then a calm came over him. His therapist had suggested meditation to control the chaos that existed within him after Kristina had passed away. He breathed deeply. Let the exhalation take its time. Let it slowly disappear out through the nose.

*　*　*

He lay in bed and stared at the vaulted ceiling. The soft bed was relatively comfortable, but he knew it would not help. He knew he would not go back to sleep, but he could at least lie down and doze off for a bit. Any rest was better than none. Nausea had diminished, and he suspected that it had to do with whatever gas they had given him.

An angry signal sounded in the room and then fell silent. He sat up. A clicking sound was heard, and to his surprise, a small section of the wall next to the door slid to the side, and a small hologram screen slid out. He stared at it and slowly the holographical image built up in front of the screen.

"Good morning, Jonathan. My name is John Vendrick III."

Jonathan grinned.

"I know who you are."

Jonathan`s pulse increased. Several seconds passed. John's face was overbearing, like an adult talking to a naughty child.

"I understand that it is you who has been here at Tabula Rasa and helped someone who has stolen from me" a long artistic pause," and I want what was stolen from me." His voice was dressed in steel.

Jonathan`s racing pulse fell as he took a couple of deep breaths, he fixed his eyes on John.

"I understand. But the fact is, that you won't be getting it back. You will neither get the holocube or my friends back. They are safe now with us."
John smirked.

"Safe? Don't you know who I am? I am John Vendrick III. And if I want to see them dead, I'll snap my fingers, and they will die within twenty-four hours. There is nowhere on Earth they can hide from me. And don't forget, you're a prisoner here on Tabula Rasa, you will not get anywhere." His voice dripped with contempt.
Anger seethed in Jonathan.

"Are you threatening me?" he breathed through his teeth and struggled to keep calm, "You will know that we will spread the discovery about the sphere and everyone will know that you already have contact with it. Everyone will find out what you have been up to."
John hissed.

"What we're up to? You can only dream about what we're doing here. We're in the middle of the greatest discovery in the history of mankind, and it was me who discovered it. Me. Not you or anybody else. Me. But it doesn't matter. Others have also discovered the spheres, it was just on the news."
Jonathan stared skeptically at John.

"The sphere is bigger than both of us. And now when the discovery is on the news, you can't do anything. The world can't handle that we are not alone. There will be panic in the streets and complete chaos in the financial markets. Can you imagine what full-blown chaos is on its way now?"
Contempt grew inside Jonathan.

"And who are you to decide that? What gives you the right to be one who decides for everybody else? It is everybody's right to know the truth. They can handle it themselves."
John laughed.

"You're either very naive or very stupid", he paused, "or perhaps both. This is not something that ordinary people can handle. Not by a long shot. Most people in the world are only interested in the most basic human urges. Eat, work, sleep, have sex, and be entertained. There is nothing else for them. That's all."

Jonathan heard how John's voice dripped with arrogance.

"That's all. People want work that gives them purpose, a reason to get up in the morning. It doesn't matter much what kind of work it is. The importance is that it gives an illusion of purpose, of meaning." John paused for a couple of seconds before he continued.

"They also want to eat good food, get stuffed on all different kinds of dishes and drink themselves into oblivion. Complete gluttony. Gluttony without precedence that makes that all so-called developed countries diseases explode. Nobody can control their intake of food and beverages which leads to all mankind quickly marching into obesity's Promised Land." He paused, "And you know that I'm right. There is nothing that I say that is not true. And besides work and food, people also want to have sex, eternal copulation where nobody can control their lust anymore. And to round it off, everybody also wants to be constantly entertained with one pointless reality show after another."

Jonathan listened while John raged.

"Everyone is as weak as you, Jonathan, who creates a nice family but then does not manage to keep it, but lets his child die and his wife leave him." He laughed hoarsely, "And to top it all, you're so weak that you have to rely on pills to get through the days."

The red-hot anger surged up within Jonathan, and he had to restrain himself to the limit to not explode

"You freak. Do you think that I'm weak? I've felt more love in my life than you've ever done or ever will."

John looked blankly at Jonathan.

"You poor thing. You pathetic little man. It takes an extraordinary man to take the next step, I'll make sure it will be a new future for mankind." He paused for a short while before he hissed with flaming eyes.

"I'll send someone to pick you up, so we can meet in person."

Space
2048-12-31

Contact. The spheres which were near the solar system had established full contact. One after the other, they had awakened after spending millions of years in a kind of hibernation.

It was a hibernation that gave them the opportunity to survive oceans of time. They had many purposes, and one of them for which they were created, was to regularly scan the area that they were in for signs of life. Especially intelligent life. If life was found, a scan was started to determine what kind of life it was. Through eons of time, the spheres had found millions of life forms on countless planets around the universe, but only a few times had the spheres recorded intelligent life.

In the beginning, there had been ninety spheres that were in a place called the Milky Way. One of them had come too close to the sun, and during an unusually powerful solar flare, it had become mortally damaged. The damaged sphere had struggled to get away but had met its destiny in the suns burning inferno. Another had gotten caught by Jupiter's strong gravitation and had been sucked down into the storming planets inner and been crushed in the violent atmosphere.

The spheres had been created a long time ago. In another time and another place. In a universe that existed before this. That universe was born in a way like the one that existed now, but even if the births were similar, their development was not the same. A grain of incredibly concentrated energy had poured out its interior and, in a few microseconds, had the grain expanded into a vast universe.

Atoms and molecules had formed and then lumped together into large gas clouds that drifted through the universe. As the gas clouds became bigger and bigger, they had begun to contract and started to rotate. After millions of years had passed, the large gas clouds had contracted so much that the gas ignited, and nuclear fusion occurred. Stars were lit. After more eons of time had passed, tiny life forms emerged, and intelligent lives had developed. Over millions of years, it had developed into entire civilizations that filled the planet that they lived on.

As the shortage of space had become acute, they had been forced out to the planets that were closest in the solar system, and as the millenniums passed, they spread further and further out. And finally, it happened. They got in touch with other intelligent creatures from a different solar system to their own. The scientific development had made quantum leaps when the intelligent races who came more and more into contact with each other.

Countless wars were fought and ended, and the technological development was so advanced that it was almost perceived as godliness. As the civilizations fought against each other, they came into a new phase. After an infinite number of deaths, they somehow reached an idea that they were involved in a game that had no winners. The only chance to win was not to play at all. So, instead of war, battle, and death, a new era of peace and cooperation began.

In principle, they achieved immortality through advanced medicine that could regenerate their bodies an infinite number of times. But even if they had de facto immortality, their universe had not. As millions of years passed, they did not age anymore, but their universe did. Clear bright stars consumed their fuel and ended their lives as either a dwarf or in a cataclysmic explosion that generated life to new stars. But there were not as many stars in the sky that shined as the time passed.

Slowly they burned out, and new ones were lit, but the amount was always less than before. And the space structure stretched out more and more, and when this process increased faster for every million years that passed, it was the final stage that accelerated against them at a terrifying pace.

Their universe was dying. It was a fact that they could not deny anymore. They began more advanced experiments to halt the inevitable development.

They succeeded with unbelievably advanced discoveries and had outstanding comprehension of their universe, but in one area they consistently failed. Time. It was this factor they could not influence or do anything with whatever experiments they performed or what discoveries they made. Time was always there. Adamant. It always went forward. Inevitably. Always forward. Relentlessly.

Eventually, they realized that it was a fight that they would lose. They would die, and there was nothing these immortal gods could do about it. But they had a chance. A chance to pass on their almost endless source of knowledge. If they could pass on their knowledge, their lives would not have been in vain. With fanatical energy that only the condemned may have.

They knew their universe would be torn apart by the invisible forces that pulled it from afar. But how this tearing apart would happen, they did not know. They had several different theories. Some of them basically assumed that it was the space-time itself that would begin to dissolve and that once that process had started, it would immediately propagate through the universe. In principle, their universe would be there one second to not exist in the next.

Other theories suggested that there was a point in the universe that would break, and from this point, the tearing would spread like rings in the water or like a filled balloon pops. It was these theories they focused on, and they started constructing intelligent machines that would search out where in the universe the next Big bang would occur. Millions and millions of sites were searched and scanned by several different criteria's that could indicate that the space in that area was especially vulnerable and, in the end, they found several candidates scattered throughout the universe.

They invented a living machine with outstanding features. They created living, intelligent spheres that might have a chance to survive a new Big Bang and thus transfer information and knowledge from one universe to another.

They were made of organic material, but they were also machines that were constructed of a newly discovered particle. A particle that had a characteristic that would be decisive for the survival of the spheres.

The particle could transform itself into radiation and back to solid. It did not make the spheres immortal. They were still vulnerable when they were in solid form but if they could make it in time to transform their body to radiation, they could have a chance to survive a Big Bang. Most of them would certainly perish in the violent forces that were triggered, but if only one fraction survived, they would have earned their purpose.

Further eons of time passed. They had put so much of their energy into developing the intelligent spheres that when the stars went out for good, they had no more energy to run their civilization. They existed now in a completely dark universe, and they began to die out. First slowly, then faster until they died in unimaginable numbers. As the living creatures died, the machines took over the search completely. Ages of time passed while the machines went to many areas where the new Big Bang would happen.

Finally, it happened. A small tear occurred, and the universe that existed began to dissolve. At first slowly, then faster and faster. The forces that tore at it were furious. And then it came. The new universe. The new Big bang. Let there be light!

The scene in front of them was so unusual that none of them could describe it accurately. The holocube was spinning in slow-motion in front of them in the air. Its shiny sides reflected the light as it resembled a disco ball that rotated around its own axis.

It had been placed on a small round study table where strong magnets created a magnetic field that it was in. The door opened, and Richard came in with his arm in a sling. He carefully closed the door behind him and walked over to his daughter and gave her a hug.

They stood silently around the table. A dull throbbing rhythm sounded in the room. Elisabeth looked in awe at the holocube, and a warm feeling spread through her chest. Rhythmic waves rolled up in her and retreated again, like water lapping against a beach. It was hypnotizing, and she began to lose grip of time.

They said nothing. The heat pulsed in Elisabeth, first slowly, then faster and faster. She glanced over at her father and was relieved that he looked healthier.

"What is happening?" She whispered.

"I don't know."

She tried to put her hands down, but the muscles in her arms did not obey her. It was as if there were invisible threads in her arms and an unseen puppeteer pulled the threads.

"I can't move, can you?"

"No." replied her father.

"Neither can I. What's happening?" Julius's voice was nervous.

Elisabeth stared at the holocube. She had never seen anything so beautiful, so different. As she looked at it, there seemed to be like a light inside it. Weakly it began to pulsate. As heartbeats that rise and falls in an eternal rhythm. She saw it in front of her. As a bright pulsating heart. It was not a cube anymore, but instead, something organic, something alive.

Julius' hand was warm, and she held a tight grip of it as well as her father's hand. After what seemed to be an eternity, something rose in her. Images that floated up inside her. In her soul. She blinked, unsure of what she saw. The images showed something that seemed to be a star system. It was something that she had never experienced before, and panic grew within her. She blinked again, harder. Shook her head to make the images go away. She moaned.

"Do you see?" she whispered.

"Yes, I see. What is it?" her father said.

A faint murmur was heard from her left side, and she turned to look at Julius, he looked pale, wide-eyed, he talked rapidly and indistinctly. Elisabeth struggled to hear what he said, but she could not discern the words.

"My God, it's so beautiful. It resembles our solar system but it's not it." Her father's voice was full of what sounded like reverence.

The images that rose up within her were breathtakingly beautiful. Solar systems that stretched across countless light-years. Brilliant galaxies that radiated magnificently in the infinite space. Nebulae in all the colors of the rainbow that slid in and out of each other in a kaleidoscopic dance.

Her own body ceased to exist. She became one of the bright stars that slid through infinite space. Her voice sounded like it came from someone else.

"I don't recognize any of these. It looks like galaxies and solar systems, but I don't recognize a single one."

In the grip of despair, there is only more desperation. They were in John's office, and Jonathan sat strapped with two arm locks in a chair in front of John's desk. John smiled and nodded towards the wall.

Jonathan saw how a wall panel slid apart, and a holoscreen slid out from behind a hidden compartment. The screen flashed, and Jonathan saw how the hologram of a terrified man slowly faded in. He recognized the man as Paco, the agent he was supposed to save. John sat behind his desk and studied Jonathan, whose eyes were fixed on the screen.

"Do you know who that is?"

Jonathan glared at John.

"Yes, I do."

John leaned forward.

"Could it be that you actually know him?"

Jonathan nodded reluctantly, John smiled.

"Excellent. We've had Paco with us for a number of days now, and since he cannot give us more information about the Amber Group, we have planned a surprise for him."

Jonathan saw how Paco was standing half bent forward, clenching his stomach.

"You scumbag. He's hurt."

John laughed loudly.

"You're really sharp-eyed you. He will be good training for my children."

*   *   *

Providence had put him there; he was sure of it. As punishment for all the bad things, he had done in his life. The heat in the room was intrusive and sweat ran down Paco Sanchez face and his eyes stung. The taste of blood in his mouth was nauseating, and he spat blood mixed with saliva on the metal floor.

He stood half-bent leaning against the wall and tried to gather his strength. He was injured, the left arm had gotten a few deep scratches, and blood trickled down the forearm and dripped onto the floor. A puddle of blood was forming where he stood. His sweaty chest moved sharply up and down, he was breathing hard, and he shook his head and tried to regain something that resembled control.

Searing pain shot through his body as he glanced up at a large window and saw a glimpse of two Asian men who looked down at him. Their faces were blank. The two men were dressed in white lab coats, and if he did not know better, he'd think he was an animal in an experiment.

The room was oval-shaped, maybe ten meters long and half as wide. The walls were made of something that looked like plastic and was completely smooth. Two small cameras sat on each side of the room and covered everything.

* * *

The doctors nodded at each other. Dr Weng-Li was pleased, he clapped his hands and rubbed them contently. The experiment had so far been a success.

"This is better than we could have wished for."
Dr Ln'geem continued looking down at the injured man who would soon fight for his life. The man was strong and in good physical shape. The good doctor made a few notes in his notebook, it was important to document the experiments properly. He looked over at the other side

of the room where two other men came in through a door that slid to the side and then closed when they had entered.

Both men were in excellent shape. Odum and his brother, Paulus, stood next to each other. They belonged to the latest generation of clones born in Tabula Rasa and were both over one meter and eighty-five centimeters tall, and when you saw their faces, you could see their kinship.

Their well-shaped legs were exceptionally strong and durable due to the dense fiber structure of the muscles. Their abdominal muscles were like chiseled marble and moved like pearls on a string. The chest muscles played under the skin and moved like a well-oiled machine. They both had a sharp nose that gave them a gladiator-like appearance.

They did not move when they stood there half a meter apart. They did not speak to each other. Both Odum and Paulus were almost completely naked. They only wore what looked like a pair of black swim shorts.

Their shining bodies stood as two Greek statues. Their hair was cut short, and they had a blindfold tied over their eyes. Neither Odum nor Paulus saw anything. And that was the main purpose of this whole test, to investigate whether the connection that the clones were designed to have was present.

*   *   *

Paco looked despairingly at the two almost naked men who came toward him. Panic welled up inside. He blinked. Sweat stung his eyes, and he rubbed them hard. His sight cleared, and Paco saw how the two men came closer.

Odum and Paulus moved like one. Their movements were synchronized. The two doctors nodded. Odum and his brother moved around Paco in different directions. Odum went right while Paulus went left. They were less than three meters from Paco. Odum started making small clicking sounds. The two doctors looked at each other.

"Do you hear that?" Dr. Ln'geem said with surprise in his voice.

Dr. Weng-Li leaned closer to the hidden speaker above them.

"Yes, it sounds like they can already use echolocation." He smiled.

"It was impressive; it seems like that part of the DNA programming was successful." Dr. Ln'geem listened to the strange clicking sound and made some quick notes in his notebook.

* * *

Paulus had been silent while they circled the man in front of them. Odum continued with the clicking sounds that he did with his cheeks and tongue. Paulus also made a few clicks and Odum stopped. After a few seconds, Paulus fell silent.

Odum re-started his click sounds. This time, the sounds came faster, and it seemed that Odum had changed the frequency of the clicks. As on a given command, the two brothers began to move faster towards Paco.

* * *

Both the doctors leaned forward.

"It almost seems like they communicate with sound?"

"Yes, somewhat unexpected. To use echolocation is something many species can do but I am not aware of any species that can use someone else's sound to orient themselves."

"Yes, and it seemed that Odum adjusted its frequency and amplitude slightly after Paulus had responded."

"Impressive."

* * *

Paco was standing in the middle of the room. His heart pounded and was close to jumping out of his body. He looked at the men who circled him, and he saw that they were blindfolded. A glimmer of hope surged through him.

He still had a chance. A minimal chance but still a chance. Strength returned to him. He would not give up; he would fight to the bitter end.

Seconds passed. The two men moved like in a soft ballet. Paco heard a weak clicking that he could not fully locate. He cocked his head and listened. The weak, soft clicking continued. He considered his chances. There were only two options. Either he could stay and wait until both men attacked or he could attack. He thought of his mother and brother in Madrid, and he cursed life for what it had become.

His mother and his brother had been his whole world, but life wanted different. The love for them welled up in his chest. He wiped away a few tears in his eyes.

* * *

324

Nausea gripped Jonathan.

"Please, stop this."

John looked at him with sparkling eyes.

"Just wait, now comes the best part."

*   *   *

The doctors who were one floor above looked interestingly at the drama that played out below them. Paco attacked with his knife. A quick thrust and the shining knife flashed.

Odum smoothly slid to the side and took hold of Paco`s arm and twisted it up. He held the arm with his right hand, and his fingers dug deep into Paco`s arm. Paco screamed. Behind them, Paulus quickly moved in, clenching his hands into what looked like a hammer, and with a lightning-quick movement, he crushed Paco's right shoulder.

A damp, crunching sound could be heard when bones were crushed inside Paco's shoulder. Paco roared even louder, and he dropped the knife from his hand that Odum still held in an iron grip. Paulus began with the clicking sounds.

Odum continued to squeeze his fingers deep into Paco's arm, and small trickles of blood began to flow from it. Paco kept shouting. His screams had shifted from pain to pure panic. Paco's eyes almost popped out of their sockets, and he began to babble in Spanish.

Both doctors looked at each other, shrugged and continued to study the event below them.

While Odum still held Paco's arm straight up, Paulus moved quickly. He bent down on one leg and spun around and kicked hard at Paco's knee in a single soft movement. Paco's knee was crushed, and his body began to twitch uncontrollably.

He screamed so loud and so intense that both the doctors thought it sounded that he would break his vocal cords. Paco's last thoughts went to Paulina and Miguel, and while his body was broken into pieces, in his heart, he heard his mother and his brother calling him.

John smiled at Jonathan when the holoscreen slid back in the panel.

"Well, what do think?"

Jonathan looked grimly at John.

"You asshole. Only a psychopath would put anyone through that."

John laughed.

"Is that all you have to say?" He paused, "My clones are my children, and they are those who will rule Tabula Rasa in the next centuries. They are part of the amazing legacy I will give to the world."

A knock on the door and John stood up.

"Just in time."

The door slid to the side with a weak hiss and a tall man with a big, crooked nose came in. The man stared straight at Jonathan and then turned to John and bowed deeply.

"You called?"

John got up and jovially clapped his hands.

"Jaap, thank you for being able to come so fast, I have a special mission for you today."

The eagle-nosed man nodded curtly and smiled fiendishly at Jonathan. John walked around the desk, stood behind Jonathan, and laid his hands on his shoulders.

"I want you to show Jonathan what pain really means. I want you to take him on a journey into hell and give him a lesson about what happens to people that defy me."

Jonathan felt his pulse quickening, and his mouth was dry. The eagle nosed assassin's smile widened, and while the smile was getting bigger, Jonathan cursed himself for not following the others on the boat.

"Bring him to the humor room and give him a lesson."

John clapped his hands and leaned against Jonathan when Jaap violently pulled off the buckles on Jonathan's wrists and pulled him up out of the chair.

"Jaap is a specialist in the universe of pain. Just wait. Imagine all the world's pain focused on a tip of a knife, and that the knife slowly and inexorable penetrates your body. That's what your destiny is."

Jonathan felt the empty fear of powerlessness when Jaap dragged him out of the office and the door behind them slid back with a hissing sound.

*   *   *

Half an hour later, John shook his head as he sat behind his desk and looked incredulously at the report that informed that Raimondo del Luis had not died on the golf course.

Jaap had failed for the first time and rage consumed him. He stood still, gasping hard and trying to regain control of himself. Focused, he took a few deep breaths and used the meditation technique he learned during his travels in the East.

But despite his focused breathing, the anger did not subside over the fact that Jaap had taken him for a ride. He stormed out from the office, slammed the door behind him, and rushed over to the side room where Jaap was with Jonathan. John heard screaming from the room. He ripped open the door.

Jaap stood in front of Jonathan with blood dripping from a small laser knife in his hand. Jonathan's face was bruised and ash-grey and John could see a long deep wound on Jonathan's upper left arm. Jaap turned in surprise when the door was torn up and took a step back when he saw the raging John rush into the room. Jaap thought John would rush over to Jonathan and beat him, so he was completely unprepared when John gave him a straight right-hand punch that sent him flying over the floor.

Jonathan saw his tormentor land hard against the wall and collapse like a rag doll. John stood over Jaap and roared.

"You bastard! He's not dead, you tricked me! Me! You asshole!"

John's strong hand caught Jaap's collar and lifted him up into the air and threw him against Jonathan. Jaap crashed into Jonathan who lost his breath when Jaap's shoulder hit him in the diaphragm. Stumbling, Jaap came to his feet and raised his arms for protection.

"Wait, father, wait! Who is it that isn't dead?"
John stared with a deadly gaze at him.

"Raimondo, of course! You said he died, but I have just read a report that he is in a hospital, injured but alive."

Jaap shook his head slowly.

"But that cannot be true. I saw him fall. He fell into the water and did not come up again."

"You get one more chance to fix this. Fix it, or you are history. Do you understand?"

Jaap bowed low, and a trickle of blood running down his mouth dropped onto the floor. John turned around and stormed out of the room, slamming the door behind him.

Jonathan had been restrained throughout the short, intense scene and now he felt something hard in his lap. He looked down and saw to his surprise, the small laser knife that Jaap had cut him with. The knife lay in the middle of his lap and instinctively, he moved his leg so the knife slid down toward his hand. It was close that he missed it, but in the last second, before it slipped further, he caught it.

*   *   *

Maria Lee tried to scream, but her lungs were empty of air. It was burning like fire in her chest. She pulled air into the nose and shouted, but only a muffled croaking came from her tied-up mouth. Her hands were tied behind her back. Her legs were tied too, drawn to the back.

She lay on her stomach on a large, round bed covered with red silk sheets and turned her head, trying to orient herself. On a wall hung what looked like a several meter-wide painting of what appeared to be naked women tied up in various sexual positions.

Pain shot through her body. She threw herself to the side and tried to roll over on her back but got stuck halfway. She struggled to get loose when the door opened and John Vendrick III came in. He smiled. His perfect teeth glowed in the light. Slowly he closed the door and remained standing just in front of it.

"You didn't break free?" he asked, "That's what's it's all about you see. That you won't break free. But you may try, my dear."

Terror gripped her. She struggled but she could not control herself, she lost control of her bladder. A dark spot formed between her legs and John looked at her and the growing wet spot. The sharp smell of urine reached him, arousing him. He noticed how he stiffened and walked toward her.

"It doesn't matter that you met Dennis. That problem is resolved." He blinked at her. Maria looked terrified at him.

"What have you done?"

John did not answer but slowly walked around the bed and sat down beside her. She trembled. He smiled.

"I don't know how you got hold of his number or what you said before I came in and interrupted you, but now he has been checked out for good, and he will not be able to help you anymore."

Maria had been locked up in John's apartment but had managed to break out. During the time she was imprisoned, she had repeatedly heard Dennis Topps name being mentioned, and when she was by herself and managed to get free, she had been able to activate the holotelephone and looked up Dennis' number.

Maria trembled when John touched her. This was the whole point of life. Being able to dominate and control another person. A shiver of pleasure raced through his body.

He stood up and took off his shirt. He knew she would be terrified when she saw him bare-chested. His powerful muscles tightened, and he slowly turned around. The glass-paved walls reflected him, and he let Maria see him in his full splendor.

On his body, a red, burning dragon was tattooed. The flaming eyes stared out of his chest and the glowing body twisted around his torso. While Maria stared in horror at him, the dragon twisted slowly and moved over his body.

It was a magnificent, living piece of art, an outstanding expression of power. He felt himself stiffen when his vivid tattoo showed up in its full glory, and when he heard Mary's despairing moans from the bed.

* * *

Jaap leaned forward toward Jonathan with an evil grin on his face.

"We were interrupted, right?"

Jonathan nodded weakly and pretended to surrender. Jaap laughed triumphantly, and he never saw Jonathan's hand quickly thrust up the laser blade that hit Jaap under the chin.

The sharp tip slid easily in under the lower jaw and further up into Jaap's middle brain. Jaap froze and stared blankly at Jonathan before his eyes rolled back in their sockets. He fell.

Jonathan pushed away from the dead killer, and it took five minutes before he managed to cut the second arm lock.

He quickly rushed to the door and opened it. He ran back to Vendricks office and heard a subdued scream coming from behind the door.

Quickly, Jonathan tore a fire extinguisher from the wall and pounded on the door to John's office and took a step to the side and waited. Several seconds passed. The door slid open, but he did not move. A few more seconds passed silently before Jonathan heard steps inside the room.

John stuck his head out of the doorway and in the same second, Jonathan hit it with the fire extinguisher which hit John in the temple, and he collapsed on the floor.

Jonathan stared at the unconscious John lying on the ground in front of him and the living, bloody tattoo that slowly moved over his body.

He rushed past John to locate the source of the screaming, but when he ran on into the hidden room, he saw a woman's naked, bloody corpse on the bed in the middle of the room.

His stomach turned, and he had to struggle not to vomit. He stopped and walked slowly over to the body. The arms were stretched out to the sides like a Jesus figure. The woman's face was frozen in a stiff cry with her mouth wide open and her unseeing eyes rolled back in her head.

Long, deep lacerations went from the shoulders down to the belly, and thick, dark red drops poured from the fresh wounds. An ice-cold shiver ran through him when he heard John moaning. He turned back and disappeared out past John into Tabula Rasa internal domains.

Tabula Rasa, Madagascar
2049-01-01

Jonathan's arm ached like it was dipped in a fire while he ran from Vendrick's office. Pounding. A tearing sensation from the wound that ran from the elbow diagonally towards the wrist. It was deep. As droplets of corrosive acid dropping on metal, and with a sizzling, bubbling sound eating through his bone.

He clenched his teeth and flexed his jaw muscles even harder. Small, colorful stars flickered past his field of vision. The metallic taste of blood welled up in his mouth, and he swallowed. The rest of his body was bruised and battered, but he did not think he had any more serious injuries besides the wound on his arm.

* * *

The amber-colored injections came to life and gushed forward in Vendrick's unconscious body. Normally, they fed on adrenaline and their power was reinforced by his anger, but now they adapted to the situation, and at the molecular level, they began to change the cellular construction of it.

The power of the injections was amazing. After a few minutes, he slowly woke up and furiously got on his feet. He stumbled into the room where Jaap and Jonathan were, but only was met by Jaap's dead body on the floor.

He roared. Wrath stormed within, but at the same time, he forced himself to savor the moment. He was alive, he had survived something no ordinary many should have survived. So, he focused his anger and enjoyed being in possession of such a perfect body as his.

No, it was more than perfect. Something alive that repaired itself. Outstanding. Perfectly outstanding. He roared again.

*   *   *

Jonathan ran into what seemed to be a service tunnel and fresh air flowed, and he instinctively knew that there was an exit further down the tunnel. There must be. The draft was stronger now. It was as an invisible magnet that pulled him forward and tried to help him out of this nightmare. He was hurt and without any opportunity to call for help. His mind fervently pondered his next move.

His left arm was in pain, and when he touched it with his hand, his fingertips were wet. He saw that his fingers had become sticky with blood.

Groaning, he sank to his knees and leaned at the wall. Weak nausea had again begun to creep up from his stomach and he had to fight down the desire to vomit.

He was on the verge of collapse. His body and mind were under violent pressure, and darkness began to sneak into his field of vision.

Small black edges approached and made his field of vision narrower and tighter. It would be so nice, so simple. To lie down here and let the darkness take over. Not to fight anymore but finally get some rest. He closed his eyes.

Somewhere in his head, an idea formed. A small, bright dot. Like a lighthouse in endless darkness. The lighthouse spoke to him. It shouted. Calling him. As a man standing in a storm. You cannot hear what he says until you will get close. He listened.

He opened his eyes. Slowly the darkness slipped back, and he was able to focus in front of him. He shook his head but stopped immediately. His head throbbed and was on the point of bursting. Images of Kristina, Chantelle, and Marie flickered past.

Slowly, he got up. His knees were shaking as if they were made of jelly. With one hand he leaned against the wall and began to move forward. The tunnel was vaulted and quite low in ceiling height. One wall was covered with various tubes and control panels. Narrow lights ran along the ceiling giving it a sterile appearance. He had only come a few steps when a voice was heard behind him.

"There you are."

Jonathan froze and instinctively raised the laser knife.

"I've been looking everywhere for you. You shouldn't have run."

Jonathan spun around. Adam walked towards him while he smiled.

"You must know now that there is nowhere to run. Don't you realize that?"

Adam made a welcoming gesture. Jonathan's body tensed for the fight and slowly nodded.

"Who're you?"

Adam laughed.

"You stupid man. My father is the greatest man of all. John Vendrick III."

Jonathan blinked.

"John Vendrick III?" he hesitated, "I didn't know he had any children?"

Adam moved slowly around Jonathan.

"That shows how little you know, and that's another reason to kill you. To free the world from someone like you is indeed a good deed."

Jonathan stared at the man in front of him who seemed to hate him. He could almost feel the hate emanating from him.

Adam smiled, moved towards Jonathan and leaped forward and caught Jonathan in a bear hug and squeezed. Jonathan cried out when two of his ribs broke and he desperately punched Adam's head. The laser knife fell to the ground and went out. Jonathan's fingers tore and ripped into Adam's face. He grabbed Adam's powerful head and pushed his thumbs into Adams' eyes. The thumbs sank softly into the eye sockets. Adam howled. But he did not release his grip but instead increased the pressure until Jonathan's body exploded with pain as the powerful arms continued to squeeze. Finally, he released his grip and staggered backward.

Jonathan fell to the ground and pain seared through his body. Adam screamed with his hands covering his bloody face.

Jonathan frantically looked around for something to use as a weapon. Adam stopped screaming and wiped his hand on his shirt. The bloody face looked like something from a horror movie.

Behind Adam, Jonathan saw what looked like a control panel with a small lever sticking out. Slowly, Adam rose up in his full length.

He made a terrifying figure. His well-trained body was dirty and bloody and shimmered with an unnatural light. But his face was worse. The eyes were gone, and sticky, bloody grime ran down his cheeks and into his mouth.

Jonathan shivered. This was do or die. He could not take on this man in combat, he had to put everything on one card. He ignored the pain in his tortured ribs, threw himself forward, and smashed into Adam.

Adam was unprepared for the violent attack and fell back against the wall and the control panel. He hit it, froze and looked down with his unseeing eyes toward his chest.

A thin, bloody handle stuck out from the chest. A narrow trickle of blood ran down from his chin when he realized that life was about to leave him.

Jonathan staggered back and watched the last breaths leave the man who hated him so much.

*   *   *

Adam's dead body hung on the wall in front of him. A dark red puddle of blood grew under it. Jonathan turned away from the body and leaned forward and threw up.

He was dizzy and confused. His brain swirled, and he struggled to understand what was happening. He tried to stay upright but his knees buckled under him. His ribs burned like burning phosphorus.

White-hot pain sliced through his chest. He fell to his knees with his back against the wall. He sat there for what seemed like an eternity, and the pain subsided somewhat when the microrobots which Marie had injected into him feverishly worked to repair his body.

As he got up and flexed his legs, he saw movement in the corner of his eye. He turned toward it, and his stomach froze.

Vendrick appeared in the dim, flickering light. Smiling. With slow movements that reminded Jonathan of a panther, Vendrick moved toward him. His body had changed. Into something else than before.

The muscles on Vendrick's body were like chiseled granite. Long, strong arms that ended in hands resembling bear traps stretched out. The huge shoulder muscles were so big that it looked like Vendrick's head rested on two small pillows.

His abs seemed hard, rock hard. His whole body resembled a well-oiled machine that had reached its ultimate limit. Perfect in its completeness and brutality. Vendrick knew that he was a formidable sight where he stood. He flexed all the muscles in his body and enjoyed his superiority. The red dragon moved over his skin and followed Jonathan with its dead eyes.

"Finally." John's voice dripped with desire.

Jonathan watched John come closer and stop in front of him. Slowly, John flexed his muscles and showed off. The bloody, terrifying body almost did not look human anymore. The veins in his legs were as thick as small tubes and Jonathan could see how they pulsed. Jonathan swallowed when John drew his lips back in a shark-like smile.

"Now you're mine. You have no idea how much I've longed for this."

Jonathan smiled faintly.

"Glad to make you happy." He paused and continued. "But it's probably too late for him." He bobbed his head toward Adam's dead body.

Vendrick glanced over at Adam, his voice low.

"Adam was a hero and my son. A true creation here in Tabula Rasa. I'll mourn his death as it is required when I'm done with you."

"And now the whole world knows about the spheres. You have nothing left. And when the world finds out that you have communicated with the sphere without informing the rest of the world, you'll see everyone turn against you."

John fell silent a couple of seconds.

"You are right that the discovery is out in the open, but it doesn't matter. That the world knows about the objects and their existence, but what does it matter? The importance is the key. How to communicate with them. That is the main thing. And that's what gives power, do you understand?"

Jonathan stared at Vendrick. The crazy man had a point. The real power lay with the one who could communicate with them. He closed his eyes. Vendrick felt Jonathan's confusion.

"Do you see? And since it is we who have the key to communicate with the sphere, it is we who have the power."

He paused for a few seconds and let the fact sink in. Before Jonathan could answer, Vendrick leaned toward him, grabbed his collar and threw him across the tunnel. Jonathan struck the wall, and he lost his breath as the hard wall punched the air out of him. It flashed before his eyes.

"We have the power, and we will take mankind to the next level. You'll see."

"The key?" Jonathan tried to laugh but stopped immediately when his ribs screamed in pain, "We also know what the key is to communicate with the spheres. The key is the Skydisc, or to be more correct, all the Skydiscs that are being found all around the Earth together with the spheres. With that, you can access the knowledge inside the spheres. Did you think that we didn't understand that yet?" he continued, "And we will make sure that the world understands how to communicate with the spheres so that all its knowledge will be for all of us."

John stared hatefully towards Jonathan while he painstakingly rose. Jonathan's body burned as if it was dipped in lava. He staggered to his feet and held out his hand against the wall to support him.

His mind raced, grasping at all the straws he could think of. Nothing. Vendrick ran towards him and before Jonathan could react, Vendrick kicked him hard on the knee so he fell screaming down to the floor. The pain was relentless.

This was the end, and images and fragments flashed before his eyes, in his mind he heard Marie call to him and he reached for her. Her voice was far away, and he could not hear what she said. Jonathan looked up through the fog and could see the outlines of Vendrick who stood over him. Vendrick was too strong.

A weak, fleeting thought flashed through his brain, the small syringe that Marie gave him on Greenland. It was still in his inner pocket. He reached for it, did not feel it, dug deeper into his pocket and found it. He remembered Marie's words that echoing warned him. He pulled out the syringe and held it tightly to his chest. Vendrick looked down at Jonathan and chuckled.

"What do you have there?"

Jonathan did not answer but pulled the cap from the syringe and stabbed the syringe quickly down toward Vendrick's foot, hit it, and the amber liquid slid into the Vendrick. Jonathan's hand fell weakly to the side. Vendrick roared with laughter.

"What was that? Did you want to give me a vitamin injection?"

Jonathan did not manage to answer, the pain within him burned away all logic and he focused on not screaming. In the corner of his eye, Vendrick's foot shimmered in dark colors. He stared in fascination at how the muscles under the skin seemed to change character from soft to something else. Dark streaks began to show on the surface of Vendrick's calf, and the veins began bulging out.

Vendrick looked triumphantly down at Jonathan and stretched a powerful hand down toward him to pull him on his legs and deliver the coup de grace.

But before his fingers reached Jonathan, he stopped. A shivering jolt passed through his body, and his eyes went blank.

He looked down at his leg and saw the dark streaks slowly propagate from his calf, over the knee and on towards his crotch, he staggered backward.

"No, no!"

Jonathan saw Vendrick starting tearing at his legs and how his sharp nails pulled up long wounds along them.

Dark blood poured out and oozed downward and met more of the thick, dark stripes slowly rising upward. Vendrick's voice yelled.

"No, stop, stop for God's sake!"

He staggered backward and nearly fell. He took a few cramped steps as he continued his fight against the dark streaks growing on his body. Jonathan watched in fascination when they grew up over Vendrick's stomach and up over his chest. Vendrick's voice now sounded more like a whining, dying animal than a human being. "No, no, stop, that's not fair, it's not fair."

Inside Vendrick, chaos reigned. The disintegration of muscles, bones, and nerves accelerated. The amber-colored liquid was in full-frontal attack on the nano-robots that he had already injected. The two different nano-robot groups were incompatible, and when they were mixed, they immediately began destroying each other with a violent frenzy and they used Vendrick's body as a battlefield.

Jonathan threw himself toward the laser knife lying on the ground, and in a sweeping motion, he turned it on and drove it deep into Vendrick's bloody chest and the dragon screamed while it slid around the impaled knife.

John staggered backward, and Jonathan saw Vendrick fall, and in a haze, he heard screaming that was turned into whimper that turned into sobs that turned into silence. Jonathan tried to stay awake, but the darkness rose from the abyss and embraced him.

EPILOGUE

After John's death, Jonathan had been taken to the hospital at Tabula Rasa where he was detained for three days. During that time, Backmann had struggled for a United Nations intervention force to get to Tabula Rasa as soon as possible to retrieve Jonathan.

The situation had required Backmann to call in several favors before the assignment was approved. The Task Force had not encountered significant physical resistance when they arrived, but a certain Derek Lamm had very much protested their arrival at Tabula Rasa and their mission. The mission had succeeded, but Lamm had submitted formal protests to several global authorities.

The months after returning to Paris, he and Marie were among the happiest Jonathan had experienced. Marie and he had reunited, and together they had bought an apartment in Houlgate which was a small, romantic village on the coast of Normandy.

His injuries from the fight had been serious, but the talented doctors that the Amber Group had access to, had soon gotten him up on his feet.

His relationship with the tablets was also over, it had been difficult, but Marie had stood by his side when it was at its worst.

It was early in the morning, and they sat together in their cramped kitchen and drank a cup of coffee while watching the beautiful sunrise bathing the rooftops in golden colors.

He glanced over at Marie as she thoughtfully sipped her coffee, there was something magical about her. Her features were soft and warm, and she smiled when she noticed that Jonathan studied her.

"What are you looking at?"
He smiled back.

"Nothing, you're just so very beautiful."

343

She giggled.

"You really know what a woman wants to hear in the morning."

He leaned forward and pushed back a lock of hair that had fallen over her forehead. When he touched her, memories poured back of his Chantelle and Kristina, and a sting of guilt washed over him.

But that was okay. He let guilt flow through him, and then, let it slowly disappear. It was ok to sit here and enjoy a second chance, there was nothing wrong or any guilt in that. It was not often a man was given a second chance, and if you got it, you better take it.

The time after the discovery of the spheres had been dramatic, but now a new kind of normal state began to present itself in the world.

Lisa and Tim had contacted the authorities in Costa Rica and informed them of the sphere they had found. The authorities had, as gratitude, let Lisa be a part of the working group that investigated the sphere.

The spheres had begun to materialize in various forms on Earth and in several places, they had managed to establish a direct connection with them. The communication with them was slow but improved all the time, and the general opinion was that they had come to help and share information.

One of the research groups that had been in contact with the spheres had been shown an artificial network that was generations before anything that existed on Earth. It was suspected that this was only the beginning.

The locked doors to amazing discoveries were about to be opened wide, and for the first time in a long time, people began to feel budding optimism that they might have a chance to solve the challenges Earth faced regarding environmental pollution and overpopulation.

John's death at Tabula Rasa had been a potential scandal, but it had quickly been swept under the rug.

The United Nations had appointed a committee that took over the control of Tabula Rasa and systematically began to audit their research programs. Both Dr. Weng-Li and Dr. Ln'geem had been forced to collaborate regarding the cloning programs. What the committee found was groundbreaking and would keep them occupied for several years. It was noted that a couple of illegal clones had managed to escape and were on the loose.

Flor Frias struggle for freedom had been lost three weeks into the New Year, and the mega-complex had come under Chinese rule. In the end, thousands of people had lost their lives in battle, but they failed at achieving their independence.

Raimondo del Luis was still in the hospital and was under constant supervision of the best doctors. It was unclear how much permanent damage he would sustain. Erik Tuva spent a lot of time by his friend's side and helped him through the difficult times.

Backmann and the Amber Group, together with Malin, Elisabeth, and Richard had continued to analyze the information they had, and they handed over their work to the authorities and received their gratitude for their cooperation; but as all work was classified, there was no official recognition. It suited Backmann just fine with keeping the Amber Group and its work outside of the public eye.

Jonathan glanced over at Marie and knew that the future for them was uncertain, just as Earth's future with the spheres was uncertain.

But in some inexplicable way, he had a feeling it would work, they would make it work. He did not know how, but he knew that he would do his utmost.

Made in the USA
Middletown, DE
24 January 2022